Staying Home and Being Rotten

Shonagh Koea is a fulltime writer who lives and works in Auckland. Her short story collection, *The Woman Who Never Went Home,* was published in 1987 and her novel, *The Grandiflora Tree,* in 1989. Her short stories have appeared in magazines, mainly the *Listener,* since 1981 when she won the Air New Zealand Short Story Award. The Queen Elizabeth II Literature Committee awarded her the Additional Writing Bursary in 1989.

OTHER BOOKS BY THE SAME AUTHOR

The Woman Who Never Went Home
The Grandiflora Tree

Shonagh Koea

STAYING HOME AND BEING ROTTEN

V
VINTAGE

The publishers gratefully acknowledge the assistance of the Literature Programme of the Queen Elizabeth II Arts Council of New Zealand.

The author gratefully acknowledges the assistance of the Literature Programme of the Queen Elizabeth II Arts Council of New Zealand in awarding her the Additional Writing Bursary in 1989.

Vintage New Zealand
(An imprint of the Random House Group)

18 Poland Road
Glenfield
Auckland 10
NEW ZEALAND

Sydney New York Toronto
London Auckland Johannesburg
and agencies throughout the world

First published 1992
Reprinted 1992, 1997

Printed in Malaysia by SRM Production Services
ISBN 1 86941 159 5

1

THE PARCEL FROM James arrived three days before Christmas when the white roses in the front garden had finished flowering. It was also the day on which ended the High Court trial of a man accused of disembowelling a woman just up the street, but as most of its residents (including Rosalind) did not get the newspaper regularly this melodrama left the neighbourhood untouched.

The area's various dogs, a brindled and motley muster of hounds with large teeth, had not howled either in unison or separately for nearly a week. For a similar length of time the police, with the usual reinforcements, had not slipped down that lane in squad cars to investigate petty larceny, domestic violence or the ravishment of women, or men, whose clothing was already tattered with lack of innocence. The whole place, it seemed, had hushed itself in preparation for the arrival of James's package, as a theatre may be quietened for the beginning of a charade. Only the postman, undeterred, had made any noise, and he had just been prophetically whistling *Hello, Dolly* as he went along the road delivering mail that day.

There was no mistaking the hand that had written her address, so Rosalind left the parcel where it was and closed the door at the back of the letter-box. The telephone began to ring at this instant — perhaps it was a kind of electronic shriek, she thought — and she went inside, into her cottage, to answer it.

'Hello? Rosie? I just wondered if you were alive.' It was Dinah ringing from across the city, from a suburb where the avenues were formed by mature silver birches and murders were committed with matching pairs of silver-handled revolvers or antique rifles with intricately worked barrels, where errant wives were bludgeoned to death with venerable Asegai clubs or drowned in tiled swimming pools.

'Of course I'm still alive,' she said, 'but only just.' They said the same things every Wednesday, and Rosalind suddenly thought that the day was an ordinary one with its usual name. It was just Wednesday.

Parcels from James, after a postal silence of nearly two years, had not arrived that day in every home to cause diffidence even amongst the brave. The alarm was not general.

'What've you been doing, Rosie?' Dinah's voice had not altered much over the years and still possessed a blameless sibilance. Rosalind and Dinah went to school together when they were five, and their chatter had altered only imperceptibly since then, mostly with regard to the size of things. In primer one they talked of dolls, boys and sixpences. Now they talked of people, men and investments.

Both owned property, tried to run immaculate cheque accounts, were treated with respect in the better department stores and cooked very well. Their repertoire of dishes was small, but splendidly presented. Dinah's cuisine ran more towards pasta and she also had a penchant for Middle Eastern cookery. Rosalind served meat cooked in a variety of wines, often Bulgarian, and she specialised in stalwart pies of the Victorian era. Of these she ate only a sliver. Dinah had never been married, but wore her grandmother's rings in a remarkable array on her right hand. Rosalind had been married, but seldom wore her own rings anywhere, in case they were lost.

'Before Roger died . . .' she sometimes used to say when they were sitting at antique sales or waiting for the menu in the cheaper restaurants, and Dinah, jolly and refreshing as a Girl Guide, would bark, 'Now, Rosie, you're not going to get all nostalgic, are you?' She would say no she wasn't, and after they ordered something that sounded nice but was inexpensive they would begin to talk about the weather.

They checked on each other by telephone from their solitary but immaculate houses every Wednesday — 'To make sure we're alive,' they told people — and sometimes during epidemics of influenza or other gripping viruses. They would both say, separately, 'I was very ill last week, you know, but

I knew my old schoolfriend would come over and find me if I died.'

All Dinah's relatives were dead. Her brother died at the age of seven, strangled in the ropes of a playground swing. Her parents died in a German aircrash on the trip of a lifetime the year before last. She had had a cousin called Mark whom Rosalind remembered well. He was a handsome, languid man who smoked incessantly and had been involved in a gangland shooting with Mafia undertones when she and Dinah were in the third form years ago. Rosalind supposed he was either still in jail learning how to make baskets, or he could have served his term and, having changed his name, might now be a tobacconist or the mayor of a small town or anybody. Dinah never mentioned him.

Rosalind had children but they lived far away, in New York, and wrote to her regularly with stories of stabbings in the lift of their apartment blocks, violence and mayhem on a larger scale than she observed through her own windows. She sent them courteously worded notes each week about neighbourhood crime, and all this passed as reasonable communication between loved ones.

'Rose? Rosie? Are you still there? Are you all right?' Patient Dinah was still waiting for an answer. 'What've you been doing? Is anything exciting happening at your place?' Dinah loved Christmas. 'Has anything nice come in the mail?' She loved Christmas cards too, and sent out more than a hundred each year.

'No,' said Rosalind, 'nothing much seems to be happening here. I've just been mucking about in the garden — you know how it is. I've just got a few cards and the odd parcel, nothing much.' It was not actually untruthful. When she had rung off she went out to the letter-box again, lifting its door with the handle of the rake this time. An odd reticence seemed to have come over her. The parcel was still there, waiting like a creature with a life of its own. It was not large, only about the size of a hand, beckoning as deep water does to people who decide to drown themselves.

The garden needed attention, so she worked for the rest of the day, weeding and pruning the rose bushes, hiding amongst the rosehips like an unfledged girl till sundown. The roses had small single flowers, each starred with only five pale petals like daisies, but there had been thousands of them so the garden looked like a generous avalanche for most of December. Amidst this beneficence and surrounded by their bitter-sweet scent that was like cinnamon, she had worked intermittently throughout the month with a sense of unaccustomed peace, and tried to do so now.

'What is your new house like?' people sometimes asked. 'You've moved, haven't you?'

'It's an old house, actually. It's a hundred years old.'

'But what's it like?'

'It's very tranquil.'

'But you still haven't said what it's like.'

'You wouldn't like it.' The truth was that she did not want them to disturb the peculiar repose that had come upon her, in the cottage and the rose garden, like a graceful and tender gift amid the sins of the lawless lanes.

'Don't you notice it's a great change from where you used to live?'

'No.' Very sharp and quick she would be then, in her fur blazer that was out at one elbow, and she would swing around and go off into the crowds or wherever they might have spotted her.

For two days before the parcel came, unseasonal rain fell, a sudden grief from an unfelicitous sky she thought now. The last of the early flowers rotted on the branches and rosehips began to form, very brown and tailored and refined. They looked like a series of fullstops as she pruned and tied up branches on the day of the parcel's arrival. No welcome thief came to steal the mail, though the newspapers were full of stories about Christmas pilfering from letter-boxes. When she returned to look at the parcel from time to time throughout the day it was always still there, waiting.

In the evening, after she had a bath and changed her clothes, she went out to the letter-box again with a pair of kitchen tongs in one hand and a glass of pale dry sherry fortifying the other; the wine was so old and notable that it nearly trembled in its bottle. It was the last of Roger's cache of liquor. A curious idea had come into her head that if she dressed for the part and behaved with inexorable grace it would all turn into a piece of theatre and would, thus, be untrue.

Over the road a line of old cottages fell down a hillside in varying stages of malevolence and decay. From these, regularly, came peculiar sounds and incomprehensible music. They were all quiet, though, that night. Once a man from the pink house had dragged his wife up the street by the hair and the dogs of the street slept in a gang on a lawn on their backs with their feet in the air. Her own appearance on the pavement with a small parcel held by a pair of tongs attracted no attention at all. The package could be opened only when she felt ready to face its contents, she thought, so placed it on the hall table with innocent, ill-wrapped but loving gifts from the children of her friends. *To Rosalind with lots of love from Imogen and Jonathan — we hope you like the ovencloth.* The cards palpitated with sincerity. *To Rosie from Phillippa,* with a line of blotted and inky kisses.

The parcel sat, disguised, amongst these ingenuous offerings for only a day when a postcard came in the mail. James's handwriting was still exquisite.

I'm coming to see you, Rosie, in February. Will let you know final details of what you have to do when all my arrangements are confirmed. I'm working on fitting you in, between Margaret and Lorraine. I hope you like the Christmas present.

Much love, James.

The card fluttered from her hands on to a Chinese rug in the hall. It possessed an indecipherable Oriental inscription along one edge and she thought that if it had been translated the sentiments might fit the occasion perfectly.

Further down the street voices were suddenly raised, and a small child began to shriek, 'Oh, Mummy, Mummy, Mummy!' The radio news at midday provided a psychologist's opinion of stress at Christmas. While she listened to this she re-read the postcard aloud. Havoc was definitely spreading.

'*"I'm coming to see you, Rosie, in February . . ."*' It was the first time she had actually spoken aloud that day, and the cat came immediately, thinking it was called for an extra dinner.

Later in the day the animal began to flick its ears as if distressed, perhaps sensing the exposure of the household. If James arrived, all small gracious acts of concealment would be stripped from them. Fringes on the Persian rugs might be tripped over and torn. Coffee would not be made by the French method. There was no air-conditioning. The cat herself might be shaved partially bald for a joke, but this was improbable, Rosalind thought, because he liked cats. The piano would be out of tune, the pieces of old music she knew off by heart would be unsuitable and too few. There would be no records to find favour, her stereo was probably by now a superseded model. All tears shed would be her own and the talk would be of other women, their beauty and talent. One of them had pubic hair of such abundance and strength, auburn as well, that it poked through her dresses. Lorraine, thought Rosalind. The one with the pubic hair was Lorraine.

'And she's a lovely big strapping girl an' all,' James used to say in London, imitating the Cockney cleaning lady, as a desperate winter came down upon them the year before last. 'Now where have you gone to, Rosie? *Rosie*!' And she would know then that he had turned round at last from his desk to her chair in the farthest corner and, finding it suddenly empty, would hear only the click of the door's latch as she found her way out on to the landing with its lift and the escape it offered to the maze of streets below.

2

THE TELEPHONE NUMBER for James's flat in London was written in a diary for the year before last, she remembered that. It was neatly printed in black ink within Morocco leather covers and jostled the name and telephone number of an elderly colonel who sometimes took her walking in Hyde Park. At the end of the afternoon he used to shake her hand and thank her for her company. She would watch him walk away towards Park Lane, where he would read *The Times* at the Lansdowne Club in a state of innocence attained only by teddy bears or the more old-fashioned toys, now collectors' items, like felt horses on wheels. The telephone number of James's flat jostled that impeccability. Afterwards, when she went through the crowds to the tube station, walked past lovely women with ageless profiles and mink coats slung around their shoulders — already the days were growing colder in every conceivable way — she wondered if they, too, were making their way home to handsome men with cutting voices that destroyed any confidence and charm given by the world that day.

The diary was at the bottom of a drawer with some letters that began *My darling Rosali —*, but those were tossed aside with hardly a glance. It was the day after the arrival of the postcard and it was time something was done about James.

The house smelt faintly of scented beeswax because she had begun to polish the furniture, and a little marble clock on the parlour mantelpiece was ticking for the first time in two years. She had had it overhauled and brought it home with a sense of minor triumph.

'Spring cleaning!' Dinah had said on the telephone. 'Aren't you good?'

'Not really.' Rosalind was referring to a wider spectrum of human behaviour, all beyond the ken of Dinah who had never married and had been insulated by her own involvement with books and learning from the wider perfidies of human nature.

The wax was drying on a burr walnut table and should have been polished off immediately, but she stood beside the telephone in the hall dialling all the codes for Great Britain, then London, then the flat in its eyrie above the High Road. The polishing could wait because with it she hoped to sweep away much dust and minor grime and the task must be leisurely to be thorough. To turn everything into an agreeable interlacing of order, prettiness and delicate scents might make the recollection of James become a myth to be forgotten.

The telephone was ringing now in the empty flat. Perhaps James had gone away. Possibly the flat might belong to someone else. It was switched over to an answering system and she heard his voice say, 'Please record your message now.' James must be away somewhere, perhaps in Wiltshire with Priscilla or up near the Welsh border with the lovely Phyllis.

'Hasn't James ever told you about the lovely Phyllis?' Priscilla said once on the telephone. 'That's a treat in store for you, my dear.'

'Hello, James,' she said when it was time to speak. 'This is Rosalind. Your postcard arrived yesterday.' She waited, but time was running out. 'I hope you have a nice time while you're here. But it isn't any use getting in touch with me because I don't want to see you.' There was no diplomatic way of putting it. 'Thank you,' she said, cursed her politeness, then hung up. The telephone was probably still in the study and the only sign that she had invaded the flat again would be a few clicking noises from the answering apparatus. It would be winter there now, the second winter since she had left, and hail might be beating on those windows again while the old tart from the studio over the landing clattered about in tattered tinsel slippers.

'I was in what you might call the theatrical world, dear,' she used to say. 'I knew ever such a lot of theatrical gentlemen. What's my name? Mrs Something? Bless your little heart, dear. You can just call me Mavis.'

The little cat was playing with a ball of paper in the hall as Rosalind hung up the receiver after the call to London, both Rosalind and the cat as wholesome as the old colonel had been. In London James always seemed to be hanging up the telephone when she went into his study. He looked like an old boy caught in a misdeed, a schoolboy red-handed with the sherry decanter, a thief with his hand in the till.

'Just chatting to someone about the bloody weather.' His hand would still be on the receiver ready, perhaps, to lift it again when she left the room. 'Going out again, are you, for one of your little walks?' The sound of the bell when the receiver went back on the hook still echoed in the room like a small gasp from a woman who might have just had the telephone hung up in her ear. 'Oh, good. You might be able to stay out a bit longer today, the weather's better for you. Shall we say I'll see you in a couple of hours?' Perhaps, she thought, the black nurse was coming to pick up her satin shoes.

Outside it would be nearly dark, though the afternoon was only half over. Dusk came now at four o'clock and the progression from sweet autumn to winter had taken a fortnight. Already cars skimming along the Finchley High Road had their lights on, Rolls Royces heading towards Hampstead and Cortinas going in the opposite direction to the *mélange* of Muswell Hill.

Towards Hampstead there was a wine shop that provided a daily selection of French wines to taste. There might be a nice Pouilly-Fuissé opened, or a Sancerre, and she used to stand there sometimes, leaning on the marble counter, sipping a glass of this or that before making her way back to James's front door. It was lacquered a red so virulent that to approach it had become a trial.

'I'll think about that,' she would say to the man behind the counter. 'I'd like to let it develop on my palate, if you wouldn't mind.' Those were Priscilla's sensible instructions.

'Oh, yes, madam?' He might look up, usually not. At that hour of the day he was polishing glasses and replenishing shelves prior to closing. Mostly he did not even glance at her, and Rosalind had an odd feeling that not only was the world probably filled with women wearing strained expressions, afraid to go home, but that she had been so ground down by contempt and anxiety that she had become as smooth and straight as an empty wine bottle. To go to London had seemed an exercise in charm at the beginning, but the time had been spent loitering in doorways, never knowing whether to enter a room was a welcome act or not.

'Don't sit there, sit here,' James would say. 'Don't stand there. You're in my way. Stand here.'

'I'll come back and let you know,' she said to the man in the wine shop.

'I'm sure you will, madam.' He had got to know her by sight in the preceding days when the weather was not so bad and a limpid English autumn gave the days more charm.

'You went out and didn't say where you were going.' That was James when she slipped in the crimson door again.

'I just went for a walk.' She always hung up her coat very slowly in the hall cupboard as if she felt at ease in that place and could take her time, could live there at a leisurely pace. 'I tasted a Sancerre at that little place down the street. I think the '89 is much better than the '88.'

'Do you indeed?' That usually stopped him, some news about wine. James like wine.

'And where do you think you've been?' he often used to say.

'I walked to Muswell Hill, to the teashop. I've been eating bread and butter.'

'You really say the stupidest things.' James despised bread and butter. She would watch him lean back in his chair. 'And you've got mud all splashed up your coat again.'

'I can take it to the cleaners.'

'It won't come out. If you had any sense at all you'd stay indoors like everyone else. It's nine days since I went outside.' His voice was as hard and mocking as the noise of churchyard rooks.

In Rosalind's little cottage in the lane, the wax had by now dried far too hard on the walnut table, a mockery of good housekeeping, and she suddenly noticed that the satinwood inlay of its top had begun to lift. That must have happened in the last year or two. Once, before she met James, the table had been perfect. Her memory of it was perfect also. The furniture was neglected, she could see that, and some of the old watercolours showed signs of foxing. The winter before last, while she had been loitering in and out of doorways at James's place, damp had seeped in — but that was in the other house before the robbery and before she moved. Water washed into the old conservatory under the french doors, then swept through the dining-room on a day of sudden flood. Amidst the smell of drying upholstery a night or two later, two men with a van and a boy to keep watch broke in and ransacked the place. They knew what they were doing, those two men who left footprints on the parquet but no fingerprints anywhere, and they might have taken the walnut table as well if they had not been disturbed by something.

'Don't you wonder what happened to your things?' people sometimes asked.

'No. I had them, and now I don't have them.' She took the loss of the Rockingham, the oil paintings from the stairwell, the smaller items of more easily portable furniture as a punishment. It was a fine by the world for her absence and must be endured.

'You could go and buy some more things the same as you had before.' This idea, she could see, cheered everyone but herself; while she thought, secretly, that the loss was her damnation by forfeiture.

The wax polished off more easily than she expected, and the inlays sank back into their slots when she glued them. The table, after an hour of work, looked perfect again. The decay in everything was beginning to be beaten back. A silver photograph frame was the right weight to hold the inlays in place while the glue hardened, and beside it she placed a tiny piece of treen, a moneybox shaped like a walnut and carved long ago from pearwood. It had a slit in the top for coins, but no trace of these, if they had ever existed, remained. It might never have been used for any sort of currency except in the dreams of careful Victorian children. There was no button inside it, or pin, or small pieces of paper folded in four that infants, who are not yet schooled in commerce, might poke in any available hole including their own ears or nostrils. It was as empty as her own heart.

The cat had followed her around the house all morning, watching the dusting and polishing, the mixing of furniture glue, and had heard the telephone call to James's answering system. It now began to flick its ears again, more seriously than yesterday. There had been no more shouting from the child down the street, the dogs were not baying, no one broke windows or bumped into lamp-posts in cars or on motorbikes, but havoc was still on the loose, thought Rosalind. A morning spent making the house smell of beeswax and furniture glue had not halted the sudden decline.

The vet examined the animal later in the day. They had been given an emergency appointment. The cat, thought Rosalind, was the first to break under the strain of waiting for trials ahead. The sole other creature made of flesh and blood was herself and, although she had a bruise on her left hip from the morning's housework, she was still upright.

'It's just wax,' said the vet. The cat was lying under an arc light on the examining table. 'They're very sensitive, some of these creatures. She's very bonded to you. Perhaps she's picked up the vibrations of some disturbance?'

'My house is very quiet,' said Rosalind. 'There's only me there. The cat and I live very quietly.'

'You've moved, haven't you? We'd better change the address on your card.' The cat was climbing back into its carrying basket now. 'She wants to go home.' Home, thought Rosalind, and thought of the looming bulk of the big house on the hill and how those french doors, so pretty and innocent always in the sunlight, must have been forced open when the moon was on the wane and the two men must have walked into the place with their empty bags in their hands.

'I've changed my address,' she told the receptionist on the way out and spelt out the name of the lane where the cottage was.

'Didn't you used to live in that beautiful place? Up on the

hill?' said the girl. 'Don't you miss it?' She did not even wait for a reply.

The beautiful house had attracted James. He had climbed up the hill from the old cricket ground one day during a summer that was nearly forgotten.

'Hello! Hello!' She had heard him calling from the lawn. 'Does anyone live here?' Blackbirds fled, shrieking, from the trees, before the sudden sound of a stranger in the garden.

'I do,' she said, taking a fatal step out on to the portico. That was how they met.

'I don't miss my house,' she told the girl at the vet's clinic. 'It was beautiful, but sometimes it attracted things that were not desirable.'

'Oh, yes, you had a robbery, didn't you? I read about it in the paper.'

'I live in a cottage now. It's very quiet, like a secret. I like it.' The robbery was something she ignored. The plunder of herself was harder to assimilate. And now the parcel had come with its very regular row of stamps and immaculate sampling of James's handwriting as a reminder of irregularity and a sullied search for love.

'I thought you loved me,' she had said the day she left London.

'Darling, I love everyone.'

'Dear God,' she said, stepping over the pink satin shoes in the entrance hall. 'Dear God, James.'

'I think it would be very nice to be loved,' Dinah sometimes said now when they dined in little restaurants.

'Loved? There's no such thing. Choose your dinner, Dinah — that's much more certain. But when Roger was alive —'

'Now, Rosie, you aren't going to get all nostalgic, are you?'

'You started it. You said it would be nice to be loved. And talking about love, what about that Air Force captain you knew once, that one you used to go dancing with?'

'I think he married someone else. I remember —'

'Now, Dinah, you're not going to get all nostalgic, are you? Nostalgia saps the strength.' A waiter had appeared beside the table to take their order. 'It's quite all right,' she told him. 'We aren't really quarrelling. We went to school together.

We've known each other since we were five. We tease each other sometimes, for want of anything better to do.' And she sat there, in that bright café, thinking how the arrival of a parcel from James might once have provoked felicity. Now the gift of James's sudden attention brought merely the malady of silent and arcane lamentation.

At three minutes past midnight the telephone rang, pealing through the night and its silence. The hounds from the street were still quiet. No barking or howling presaged the interruption to sleep. The house still smelt faintly of beeswax and a card from the restaurant lay on the trunk at the foot of Rosalind's bed. The little cat, which had been asleep beside Rosalind's pillow, stood up immediately with its fur on end. The sky, viewed through the bedroom's sole casement, was brooding and filled with scudding cloud. There were no distant fireworks, no sky rockets. No stars had come to light the message through the air waves.

'I've had a bit of trouble finding you,' said James. 'Hello.' He spoke with confidence, like a man reaching the successful end of a long journey. 'You're a bit elusive, aren't you, Rosie? I've had all those telephone girls looking for you all over the place.'

'Have you, James?' She stretched out a hand to soothe the cat. It turned slowly round and round in circles, like a creature mazed, before falling over again and going to sleep immediately.

'Where the hell do you live, Rosie? How could you leave your other place? I can't imagine you in the city.'

'Can't you, James?'

'Anyway, how are you managing, Rosamund?'

'Rosalind.'

'Rosalind—Rosamund, what does it matter?'

'What indeed,' said Rosalind.

'How can you survive in that ghastly place, Rosie? I've always thought it's one of the most horrible cities in the world.'

'It is, James, it is.' And she curled herself up on the bed, grinning. 'It's a very ugly city, James. There's a lot of crime, and the streets are filthy.' James hated dirt, she remembered that. 'I live in a tiny house,' — he liked space — 'right slap bang in the middle of everything. The noise is really awful.' She listened to his silence. James liked footsteps to be muffled by deep carpet, preferably other people's, for motorcars all to be silent, for people to use well-modulated tones. 'Even the people round here scream and shriek quite a lot, James. You'd hate it. I live behind a shoe factory. Well, sort of behind a shoe factory.' The factory was a kilometre away, at least.

'I knew there was a recession,' he said after a delay. She thought he might be flicking over the pages of his black notebook to see if he had better addresses to call upon. 'But I didn't really realise it was as bad as all that.' His voice had become anonymous. 'Whatever happened, Rosalind?' He sounded like a doctor in a hurry, someone who had only two minutes to spare.

'You know how it is,' she said, stroking the cat till it began to purr in its sleep. 'It's a worldwide thing: dropping interest rates at the banks, shares suddenly worth only half as much if that, loss of value in capital items like paintings and silver because the market can't sustain their purchase.' None of it had seemed like a benefit before that moment, but she sat on her bed then luxuriating in the paucity of her outcry.

'What a pity for you.' His voice sounded far away, as if he had removed himself from the telephone receiver.

'But I like it here,' she said, a small finality. 'I'm happy here.' Another one, undetected.

Outside the crushing silence continued, like the hush before or after a play. He always provoked that thought.

'Anyway,' said James, 'I just rang to wish you a happy Christmas.'

'Thank you, James.' But she did not wish him one in return. The lack of reciprocity was almost shaming, but she still said nothing about the festive season and her hopes for him because she possessed none. 'I rang you today. I left a message for you on your answerphone. I told you I hoped you had a nice time when you came out here, but I wouldn't be able to see you.'

'Won't be able to see me?' His voice suddenly echoed in her ear with a resonance that was nearly frightening. 'What do you mean by won't be able to see me?'

'I mean I won't be able to see you, James.'

'So you've got my postcard.'

'Yes, James.' She was sitting on the very edge of the bed now, like a schoolgirl in a dormitory. The little bedroom looked like a lodging in a small but exemplary hotel frequented by people who had never committed a sin, and possibly mostly elderly as well, she thought.

Rosalind is very old for her age, the teacher had written on her report when she and Dinah were both in primer three, and she could see now that the remark was perfectly true. Her bedroom smelt of roses, and the sheets were white and trimmed with old lace. Her hairbrush was silver and bore the hallmark for 1864, and the Persian rug beside the bed was so old it had a hole in it. The whole effect was inexpressibly quaint and ancient and suddenly nearly made her weep.

'I think you're being very silly, Rosie,' said James. 'You could forget all your troubles and we could have a good time.'

Perhaps, she thought, the black notebook contained names that were suddenly unusable. Had great swathes of James's women died of cancer, or run away to be happy waitresses in provincial hotels where they might marry the publican, or got themselves hitched up, second time round, with sensible reliable accountants? Or perhaps, she thought, they had folded themselves up with all their possessions and had fled quietly, as she had done, to the inner reaches of an anonymous city. There crowds might disguise and camouflage them, and amidst faceless assemblies of human creatures they might be lost for ever amongst the broken-hearted.

'Are you still there, Rosie? Did you hear what I said about having a good time? If you won't come I'll have to get Lorraine, won't I?' The threat was unmistakeable.

'You will, James.' So was her own.

'She's a lovely, big, strapping girl.'

'You've already told me that, James.'

'And she's got this ginger pubic hair that pokes through her dresses.'

'She sounds really lovely, James, very suitable. I think you should ask her.'

So she had extracted herself from that lengthy conversation in the black heart of the night and stood for a long time afterwards watching the cat sleeping peacefully, the fur round its ears slightly matted from the vet's drops. The old clock on the mantelpiece struck one in the morning, as loud as a bang on the head.

'I can't believe you just live by yourself, Rosie,' James had said, the laughter like a jeer and a gibe or a pie in the face.

'I've got a cat. I live very quietly with the little cat.'

'Sounds boring.'

'It's very peaceful, James. Nobody shouts at me or makes me cry. Nobody says, "Get out of that chair. That's my chair," or, "You're always in the way, nuisance." I'm not frightened.' I have gone too far, she thought.

'What a waste.'

'It was,' she said, but thought they were referring, separately, to different things.

'Happy Christmas, anyway, Rosie. I should ring you on the proper day, but I won't be able to get to a phone then.' The voice lowered. 'I'm down in Wiltshire at the moment, staying with Priscilla. She's just gone out.'

'Oh,' she said, just a light, innocent, little sound like a child might make. Priscilla was the one she used to talk to on the telephone in London, the one with the nasal, high-pitched voice that sounded as if it resonated within a thin and arched nose. The friendly one. That had been Priscilla. And she was the one he said had gone off with someone called Cruikshank, a name something like that anyway. But he had got Priscilla back again, had not really let her go at all. James seldom let anything go completely.

'I've sent you a parcel, Rosie. Have you got it? I got your address from that mad old colonel you used to know, that old lunatic you used to go for walks with and have afternoon tea with — all those sticky cakes. I don't know how you could eat all that stuff. You should have been home with me letting me make your nostrils flare. I rang the silly old bat's club and got hold of him.'

She let a silence lengthen.
'He's not mad, James. He's not a lunatic. We didn't eat sticky cakes. He's a dear old friend, that's all. I've known him for years. We knew him for ever.' If Dinah had been listening she would have said, 'Now, Rosalind, you're not getting all nostalgic, are you? Talking about Roger and the past?' when she mentioned old chivalry.
'Have you opened the parcel yet, Rosie?'
'You know I never open parcels before the proper day. I'm saving it till Christmas morning.' Or till strength came.
'So you haven't read my letter. You're really the most irritating woman, Rosie. I've put a letter in it explaining exactly what you have to do in February.'
'I'm not doing anything in February, James.'
'I'll simply get Lorraine, then.'
'Do that.' From far away, at his end of the line, she suddenly heard the sound of footsteps, sharp and clear, on a wooden floor.
'Just wait a minute. I'll ring you back in a moment.' James's voice dropped to a whisper, and the call ceased with the sound of breaking china. Presently the telephone rang again.
'It was just the postman,' said James.
'Do postmen come inside and break things, James? I thought I heard something break.'
'If you must know, the postman arrived, and Priscilla came back for a moment to collect something she'd forgotten and the cleaning lady dropped a jug in the kitchen.' It had sounded closer than that, though. 'I'll try to keep ringing, Rosie, it just depends when I'm free to make a few calls, and by then you'll have read my letter and you'll know what I'm talking about.' He spoke too quickly, she thought. He might be looking over one shoulder at a door through which Priscilla might come at any moment. 'I want to get everything set up, darling. Must rush. Byee.' He almost sang the last words.
When the conversation was finally over she walked through the cottage, past the old portraits that were too large for the entrance hall but attained a lost glory in its miniature splendour, past the table that held the remnants of the

Rockingham left by the burglars and also the Christmas mail. James's parcel still lay there unopened. It was small and immaculately put together. Even the pieces of Sellotape were parallel and exactly the same length.

Rosalind did not doubt that, like an involved piece of calculus, there would have to be an answer somewhere. On James's imaginary abacus filled with named beads there would be much addition and subtraction. There was herself, Rosalind the escapee hidden in arcane byways, there was Lorraine with the wild pubic hair, Priscilla who ran away intermittently according to James's falsely inflated accounts and who returned to throw china when she found James talking on the telephone to other women. There were also recalled fragments of James's other conquests, all of whom had become revealed to her as day followed day in London the year before last. Wasn't there a university professor in Adelaide? 'I do like them with brains,' James used to say. And there was someone who had been married to a diplomat and never wore underwear. The mixture was a fruity one and this, she thought, was only the beginning. The parcel was not opened yet. The letter it contained had not been read. Margaret, she thought. The one in Adelaide was called Margaret. 'She's got a lovely mouth,' James used to say. 'She's got beautiful lips. Very sensuous. Rosalind? Where are you? Have you gone out again?'

3

A MILLIONAIRE HAS come calling at Rosalind's cottage. It is after Christmas, but before New Year, and she supposes he has nothing much to do between parties. The Christmas cards are still lying about, and she watches him, this neat and dapper man, as he walks past James's postcard and the untouched parcel. There are disguising messages from friends, though, to mask this postal squalor. There is also herself, like a well-framed but foxed watercolour, positioned in her own small parlour saying, 'How nice to see you. And did you have a good Christmas?' He notices nothing amiss. His own difficulties fill his mind.

His *de facto* wife has misbehaved at Christmas and has given him several pieces of her mind and much else, including a dinner plate applied to his head, from a distance. He shows Rosalind the wound. His *de facto* wife's father has also misbehaved and has given him several pieces of his mind and has drunk all the Moët in the house, not that there was a lot. His own mother dropped the teapot he had given her, so by Boxing Day his gift was severely dented, the spout crooked.

'But it was only silver plate,' he says, sitting down in the best chair, 'even though it was quite a pretty piece. A two-cupper,' he adds, 'and just the thing for her.'

'Oh,' says Rosalind.

'Just what she wanted,' he says.

'Oh,' says Rosalind again.

'My God,' he says as she sits down in a chair beside his. There are only two chairs in the parlour — there is no space for any more — and they are side by side because they have to be. There is no other way they can be placed. One of his hands slips to her nearest knee. 'You're an attractive woman, Rosalind. A very attractive woman.'

Rosalind excuses herself to make a cup of tea, pours the

boiling water carefully into the old Sheffield plate teapot, which, as he has often told her, is very charming but valueless because there is too much copper showing through. There is hardly any silver plating left on the pot at all, but the shape is agreeable. It is a melon-shaped pot of remarkable size and has a family crest on one side. Its handle is made of pearwood, but the greater value of the whole article departed long ago, with the plating.

'Made about 1820, I should say. Did you pay much for it? No? Oh, good.' He is a careful man and his presents are usually small and infrequent. Do they exist at all? she wonders, teapot in hand. Has he ever given her anything? She cannot remember a single thing.

'Rosalind?' He is speaking again. 'Are you going to finish pouring the tea?'

'Oh, sorry. I went into a dream.' She has put milk and sugar in his cup, and is sure she has remembered that correctly, or was that how James took it? Worry about James has exhausted her.

'You could get it renewed,' he says now, this millionaire who collects beautiful things whilst dealing in bankrupt stock stored in his commercial premises encrusted with racist graffiti over the luminous pink paint. 'That silver plating — you could get it re-done, Rosalind, but you'd destroy the value of the pot as an antique.' Together they both study the teapot, and each other. She notices his handmade shoes, which are burnished to a colour approaching bronze. 'You're a fine-looking woman, Rosalind,' he says. Presently, as she sits down, she feels one of his hands slide up her silk camisole.

'You seem to be in an uncharacteristically sociable mood today,' she says, watching him laugh soundlessly. He is economical with everything — 'The key to riches, Rosalind,' he always says, 'is vigilance and frugality,' — including his own sounds. She continues to pour the tea. The cups and saucers are willow pattern, which he admires.

'Quite valuable,' he says now, and she follows the thread of this lack of conversation without effort. 'Unusual,' he says, 'in the very pale blue.' Like his eyes. 'And the can-shape for a teacup — very unusual. You've got some value there, Rosalind.' The hand, meanwhile, continues its journey inside the camisole.

'I remember,' says Rosalind. She is still thinking about presents. 'Didn't you once give me a roast of beef?'

'I think I did.' He looks puzzled. 'I thought we were talking about your teaset, Rosalind.'

'We were. But I was also thinking about presents.'

'Oh, well,' he seems to shift in his chair a little uneasily, 'It wasn't really a present, Rosalind, the roast of beef. Don't you remember? I admired a book you'd bought and you said I could have it if I gave you a roast of beef.'

'Oh, yes,' says Rosalind. 'I must have been hungry that week.'

'Ha, ha, ha.' He laughs again, quite loudly this time, and Rosalind is shocked that she has provoked him into such luxuriance. 'It was a standing rib roast and cost thirty-one dollars,' he says.

The teatray is peacefully and abundantly painted, in oils, with suitably full-blown, pink roses. Amidst this plenitude he asks her age, and when she tells him he says, 'My God, Rosalind, you're a very lovely woman. You've got the flesh tones of someone half that,' and he quietly clasps her left breast, peeking down her front for a sliver of a view. The value of the glimpse, if it were a commercial proposition, could be, say, anywhere between five and fifteen dollars, depending on the market. She looks at him and thinks of this. The hand is difficult to cope with.

'You're gazing at me very fixedly, Rosalind.'

'Am I?' Fifteen, she thinks.

It is four o'clock in the afternoon, the sound of lawnmowers is in the distance again. People are cleaning up after Christmas, thinks Rosalind. She has left James's parcel tossed on the hall table and it is surrounded by a neat circle of dust. Her hand, faltering with the cleaning cloth, had avoided contact and had just circled the slovenliness engendered by James and the arrival of his gift.

'Your house is immaculate, Rosalind.' The millionaire looks round with approbation. He likes tidiness, cleanliness, order, organisation, calculation, all that. He often says so. 'Roberta isn't much of a housekeeper.' So the woman he lives with is called Roberta, thinks Rosalind. She has not been mentioned before in any detail. 'Mind you,' he says, 'she has a career.'

'What does she do?'

'She's a sort of lawyer.' He coughs. 'Well, actually, she's not a proper lawyer, but she can do a lot of the work. They leave a lot of it to her.' He coughs again. 'She could be a lawyer if she wanted to be one.'

'But she isn't one.'

'No.' He is reluctant about this. 'But it's a great strain for her. There's a lot of pressure, that's why she gets bad tempered.' He fingers the stitches on his head. 'They're a very highly strung family. The mother's out of her tree, wouldn't even know what day it is.'

'Oh, really,' says Rosalind. 'I used to be highly strung as a child.'

'And what happened?' He is laughing again. 'I've never seen you out of sorts.'

'I gave it up. You can't be highly strung if no one takes any notice. You can only be highly strung if there's an audience.

'I see.' He is suddenly pensive. 'Anyway, Rosalind, your house is immaculate, and I think you're a very kind girl.'

'Thank you.' She refills his cup of tea, wondering how he will manage to balance the cup and saucer while keeping one hand up her camisole. He does so very well. Perhaps, she thinks, he knows a lot of women and handles them all, assessing their value and their virtues.

'Do you know a lot of people, Ben?' It is the first time she has ever used his name. It is a secret form of undetected shyness, this lack of facility with people's Christian names. 'Ben?' She is holding out the silver bowl of sugar. It does not match the teapot and is in a much later style, somewhat Adam in influence but definitely Edwardian. The hallmark, London 1909, is clearly marked on the side where the spoon rests. The spoon is only silver plate but is Victorian, a respectable collectors' item with an acorn finial. Without the acorn it would be nothing. It is a day for detail.

'I know quite a lot of people, Rosalind.' He is proceeding with caution, and declines the sugar. The first cup of tea was a mistake, thinks Rosalind. It must have been James who liked his tea sugared.

'Do you know many women?'

'Quite a lot,' he says, and as she wonders how many of them could be compared with the roses on her hand-painted tray the telephone rings.

'Just excuse me for a moment,' says Rosalind, and suddenly the hand has gone, enabling her to walk without hindrance out into the entrance hall.

'Hello? Mrs Wentworth?' It is the jeweller up on the main road. His shop is small and plain, and she has latched on to him as a worthy recipient of her jewellery repairs. This seems a suitable telephone call to interrupt the millionaire, so she leaves him for a minute or two alone in the parlour with the rose tray and the pale blue, valuable willow pattern china while she talks to the jeweller about her turquoise necklace.

'How very kind of you to ring,' she says.

'Not at all. I thought you might want the necklace by this Friday, but it won't be ready till next Friday. A shame for you to drive all the way up to the shop and get a carpark and then find it isn't done.'

'How good of you to tell me.' She thinks the jeweller is a kind man and has given her the benefit of imagining that she is still driving her car. It, actually, nearly ran out of petrol two weeks ago, and she has not bought any more. The car remains in its shed, and Rosalind walks or catches the bus most places. 'Please don't worry about it, Mr Gray.' The jeweller's name has suddenly come into her mind. Rosalind is not good with names. Even her own escapes her sometimes since the arrival of the postcard and the parcel and the telephone calls from James in the middle of the night. Her sleep, never reliable, is not resumed, and Rosalind arises at dawn not knowing her own name but remembers, always, the name of the cat. *Mr Gray,* she thinks now and imagines that it is a suitable name to use on that day. 'You see far too much in black and white,' Roger used to say. 'Life is not made up, Rosie, of clearcut issues most of the time. Much of life is a grey area.'

'It was just Mr Gray, that jeweller up on the main road,' she tells Benjamin when she returns to the parlour and the teatray. 'More tea?' She waits, almost like a geisha now. 'He's fixing up my turquoise necklace. The catch broke, but he doesn't have to restring the whole thing. Isn't that lucky?' She is thinking of the expense.

'Nice for you,' he says, 'to get your beads back sooner than you thought.' He is smiling, and she suddenly thinks that he may wish to please her.

'Oddly enough,' says Rosalind, 'the job will take longer. Mr Gray's waiting till he gets part of a catch in, secondhand, on some other piece of jewellery, so that will make it cheaper for me. But I must wait.' Like a true geisha now, she nearly bows before his approval.

'No need to waste money,' he says, watching the cat run across the patio chasing a leaf that has fallen off the 'Peace' rose. Three buds, placed perfectly on that bush, await heat from the sun or prompting from nature to open fully. Neat as miniature, furled umbrellas, they await the final push.

'Rosalind, you're a beautiful woman.' The millionaire speaks. He, too, is neatly furled, on a blue velvet chair. They have known each other for years. She has seen him through the big stockmarket crash and other related, smaller financial falls that followed, the bankruptcy of his cousin Leonard who was something big in textiles, the insolvency of his Uncle Fred who was more into car parts and tyres, the divorce from Sybil, his subsequent meeting with the woman who later went to live with him, the bankruptcy of the business next door to his own, the final failure of the firm on the other side. He has been for years surrounded by doom and business disasters and she has heard it all. The hand is back on her left breast.

'Your tea.' She hands him the pretty cup and offers shortbread. He seems to consider this, as if it may be a speculation. 'It's homemade,' says Rosalind. 'I made it myself yesterday.'

'Too rich for me, Rosalind,' — he watches his weight — 'but thank you. You're a kind girl. I don't know what I'd do if I didn't have you to talk to.' She feels the approval again, sees the smile.

They continue to talk of money, and the hand remains under the camisole. It is eloquent, she thinks, that she has left it there, but he is probably thinking about money and has forgotten all about the hand.

'. . . and the whole empire suddenly went bust,' he is saying now, 'absolutely overnight. It was the fault of the Japs. The blame for it can be laid squarely at their door. The Japs pulled out overnight and by morning everyone was ruined. House for sale, auction notices everywhere, the receiver called in by lunch-time — that bastard Finnigan. You know him, Rosalind.'

'Do I?'

'Everyone knows that bastard Finnigan.'

'Does he deal with ordinary people?' She is thinking about her last bank statement, which showed her transactions to be completely overdrawn. The situation was due to a fault in her own arithmetic and also a bank error. But it was alarming, nevertheless. 'If an ordinary person, say, got overdrawn at the bank, would this Finnigan get on to them?'

'Oh, God, no. Finnigan's in the big time. Finnigan's called in when the carcasses really stink and this one's a stinker.'

'Just excuse me for a moment.' She goes to the chiffonier and places her bank statement in the drawer. He seems hardly to notice her brief departure, and his hand returns to her breast when she sits down again.

'You've got a very lithe and sinuous walk, Rosalind.' So he had noticed she had gone. 'Their bubble just burst,' he is saying now, so they are back on the latest bankruptcy.

'My bubble's burst,' says Rosalind.

'Don't be silly, Rosalind. Now, what was I saying —'

'It's true. My bubble's burst.'

'Rubbish, Rosalind. You haven't got a mortgage. You get a bit of income from here and there. You've got no worries. You're a very lovely woman.' The hand tightens. Rosalind arches her back, a little.

'I'm not all right. I've been crunched by the interest rates. I get so little in interest now that I can't draw any till every third month. This means my income's cut effectively to one-third.' He is a businessman, would probably like to have things explained succinctly. 'Four years ago the banks were paying more than twice what they're paying now to people like me, people living on trust funds.' In the catechism of her own disaster, she knew the facts as well as he knew his own dealings. The terminology of calamity, well known from her conversations with him, sprang easily. 'I need cash in hand. I can't pay the gas bill, or the electricity.' The cat is running round the patio unaware of the stillness within the cottage. A light breeze must have sprung up in the last half hour, ruffling the blue salvias, rippling over the lawn, rattling spiny branches of the bougainvillaea against the roof of the garden shed. 'I feel very exposed,' says Rosalind. 'I'm frightened.'

The hand is still on her breast, but feels cool now, her own rose unassailed. The day is suddenly chilly.

'You're a lovely woman, Rosalind. I don't know what you're worrying about all this for.'

'You could have me, Ben,' says Rosalind, thrashing his name again. 'You'd have to pay, of course.' They might be discussing the price of a Windsor chair or a mule chest, thinks Rosalind.

He bought well at the better antique sales and hinted delicately at possessing a Georgian drop-leaf dining-table that could seat eight without effort, a set of Sheraton chairs, a corner cupboard of museum standard, cases of Rockingham in rose pompadour (her own had been cobalt blue), a Napoleonic sleigh bed. All in storage since the divorce from Sybil. But he likes buying things, and says so.

'How much, Rosalind?' His laughter, spontaneous and ebullient, is seldom heard. The mirth, if it exists at all, is silent and economical. 'So, you're going on the game, are you, Rosalind? Ha, ha, ha.' This laughter is unusual. He deals in bankrupt stock during the day and at night merely smiles a little.

'Only as far as you're concerned,' says Rosalind.

'Ha, ha, ha.' The cat is staring in the french doors, attracted by the noise.

'Five hundred dollars would be a useful sum,' says Rosalind.

'Indeed it would, my dear. We could all do with five hundred dollars from time to time. Tax free.' So his mind is meticulously on the dollars, she thinks. Everything has been summed up. 'Ha, ha, ha.' There is the laughter again.

'More tea? Shortbread?' He removes his hand from her camisole and takes a biscuit instead.

'Perhaps you can tempt me after all, Rosalind.'

'I think not.' Her own words fall now with a mirthless clarity learned from him on other occasions.

'This tea tastes different today, Rosalind. What brand is it?' He is fussy about food. Everything must be the best. Once she gave him a sandwich made with a slice of homemade meatloaf in the middle, and he said, 'Rosalind? What is this? What is this meat? What have you done to this meat, Rosalind? Half sausage meat and half mince? In a loaf?' And she had taken it away, as though it were in disgrace, and threw it all out on to the lawn. 'This tea tastes different,' he says today.

Woolworths's own brand, she thinks. In a plain packet.

'I've just forgotten, Ben. I think it might be something new I'm trying.'

'The other's better,' he says. 'You can't go past Twinings. You can't better it, Rosalind. You always must have the best.'

'Thank you,' she says, 'I'll remember that, Benjamin.' There is his full name now, as big as a slap.

'I think your telephone's ringing again, Rosalind. You seem to be in demand today.'

'I don't think I'm in demand at all,' says Rosalind, but she answers the telephone.

'Hello? Hello? Is that Mrs Rosalind Wentworth?' The voice is elderly, masculine and emphysemic.

'I think it is,' says Rosalind. She is beginning to feel very tired.

'This is Eaglinton Baker speaking,' says the caller. 'I don't know if you'll remember me.' Rosalind doesn't. 'We met last year at that annual general meeting, do you remember? I sat beside you during the chairman's report to the shareholders, and he said we weren't getting a dividend.'

'Oh, yes,' says Rosalind. 'I remember that very well.'

'And I told you about my grandfather, W.G. Baker.' He waits. 'The well-known artist.' He waits again. 'One of his pictures fetched a world record price last week, did you see that in the paper?'

'I did,' says Rosalind, though she hadn't as she no longer dared to spend money on newspapers. 'Of course I remember you now.' She places one hand over the telephone's receiver. 'It's just someone I know,' she calls down the hall to Benjamin. 'A grandson of W.G. Baker. One of his pictures has just fetched a world record price.' She has innocently recast the truth.

'I think I went to sleep during that meeting,' says Eaglinton Baker when she returns to the telephone.

'Not at all,' says Rosalind. *You're a kind girl,* the millionaire has said many times over the years. *Golden-hearted.* Like a tart. 'I don't remember that.' But she does. She remembers the even breathing, slight snores, the sudden awakening.

'Oh, dear.' He had roused himself during the scraping of chairs that announced the end of the chairman's speech. There had been no applause. 'Did I drop off for a minute?'

'Not at all,' Rosalind had said.

'I feel sure you're misleading me, my dear,' the old man said, and when the meeting ended he held out his arm to her with a gallantry she had not seen for a long time, and they went into the supper room together.

'Champagne?' said the old man with pride as if the party was his own. 'A cracker? Some caviare?'

'I've spent the past ten months researching my grandfather's life,' says Eaglinton Baker now, 'and I've run across some very interesting facts and figures. I feel sure you'd find it fascinating.'

'Yes, indeed,' says Rosalind. The millionaire is walking round the parlour now. His footsteps are clearly audible because of the wooden floor. The Persian rugs are scanty and do not cover a wide area. She hears the door of the big bookcase open. He will be examining the first editions, she thinks. Perhaps some of them could be sold. What a good idea.

'Perhaps I could meet you at the annual general meeting again, Mrs Wentworth.' Eaglinton Baker goes on talking. 'I don't know if they'll pay a dividend this year, but the supper's worth having, though last year I noticed they'd cut the vol-au-vents. They usually have very nice vol-au-vents. I'll wait by the main doors and we could go into the meeting together, and while we're having supper afterwards I can show you some of this material about my grandfather.'

'Very well,' says Rosalind. 'It's a date then.' She returns to the parlour. 'Sorry to keep you waiting.' The books are slightly disarranged, she notices. 'I was just talking for a moment to someone I know — Baker, the painter's grandson. They seem to be a very interesting family.' The word *grandson* introduces a juvenility to it all, the hint of a middle-aged yachtsman or a man aged fifty who still drives in rallies.

'Do you go out with him, Rosalind?' The millionaire is watchful now.

'I don't know what to say,' says Rosalind. Well, she doesn't.

'I see.'

'I'm very interested in art, Ben. You know that. He's a grandson of quite a remarkable figure in the art world. It gives one an interesting insight.'

'I take your point, Rosalind.' There is a lengthy pause. 'Has he got many of the old boy's pictures? Is there much family stuff?'

'He's got eight very large canvases,' says Rosalind, 'all beautifully framed and presented. He's had them all professionally documented.'

'I see.' The millionaire is repeating himself now. 'So you've seen all this.'

'And what are your interests?' the old man had said last year as they took their third glass of champagne from the waiter's tray. 'They're keeping the bottles out of sight, do you notice that?'

'Sometimes I don't think I've got any interests,' Rosalind said, and the old man, gallant again, said, 'Oh, come now, come now. . .'

'I like anything beautiful. I like music and I like paintings, art —'

He had interrupted then.

'Paintings? You like paintings? Let me show you some pictures of mine,' and he had fumbled in his wallet for photographs. 'I've just had these taken for insurance purposes.'

'But don't you think you should be careful. I could be a robber.'

'Ha, ha, ha.' The world was full, she thought now, of men who went *ha, ha, ha* at her. 'With that face? I feel sure you're a very good-hearted girl.' So she took the photographs of his art collection, saw the sweep of landscape, the glimmer of mountains held in gilded frames.

'How very beautiful.'

'Yes indeed, my dear. Perhaps I could tell you about my grandfather sometime?'

'Perhaps,' Rosalind had said. That was nearly a year ago.

'You've got one or two nice little pictures yourself, Rosalind,' says the tea-drinker now.

'Are they worth anything to you?' Her sharpness is shocking, she thinks. 'I know what they're worth, but are they charming enough for you to buy?'

'Well — ho, hum. Their charm is the way you arrange them. Roberta's hopeless at anything in the house.' But his face lights up. She notices that. 'The whole place is like a barnyard. She doesn't take any interest. That's why I've left everything in storage.' But he seems cheerful and smiles while he says this. 'There's her career to think of,' he says. 'It takes a lot of her time.'

'Being a law clerk?'

'They're not called that now.'

'But that's what they are.'

'She could be a lawyer if she wanted to,' he says.

'But she isn't one.'

'She can do a lot of the work,' he says.

'But she isn't one.' There is a long silence after that.

The clock in the hall shivers out the chime for four-thirty.

'That needs an overhaul,' he says still clasping the pale blue willow pattern cup and saucer with one hand and her left breast with the other. 'It doesn't pay to let these things go. It's quite a valuable timepiece, Rosalind. They don't come two a penny, you know, not these days.'

'Would you like to buy it?'

'Rosalind, I've got enough clocks, and they're all in storage.'

'Sorry.' She waits for a moment. 'I had the little clock on the mantelpiece overhauled.' She is as cold and precise as the hall clock should be. 'It cost sixty-five dollars. I thought I'd leave the other clock for a while.'

'Sixty-five dollars,' he says. 'Dirt cheap, it sounds like a steal. Jump at it.'

The sky has become overcast in the past half hour. There is a hint of rain in the air. There have been electrical storms in the night lately, thunder booming through the small hours to rattle all the necklaces in the drawers and make the old clock shiver. James has telephoned several times on these nights.

'Is it three in the morning where you are, Rosie? Oh, sorry. I suppose I've woken you up, have I? Never mind, you can go back to sleep again. Now I won't take no for an answer about Sydney. If you don't come you'll ruin all my plans. It's dovetailing very neatly. I must say that Lorraine and Margaret and Priscilla have been wonderful about it. There's only you, Rosie, being rotten —' She hangs up. The telephone has been removed from the trunk beside her bed and sits on the floor, a small but ultimate disgrace. It is shrouded in a white bath towel that has a medical look about it, like a towel in a hospital where small operations are done. The numbers on the telephone's dial look like arithmetic gone wrong.

'You're very quiet today, Rosalind,' says the millionaire.

'Am I?'

'You mustn't worry about your clock. You just need to look after things. We all have to keep an eye on things.' Yet again he peeks down her camisole.

Fifteen dollars, thinks Rosalind. A bargain.

'You've got lovely flesh tones, Rosalind, did anyone tell

you that? For a woman of your age you've got the tonings of someone only half as old.'

'If that were so,' Rosalind listens to herself rising to her own defence 'the person concerned would be hardly more than a child.'

'Ha, ha, ha.' The millionaire laughs out loud again, an unfamiliar abundance of sound, a generosity. 'Anyway, what was I talking about?'

Rosalind has forgotten.

'Finnigan,' he says. 'I was telling you about that bastard Finnigan.' So they talk about Finnigan, he with observed horror and relish, she with terrified anticipation.

'Do you think Finnigan might deal with me?' she asks. The room is very pretty with numerous small items, hallmarked, in silver. There is even a gold spoon somewhere. She suddenly thinks of that golden spoon and resolves to find it as soon as possible. Perhaps the golden spoon can be sold.

'Why would that bastard Finnigan know anything about you, Rosalind?' He laughs again. There is a lot of laughter this afternoon. He lolls back in his chair. 'These are very comfortable cushions, Rosalind.'

'I had them made out of an old Persian rug. It was too ragged to put on the floor. You could buy one or two of them, if you like. Or even several.' This last remark seems to turn it into a joke, because he laughs again.

As he goes up the hall to the front door, he admires the Baluchi rug in front of the umbrella stand.

'You can buy it, Benjamin.' Even to her own ears her voice sounds passably careless. 'I'm a bit tired of it.'

He stops walking immediately. A business deal might be in the offing, so she has his complete attention. He kicks the rug with one bronze toe.

'It's a bit worn. Quite a pleasant little rug, Rosalind, but it's absolutely gone, really. Look at the edges. It's lovely just there. Leave it where it is, it's your talent for arrangement that makes everything look nice. Now, that's a nice rug.' He points to an old Chinese rug that Roger died on. Its receipt of a body in the throes of a fatal heart attack has not dimmed its colours.

'You can buy it if you like,' she says again. 'It's a good size.' She does not say what for. 'The colours are pristine. You could have it for, say, a thousand dollars. Well, make it eight-fifty.'

'You're having your little jokes today, aren't you Rosalind?' He is making steadfastly for his red hatchback now and has taken a mobile phone out of his pocket. Already the aerial is up. 'Nice to see you looking so well and cheerful. You're a beautiful woman, Rosalind. Did I wish you a happy Christmas?' He has gone.

In the evening Rosalind dines with Dinah in a small Thai restaurant before going to a concert.

'It's Skriabin tonight, Rosalind. Isn't that exciting?' Dinah is eating her beef and cashew nuts slowly but with great enjoyment. 'What's your lamb like, Rosalind? I never have lamb, but it's usually the cheapest thing on the menu.'

'It's okay,' says Rosalind.

'I must try it sometime. I'm looking forward to the Skriabin, aren't you Rosalind?'

'No,' says Rosalind. 'Skriabin always sounds to me like people worried to death having all their nerves torn out by the roots.'

'Oh, Rosalind.' Dinah takes a few mouthfuls of the beef. 'This is delicious. Anyway, what have you been doing today?'

'I applied for a job.'

'Did you, Rosie?' Dinah's fork remains poised over the plate for a moment. 'What sort of job, and did you get it?'

'I applied for a job as a tart, and I didn't get it.'

'Rosie, I'm going to tell you something. Now this is quite off-the-cuff and I mention it only socially.' Dinah is a psychiatrist. 'You have this tendency to kid people all the time. Now, I've known you for years and I don't take any notice. I know you wouldn't have applied for any such job, Rosalind, so it's no use trying these things out on me. Now? Are you going to talk to me properly or not?' There is a long silence. 'Well, we'll talk about the Skriabin then,' says Dinah. 'It's a very unusual programme and contains a work never performed before.'

'Right,' says Rosalind.

Thus ends her first attempt to find a job.

She said 'Right,' when Benjamin had finished his cup of tea between Christmas and New Year and, spying the unopened parcel, held it out to her.

'Rosalind,' — he always called her by her full name — 'Rosalind, do you know you've got a parcel here that you've forgotten?'

'I haven't forgotten it, thank you. I've just left it for the moment.'

'You're a funny girl, aren't you, Rosalind.' He was putting the package down again on the hall table.

'Right,' she had said.

'I don't know how you could leave a parcel like that, Rosalind.' He shook it gently. 'It feels like a book.'

'It does, doesn't it?'

'And you're not going to see what it is?'

'No, Benjamin.' Another slap, if he only knew it.

'You really are the funniest girl, Rosalind.'

'Right.'

'I'm really glad, anyway, that you had a nice Christmas, Rosalind.' He has imagined this, she thinks.

'Right. Thank you, Ben.'

4

ON CHRISTMAS MORNING she had regarded the parcel again with a practised prudence now. Perhaps things had not been going well and James was marshalling the forces at his disposal to recoup lost ground. Jealousy, curiosity, mastery, acquisition and advantage: he used all those.

'I've sent a parcel to Rosalind,' he might have said to Priscilla. 'You remember Rosalind? You used to talk to her on the telephone. I thought it was time I sent old Rosie something for Christmas.' Then he would watch Priscilla bridle.

'Here's a parcel for Priscilla,' she had said herself before she left London. Perhaps Priscilla was a person who prompted the giving of gifts, she thought now with James's own gift in her hands. 'You could give this to, um, Priscilla, if you thought it was appropriate.' She held out the wide flat parcel to James. 'She's been quite kind to me.'

'What's this? A parcel? For me?' He turned round from his desk and she saw she had gauged the time accurately. It was exactly a quarter past eleven in the morning, and he always stopped then to have a glass of wine. 'Something from the Tate for me?'

'It's for Priscilla.' She stood in front of him with her black trenchcoat on, a red scarf and beret in her hand. She hoped these carmine garments might act as a small defiance for the weather. The early forecasts definitely promised snow by mid-afternoon.

'Priscilla? What are you giving presents to Priscilla for? I didn't know you even knew Priscilla.'

'I don't know Priscilla, but I often talk to her on the telephone.'

'I didn't know that. You never told me that. How do you know Priscilla's number?'

The day had grown suddenly darker, the chimney-pots

of the houses over the road disappeared into the gloom. Standing there, like a girl on the mat in the headmaster's study, she thought it might not be possible after all to walk to Muswell Hill and see other people happily shopping or talking to each other in teashops. The weather, like everything else, might be closing in.

'You still haven't told me how you know Priscilla.'

'It's quite simple, James. Sometimes Priscilla rings up from where she lives in the country, since she ran away with that man you told me about, that Cruikshank or whatever his name was —'

'Oh, that's all broken up now. We've got that all sorted out.' Avuncular and smiling, he went out to the wine rack in the kitchen, still holding Priscilla's parcel. 'What a kind girl you are, Rosie. We must get you a nice little glass of wine, mustn't we, darling? What do you feel like having? Would you like me to open another Sancerre?' He was pleased with the parcel, she thought. Delighted she had sent something to Priscilla.

'I'm going out for a walk. I'm just on my way. I won't stop.'

'Nonsense.' He clasped her right buttock through the coat. 'I insist you stay, darling, I insist.' He was drawing the cork carefully from the wine now. 'I'm very intrigued you've got to know Priscilla. Friendly little thing, aren't you? Get on all right, do you, you two girls?'

'Priscilla,' she said, 'is not a girl, and nor am I. We're a long way from being girls.'

'You're all girls to me, darling, and here's to your very good health.' He raised his glass to her. 'Next time I go down to Wiltshire to see Priscilla I'll take this with me. What is it, by the way, a piece of cardboard?'

She waited till he stopped laughing.

'It's a picture, James, a print. It's something by one of the Pre-Raphaelites. Nymphs cavorting in a forest with a satyr or a shepherd, I forget which.' A melancholy and suitable gift.

'I'll look forward to seeing it. And you still haven't really told me why you're giving Priscilla a present and how you know her so well.'

From out on the landing she heard the lift doors close behind someone. Perhaps lucky Mavis was going to the shops with her shopping trundler for a tin of sardines and the smallest loaf of bread.

'Priscilla just rings up for you sometimes, and if you aren't here I answer the telephone and talk to people. There's a man called Robert Something who rings sometimes from Eaton Square. He's something to do with publishing, and I just tell him you're away in Wiltshire and you'll be back again on Monday.'

'Oh, God,' said James. 'You've been talking to Lawford.'

'Yes,' she said, 'that's his name. Old Bobbity Lawford.'

'Old Bobbity? Do you mean to say you call him Bobbity?'

'You know how I always call people nicknames, James. He's all right, isn't he, old Bobbity?'

'Oh, God. How do you get talking to them all, Rosalind? I thought I'd switched everything over to the answerphone.'

'You had, James. You do. But it gets very quiet here sometimes, and lonely, so I just turn the telephone back to being ordinary again. It's really quite all right, James. I don't mind answering the telephone.'

'Oh, God,' said James. 'And you've been talking to Priscilla. How did you get talking to her.'

'I just chatter away to people, James. I tell them to ring back when you're here.'

'Hello?' she had said, careful as a valet the first time the telephone rang. The day was wild and empty, and James had left early in the morning. She watched his white Peugeot slide away through showers of drenching rain. 'Hello?' The voice she heard was clear and nasal, resonating slightly in the bridge of a distant, and female, nose.

'Who the hell are you? I want James.'

'James isn't here. He's gone away.'

'I know he's gone away. He's coming to see me and he hasn't arrived.'

'He left about an hour ago. It was raining.'

'I see.' The woman thought for a moment. 'And who are you?'

'I'm Rosalind.'

'But I thought he hadn't seen you for years. I thought he had dinner with you once in a some God-awful place and never saw you again.'

'He's a bloody liar,' she had said. 'And who are you?'

'I'm Priscilla.'

'He told me he didn't have anything to do with you any more. He said he hadn't seen you for months and months. He told me you'd gone off with someone called Cruikshank, some name like that. He said it was all over.'

'Isn't he a bloody liar?' said Priscilla. 'So, you're in London. So James has brought you to London. Well, well, well.'

'He said he was lonely.'

'Well, well,' said Priscilla again. 'James doesn't change, does he?'

Rosalind had listened to the lengthening silence.

'Hello?' she said. 'Hello? Are you still there?'

'And it was *Crookbain*,' said Priscilla at last, 'with a double *o*, not Cruikshank or Ramsbottom.'

'I don't think I said Ramsbottom, did I?'

'No, but he told somebody else Ramsbottom,' said Priscilla. 'How like James. He told the bank manager it was Ramsbottom.'

'He told me he was getting old and just wanted a quiet life.'

A gust of noise came from the telephone receiver. Priscilla's hysterical laughter was drowned out by the barking of a dog, and she shouted, 'Down, Ollie, down.' Presently she returned to Rosalind and the telephone. 'So he's back on that old chestnut again, is he? Well, I've just about had enough of James. I've got smoked salmon for his lunch, but I'm going to tell him I haven't been able to get anything ready, and he'll have to take me over to the pub for something. And how are you getting on, anyway?' The voice showed signs of thawing.

'I'm all right,' she had said. 'But I can't seem to find things I need. I want to go right into the city, as far as the Thames. I want to go to the Tate Gallery, and I can't find the tube station to catch the train.'

'Hasn't James told you?'

'He says he never catches the train. He says he hasn't been

on the tube since he was four years old and he doesn't know anything about it.'

'Oh, isn't he a bastard?' Priscilla's tone was fervent. 'Haven't you asked anyone else?'

'I don't know anyone who can help. I asked the only other person I know, an old colonel, but he only takes taxis. I asked an old Irish lady sitting on the seat by the bus stop, and she said she didn't know. She only catches buses. That's what she said. And I asked a man in the lift one day, and he said he couldn't talk to me because of how it would look if his wife saw —'

'Oh, for heaven's sake.' She could imagine Priscilla's narrow, arched, little nose and the air fairly seemed to whistle through it that day. 'The English are bloody mad, my dear, you'll have to learn that. Just go down the High Road and walk along to the left till you're nearly under that overbridge thing at the bottom of the hill. If you cross over with the lights there, you'll be in front of a big artificial hill that's all paved with orange bricks. The tube station's behind there.'

'Thank you, Priscilla.'

'Not at all, Rosalind.' So they had rung off, almost conspirators, she and Priscilla. The telephone rang again immediately.

'And while I'm about it,' said Priscilla from Wiltshire, 'if you want a good drycleaners go to that one in the High Road with the big red sign. It's run by Cypriots, and if the girl's there she hardly speaks a word of English. I don't know how they manage, I don't really, but just point out any marks to her and make sure she understands. Don't go to that place over the other side of the road. It looks better but it's very expensive and they're no good.'

'Thank you, um, Priscilla.' There was that difficulty again with saying names.

'And if you get sick of him shouting at you, there's a nice little off-licence just a block away. The man there opens a new French wine to taste every day. Go in there and say you want to taste something, and have a glass of wine at someone else's expense. Tell him you want to let it develop on your palate. Don't be intimidated and don't buy anything, do you hear?'

'All right.'

'I think the man's called Harold. Something like that. I always call him Harold, anyway.'

'Thank you.'

'And there's quite a nice little teashop in Muswell Hill – it's the one with the green gingham tablecloths. They make very good homemade bread. Sometimes you feel like having a nice piece of bread and butter, don't you, at James's place? He hates bread, won't have it in the house, but I suppose you've noticed that?'

'Yes,' She listened to that dog barking in the background again, far away in Wiltshire. 'Have you got a dog? James said you had a cat. He seems to really miss your cat.'

'James misses poor old Rags? But James always said he hated Rags. James loathed Rags.'

'Oh, no. He loved Rags. He's always going on about how he misses seeing Rags sitting on his desk and how, when he steps in the front door, he thinks he sees Rags waiting for him by the bookcase, and when he looks again the cat's not there.' She listened to that barking, and the high-pitched whistle of air coming through those little nostrils. 'He really seems to have liked your cat.'

'Good God,' said Priscilla. 'Now I've heard everything.'

'He seems to be really sorry you took the cat. He says he might go to the RSPCA and get another one.'

'I don't know,' said Priscilla. 'I don't, really. Anyway, I've got a dog now too. Ollie came with the house. My aunt left me the house, and her dog – so there you are. That's how I got the dog and that's how I came here to live. I'd better go, though. He might be here any minute, unless he's stopped to telephone Phyllis. Has he told you about the fat and lovely Phyllis? My dear, you do have a treat in store.' So they had rung off after that first conversation.

'How often do you talk to Priscilla?' he asked that day, later.

'Lots of times, I suppose. We just talk about ordinary things like the best drycleaner, and I told her about the Gainsborough portrait of Giovanna Baccelli at the Tate. She's going to see it when she comes to London.' That was a mistake.

'Is she coming back?' He suddenly sat up very straight. 'Is Priscilla coming back?'

'Just for the day — when all the sales are on.'

'Oh.' He sat back again.

'She wants a new umbrella,' she had said, 'and a few other things, but she's waiting for the sales.'

'And when', he asked, cunning as a spider, 'do the sales start, did Priscilla say?'

'You'll have to ask her that yourself, won't you, James?' She was beginning to learn, then, about their games and when it was best to play or withdraw.

'If you're determined to go for another silly walk you'd better go, hadn't you, nuisance.' He had turned away now to his work at the desk. 'It's getting late, and I can see mud on your coat.'

The shops down the High Road held a vaunting abundance of holly and Christmas decorations. It was late November and the festive season was starting. She stared at her own reflection in the window of the drycleaners, wondering about the mud on her clothes.

'If he gets into one of those picky moods,' Priscilla had said, 'you know how he picks and picks at you, well, don't take any notice. Just go away and read a book or something. Or go down and see old Harold and drink a glass of wine.'

It was only just midday, but the rain had made everything dark. She set off for Harold's shop, two blocks down the street.

'Good afternoon, Harold.'

'Good afternoon, madam.' He knew her by sight then, knew her quite well.

'What have you got open today, Harold?'

'Same as yesterday.'

So she went over to the marble bench with its stone sink, took a glass from the shelf and poured some Sancerre. Harold was replenishing the shelves, walking along with half-a-dozen bottles of wine in his arms like a sheaf of wheat, placing a bottle here and there in the empty spaces. He was, she thought, like a gardener going about his little plot to place an extra plant of some reliable and stalwart annual in blank spaces in a flower bed.

The Sancerre was golden with promise and lay in her glass like a jewelled recollection of a distant summer, and she thought then of the previous year in her own golden garden around the big house, and wished she had said when she had first set eyes on James, 'I think you might be trespassing, mightn't you?' in that polite, shy way she had had then. 'Perhaps I could show you the way out. The gate is this way. This is private property.'

'Is this a good year?' she said to Harold, holding up the glass.

'So-so' said Harold. 'The year before was better.' He was rustling round behind the counter now like an old mouse amongst the boxes. 'The vintage from this year's no good at all, madam. The rains came too early and then there was blight.'

'I seem to recall that, Harold.' Blight was known already.

'Don't buy this year, madam. Don't touch it.'

'Thank you, Harold.' She took another mouthful of the Sancerre and felt it begin to grip her stomach. 'Have you had many customers today, Harold?'

'So-so.' He waggled one hand back and forth. Perhaps, she thought, he was fond of saying 'so-so'. Outside the road was black with sleet, and the cars had banked up for five blocks as far as the roundabout. 'The weather's too bad to bring them out.'

'And this year's not a good year?' I am babbling, she thought, turning into a woman who talks too much, and in wine shops too.

'Not a good year at all, madam.'

'I'll remember that, thank you. I don't find, myself, that it's a very good year. In fact I think it's one of the worst years I've ever had.'

'Perhaps next year might be better.'

'Perhaps,' she said and went out into that dim and bitter street with all its traffic. The winter chill had come down suddenly in the last few days. Earlier there had still been the idea of a lovely spell, the air faintly misty with a promise of an Indian summer, like this year at the cottage when the blue salvias grew higher than Rosalind's head, when the little cat slept in a bed of dried bougainvillaea flowers beside the mint as another more tranquil Christmas approached. The silence now was glorious.

On Christmas morning the lane had been perfectly quiet. A torpor fell on the neighbourhood, which had never fully recovered from the noisy excesses of the general election back in November. Then large women drove up and down the maze of narrow roads while men with megaphones shouted happy political messages from the back seats of cars that matched their parties in colour. They wore bright clothes and smiled a lot as if the area was populated with simpletons.

After the election a silence, like that following a war, fell on the lanes, except in the evenings when people from the council houses at the bottom of the hill played cricket in the street. They used a board taken from a fence to be the bat and had a lump of newspaper tied with string for a ball and they asked anyone who passed to play. Their laughter, always from a distance, had given an atmosphere of harmony everywhere, and it was into another day of this luxuriant and honeyed hush that Rosalind stepped on Christmas morning to water the rose garden.

Even James with his parcel and his card and his telephone calls had failed to ruin the stillness completely.

'Isn't it lucky, Rosie, Priscilla keeps going out so here I am agai—' She hung up, looking at the clock. Three in the morning on Christmas Day. Sleep was fitful after that.

The parcel had now been lying on the hall table for three days, its line of stamps chosen to attract her attention, like bunting. There were nine of them in a brilliant series of values and colours. Virulent emerald green, blood red, bishop's purple, sallow yellow like bile from an upset stomach, garter blue, they insinuated themselves across saffron paper.

'Do you mean to say you haven't even opened my parcel?' There was that cutting edge to James's voice again, and her hand was already moving to replace the receiver on the

cradle. 'I don't know how you could leave a parcel like that.'
'Quite easily, James.'
'I went to all that trouble. What is the use, Rosie? What is the use? You haven't even read the letter. You're mad, Rosie. You're rotten — ' She had hung up again.
'What do you want for Christmas, Rosalind?' Dinah had asked. 'Give me some hints.'
'I like soap, Dinah. Any nice soap.' So she could lie in the bath washing away this recurrence of the idea of James.
'I don't understand you, Rosalind.' But there was no malice in Dinah. She was laughing like an old girl. 'When there are so many interesting things in the shops, why do you want soap?'
'Soap', said Rosalind, 'is wonderful.'
'I don't understand you, Rosalind,' James used to say, 'I don't understand what you're looking for in life.'
'*Tendresse*,' she had said. Outside darkness was falling on the High Road again, even though it was not long after three in the afternoon. It was too late to go out, away from James, for a walk. 'What I'm looking for is *tendresse*, James. I want something better.'
'Torn dress? I never tore anyone's dress. I've never torn anyone's dress in my life, Rosie. You girls don't even have to take your dresses off for me, Rosie, you know that. Shame,' he said, 'you don't like all that lovely stuff. Won't even let me give you lessons, naughty, boring girl. It's so much better than the other dull, old things. Yum, yum.'
'I've made some French onion soup, James.' Her sudden practice of self-effacement and changes in conversational subject might lead, she hoped, to survival of some sort.
'You've made some French onion soup.' James sighed and put his head in his hands. 'Oh, Priscilla, why did you have to go away and leave me?'
'Do you want some soup for dinner, James? Later on?'
'Do I want some French onion soup for dinner?'
'Yes, James.'
'You're a very boring person, Rosamund. Now Priscilla, she's a very naughty little thing. Priscilla just loves having me for afternoon tea or dinner. Sure I can't tempt you?'

'Yes, James, but do you want some soup?' By now she had her hand on the front door and it was half open. From under Mavis's front door came a line of light — the bulb on the landing had gone again — and a faint sound of enviable singing and sweeping. Mavis was doing a few chores.

'Go away, Rosie, I might hit you.'

'What's going on out here?' The front door opposite opened, and Mavis stepped out on to the landing. Her green locknit housecoat and satin slippers matched impeccably and she carried a small broom. 'Did I hear shouting again?'

'Oh, God,' said James, 'not that old troll,' and Rosalind felt his hand on her shoulder, pushing her out of the door. It slammed, the decisive sound echoing down five floors of the stairwell and back again. 'Oh, Priscilla, why did you have to go away and leave me?' Rosalind heard his voice, muffled by the wine racks in the hall and the dog-leg bend just outside the bathroom. He was going back to his desk, she thought, and the sitting-room with her empty chair and the merciful absence of any intrusion she might make.

'Hello,' she said to Mavis in the murk of the landing. Someone had tipped over the potted plant by the lift doors again.

'Hello, dearie,' said Mavis. 'Been shouting at you again, has he?'

From right down the bottom of the stairs came the sound of dragging footsteps, a slow and shuffling walk. The porter was down in the entrance foyer doing some cleaning. Faint and far away came the sound of water and stealthy noises. Perhaps, thought Rosalind, he was doing some mopping with someone's severed head on the end of a stake.

'He's got a very short wick,' said Rosalind, and wondered if this was a suitable term to use, for James. 'I mean, he gets tetchy.'

'I found a girl out here once,' — Mavis was not to be stopped — 'a black girl, told me she was a nurse. I found her out here ever so upset. She'd no shoes, dear, or anything, and he'd been shouting at her. I heard him through the wall. Had a very pretty satin dress on. Pink. Quite a pretty girl, if you like them like that. If you see what I mean, dear.'

Rosalind said she did.

'I called her a mini-cab. Off she went. No shoes or nothing. She came back the next day and gave me the money I lent her. She'd no purse with her. Left it all behind I suppose.' Mavis looked watchful. 'Would you like me to call you a mini-cab, dear?'

'I don't think so,' said Rosalind. 'I think I'll just go for a bit of a walk round the block and come back.'

They regarded each other carefully in the gloom.

'You're not the first, dear, and you won't be the last,' said Mavis. 'Sure I can't get you a mini-cab, dear?'

There was no gloom on Christmas Day. It was bright and sunny and beautiful. There was no sound of slamming doors, nobody in a green dressing-gown appeared as Rosalind stepped out of her own door, past the parcel, just after the sun rose. The flowers on the pink and white daisies were freshly open, and one damask bloom glimmered on a 'Josephine Bruce' rose beside the steps that led to the lawn. Bushes of Victorian salvias tossed up improbably blue spires of flowers as bright as the sky promised to be.

As she mixed liquid fertiliser in the watering-can, the first of the bees began to blunder into bushes of red geraniums. The Queen Anne's lace was going to seed, but the yellowing staffs that held the flower heads were unbowed and presented upright fingers to the wide, clear sky. There was colour everywhere to reflect the enrichment of James's vivid stamps. The garden, too, had readied itself in preparation for the arrival of the parcel, she thought. The water from the hose soaked into the soil immediately when she turned the sprinkler on, just as people who live without love or compliments might absorb unexpected admiration from a stranger.

'Hello! Hello!' James had called the day she heard his voice in her garden and stepped outside to see who was there. 'They told me down there' — and he nodded his head towards the old cricket ground in the park below — 'that a lady lived here all by herself.' He made it sound like a greeting for a beauty.

The telephone began to ring that day, and when she had

found it was a wrong number she went back over the old quarry tiles to find James leaning against the french doors.

'Lovely place you've got here,' he said. 'I used to be an architect.'

But today, Christmas Day, someone else owned those french doors with their jemmy marks and new panes to replace those broken by the burglars. The french doors at the back of the cottage were small and worn by weather, undistinguished.

There was no figure, either, lounging in the doorway, but the telephone was ringing just as it had done that day a long time ago when James appeared in the other garden. This time it was Dinah.

'Merry Christmas, Rosalind. You're up early.'

'I'm watering the garden.' She let one of her pauses blossom then. 'I'm watering my garden and my roses.' Thus she stated her boundaries and territories clearly in preparation for the opening of the parcel. Perhaps tomorrow, she thought. Or next week. Or next year. The parcel might never be opened. 'The old pink rose out the back's covered in flowers.'

'It will be till June.' Dinah was an expert on gardening. 'July if you're lucky.'

'Let's hope I'm lucky then,' said Rosalind. This small conversation was the first one in which she had spoken with any pleasure that day. Upon these sincere and guileless remarks the quandaries of Christmas began.

'Have you got any nice presents, Rosalind?' Dinah had always been cheerful and loved gifts. When they were both in primer one she said, 'If you'll just stop crying, you silly little girl, I'll give you a nice biscuit from my lunch. What's your name, cry baby?'

'I got a book from America and a tartan scarf from my aunt and I got your nice soap, thank you.' She waited. 'And there's another parcel from England, but I haven't opened it yet. I think it might be another book, but I'm not sure.'

'I know what you could do, Rosie,' James had said in London. 'You could write a book, a real book — not all that poetry and stuff you waste time on. There's no money in that, Rosie, none at all. Everything about you needs to be more gaudy. If you wrote something really gaudy, something disgusting, if you wrote something filthy you could make a fortune. You've got some brains, haven't you?' She had said nothing, and he tapped on her forehead with the knuckle of one finger. 'Knock, knock, anyone home? Got a few brains, have you? Well?'

'The trouble is' — and she spoke very slowly — 'that I don't seem to think like that. When there was a murder round the corner once, when some man stabbed someone on the pavement, I thought it was cochineal — the blood. I thought someone had dropped their shopping from the supermarket. I don't seem to have a mind that thinks of —' and she stopped there. Thinks of what? 'Thinks of evil,' she said at last, and knew that was not quite right. Outrage, she thought hours later, long after James had gone out somewhere. That would be a better word. Hurtfulness. Bane. Peccancy. All of those could have been used, and she thought of them as, towards midnight, with the light from the bedroom blazing out on to that London balcony, she began to pack. The clothes that had taken her through Cape Town and Johannesburg were neatly folded in creases that had been there for a fortnight. It was only two weeks since they had flown from all that heat to the chill of London, she and James, and he had said, 'What I really need is a good nubile girl of twenty-one, not any older than that. You don't do a thing for me, Rosie. But if we make an effort we might be able to get through the next two weeks.' The bookings could not be changed.

'I'll go to a hotel, James. I'd rather do that.'

'Don't be ridiculous, Rosamund. Don't be stupid. You can knock about the place, make yourself useful doing this and that. And I've got your tickets anyway,' he patted his pocket, 'and your passport. You can't go anywhere without those.'

'My tickets and my passport are in my bag, James. I put them there myself.'

'No, they aren't any more, Rosie. When you went up the aisle to get a drink of water I thought I'd better mind them for you.'

The air hostess came along then with a trolley of drinks,

and James said, 'Darling? Would you like a glass of champagne? Darling?' She had turned away by then, and when the hostess handed her the glass she saw in the girl's eyes that she thought them a wonderful couple, so handsome and well presented, James so punctilious and courteous about looking after her.

'Give me my things.'

'No, darling.' James wore a feral grin. 'Haven't I ever told you the funny story about the time I took away all someone's clothes so they couldn't leave? Silly girl didn't know when she was having a good time.'

He watched the hostess as she walked up the aisle.

'What a lovely bum,' he said. 'I'd like to slip one up there.'

'You could probably do quite well there,' Rosalind had said. 'If you tried. She seemed to like you.' By then she knew him so well.

'We know each other so well,' Dinah sometimes used to say in small cafés when they dined before concerts. 'We can sit here, and we've known each other so long that there's a lot we don't need to say or explain.'

'Yes.'

'You're very quiet tonight, Rosalind. Very monosyllabic. Not like you.'

'I'm just a bit worried, Dinah, about this and that. I'm just a bit tired.'

'I saw a job advertised in the paper this morning.' Dinah is proceeding with caution. 'You mentioned something about a job when I saw you last. I know you don't speak Mandarin, but one of the schools wanted a Mandarin speaker for two hours a day, just for translations. If you spoke Mandarin, wouldn't it be a wonderful job, Rosalind?'

'It would, but I don't speak Mandarin.'

'I'll keep watching out, Rosalind. I'll let you know if I hear of anything.'

'Thank you, Dinah.'

'Do you want to have some of my wine?' Dinah has bought a half-bottle of claret.

'I don't think so. I think I'll just have a glass of water.'

'The trouble with you', James had said in London, 'is that

you drink too quickly. You should savour each sip, Rosamund.'

'Rosalind,' she had said. 'And I'm not merely drinking. I'm seeking swift anaesthesia. A bang on the head would do just as well,' but by then he would be on the telephone again saying, 'Priscilla? Darling? Guess who this is? Yes, of course she's still here, but the nuisance is going home soon.'

'Priscilla thinks you sound a nice girl,' he used to say. 'Of course, she's furious you're here. Priscilla's got a very jealous nature, suffers from the green-eyed monster quite a lot, does Priscilla. I've told her you're going home at the end of the week. But she thinks you sound a nice girl.' He went away, humming a little tune, into the kitchen. 'I must give you something nice to drink before dinner, darling. I'll open a bottle of that French stuff you liked last week. Would that be nice?' He was oddly pleased, in a gleeful mood, as if she had done a difficult task and must be well rewarded. 'Tell me where you went on your walk today, darling. Did you go to the Tate again?' And she had sat there, in the chair in the farthest corner, knowing that all the pieces of her puzzlement were fitting together admirably.

'Cough, cough, cough.' He returned with the glass of wine. 'Drink this and stop coughing. If you'd only stay indoors you wouldn't catch cold. Come on, Rosie. Drink up.'

'Come on,' he had said. 'Live a little, Rosie. Come to Africa with me. Meet me in Johannesburg on the fourteenth. And come back to London with me after that. Won't it be fun, Rosie?' and it had rung in her ears, joyfully, like the sound of bells over the telephone. 'You're so lovely.'

'You sound so close, James. Isn't the telephone a wonderful thing? I wonder what people did when the telephone hadn't been invented.'

Now silence merely seemed like glorious solitude, loneliness like space, isolation a curious benediction by absence of violence and cruelty, grief a sad kind of joy.

'I suppose you learned a lot in Africa,' people sometimes said.

'Yes?' Her voice had become so quiet and dry it concerned her.

'You wouldn't like to come and be our monthly speaker, would you? Give us a little address? About your travels?'

'No, thank you.' Rosalind the bait. What could be said about that?

'Thank you for giving me my things back, James,' she had said as she left London. She held her passport and tickets carefully in a hand that trembled a little, but no one had noticed that. 'Don't bother to come to the airport. I can manage perfectly, thank you.' She shook his hand like an old maid at a tea party. 'You've taught me a lot. Thank you, James'. When he looked at her as if she might be mad she said, 'Well, James, you've taught me how to eat artichokes, haven't you? And how to open giant prawns,' and went away across the landing to the lift laughing and coughing at the same time — an eerie Rosalind who frightened even herself by seeming to be two people at the same time. There was calm Rosalind who knew the way to the tube station for the train to King's Cross. And at King's Cross she would find the airport shuttle and the shuttle would take her, eventually, to the plane and the plane would, eventually again, take her home. There was that Rosalind. There was also another Rosalind who coughed and walked and held the suitcase only by an effort of will, an ill Rosalind with a pain in her chest. Another person who thought she might not make it on foot even as far as the High Road. Rosalind ailing. Rosalind stricken. Rosalind at the very beginning of her inexorable and inevitable journey to the lost lanes.

'Goodbye,' she said, and pressed the lift button marked *Down*.

5

THE SILENCE IN the neighbourhood was profound, as though everyone was actively quiet in unison. This idea gave a solidity to the peace, and even the distant motorway provided only a swishing sound like that made by dolphins in a silver sea. Kind people with clean bright faces might be driving along in limousines to deliver parcels containing *objets d'art*, she thought, and knew immediately this was ridiculous. Her thorough and imaginary clean-up of her own small world could not extend everywhere. The sound was probably made by stolen cars, fuelled with siphoned petrol, hastening into hiding with booty from a night of crime. The robbers and plunderers were decently taking cover for the day, unlike James who remained undeterred, unchastened and very much out in the open.

'What sort of area do you live in now?' he had asked on the telephone. 'I mean, you are comfortable, aren't you, Rosie?' It might have been sweet to think this question pertained to herself, yet his known self-interest made it an inaccurate notion, a ludicrous absurdity. Already his hand might be on the black notebook to find the telephone number of someone else.

'It's a very quaint place, James, if you like that sort of thing.' He did not. She knew that. James liked large swathes of luxuriant lawn mowed by someone else. He liked to have the best of everything. 'It's slightly sinister, the police patrol round the lanes all the time looking for people breaking into houses. Someone was disembowelled a while ago.'

'Disembowelled? How do you mean disembowelled, Rosalind?' So he really did know her proper name, she thought.

'It was just a crime of passion,' she said. 'It was nothing. The area's very up and down.' Next door to the place where the woman had been murdered a Rolls Royce had suddenly appeared in the last few days, a Christmas purchase by a young stockbroker on the way up. In-depth articles in the newspapers claimed the area was being gentrified, but she did not tell James that. 'Definitely up and down would be the best way to describe where I live, James.' Her laughter echoed oddly on the line, the resonances of long distance multiplying it into weighty mirth. He would think it was hilly, she thought.

'I'm not good on hills, Rosie. You know that.' The clamour of her laughter echoed again. 'We're none of us getting any younger. Just wait a moment, will you?' There were distant footsteps, on parquet again, and they clattered faintly in her ear while she assessed the distance of the walk. Only a few steps, she thought. It was the flat in London where the tiny sitting-room had a wooden floor. Priscilla's house in Wiltshire sounded larger.

'Are you in London, James? Have you gone back to London from Wiltshire?'

'I wanted to check my answerphone. I got your message, by the way.' But he sounded abstracted. 'Hang on a minute, will you, Rosie? Don't hang up.' There were those footsteps again and she wondered which of James's women it was.

It might be Priscilla herself as he seemed to have got her back more or less permanently, in an impermanent way.

'You've done one or two good little jobs for me, Rosie,' he had said as she left London the year before last. 'I mean, for one thing, Priscilla's come to heel very nicely. Gave her a fright, your being here.'

It might even be Phyllis. The whole business of buying out James's share in the country house could have fallen through. She might have come to London to buy mixing bowls or diverse herbs for the tender and exotic dishes she beguiled James with.

'She's a wonderful cook,' James said once. 'And she's got a great big — well, never mind. Don't shrug like that, Rosie. It doesn't suit you.'

'Jamie? Jamiekins?' Phyllis had once come through on the carphone when he pressed the wrong button during a journey to Oxford.

'You can make yourself useful,' James had said back in London a couple of hours before. 'Throw a coat on and you can come with me and navigate, and you can see a bit of the countryside, Rosie. Hurry up.' She had sat with the map on her knees and watched the snow close in. 'Gawd,' said James. 'Look at that.' They passed another burnt-out pantechnicon. The motorway out of London was littered with pile-ups. 'I'll see if I can get a weather forecast from somewhere,' and she saw that hand in its pigskin glove dart out to the wrong button on the dashboard.

'Jamie? Jamiekins? Is that you, dwarling?' It was then they heard that gustful and tremolo voice. It possessed a richly juvenile vibrato that was at once saddening and ridiculous. 'Guess what I've got for your dinnydins? Daddy's sent you a lovely salmon from Scotland.'

'We'll just get rid of that mess.' James's hand darted forward again and cut her off. 'Now what I want is the radio. Let's find the radio, Rosie. Can you turn the radio on and find me a weather forecast, no you can't' — there was not even a gap for breath — 'because you're hopeless at finding things and even more hopeless with machinery, not that a radio's machinery, but Rosie thinks it is, doesn't she? Here we are now. James has done it all himself.'

Miles up the road, when the snow was even thicker, he said, 'I suppose I'd better stop somewhere and get you some lunch, Rosie, hadn't I? What do you think you'd like?' One of James's apologies.

'Not fish,' she said, thinking of Phyllis and the salmon.

The footsteps on the parquet sounded too dainty for Phyllis, thought Rosalind.

'Somebody's at the door,' said a woman 12,000 miles away in London. 'Somebody's asking for you, James.'

'Well, tell them to go away. Can't you see I'm busy?' Rosalind sat down on the floor and the cat climbed on to her knee. James's temper was horrible, even from a distance.

'But they particularly want you, James. It's a parcel and you have to sign for it.'

'Take the parcel and sign for it yourself. Tell them I'm out. Do anything. Just deal with it.'

'You've got a new girl,' she said when he returned to the telephone. The voice had not been familiar.

'No, I haven't.'

'Yes, you have, James. You've had her for about a week and you're getting sick of her. She weighs about sixty kilos and you've been shouting at her and you've made her cry.'

There was a silence and she could imagine how he would lift his pen and poise it over her name in his notebook, how he would make preliminary little flourishes of his wrist prior to crossing her off the list. Silent and discomforting Rosalind. Rosalind who had packed and left. Subversive Rosalind who had possessed the passivity of a prisoner sitting out a sentence, and had gone when it was over.

'You're bored, James.' His silence was daunting. 'And she might be a nurse. You've got a taste for nurses. Priscilla told me.' It was the authority of the uniform, she thought, that attracted him and the fob watch that dangled on each medical chest like an extra magnetic miniature bosom with seventeen jewels. 'And she could be black.'

'I love black women,' he had said once when they were dining in a little Greek restaurant over in Camden Town. 'When they open their mouths their tongues are so pink. All their mucous membranes are so pink.' He was gazing now at a black woman eating olives and salami, which was very red as if to nourish the obscure pockets of her rich flesh. 'I love black women. You're so bloody pallid.'

Outside, the streets were thick with greasy rain that night and a promise of fog for tomorrow. She pushed aside her plate of calamari then because everything about the dish reminded her of bodies — of nostrils and parts of the inner ear and other things which, as her politeness and reticence was a recognised and mocked excess, she did not even care to think about. As she did so he began ravenously to attack his Dover sole. It lay flat on its back, lightly sauced, on a bed of shredded ginger.

'What are you going to do tomorrow?' he asked when he had consumed the upper side and was taking out the backbone. 'More walks?' She thought his eyes on the black woman opposite were speculative. Perhaps he might send her a note, she thought, or get the waiter to arrange a meeting somehow.

'Women are an illness with you, James,' she said.

'You've lost me, darling.' He spoke with such rich concern and glorious affection that she suddenly did not doubt that he would send the black woman a note with his telephone number, his unctuous attention to herself merely a smokescreen now to hide proclivities. 'I thought you were saying you were going out tomorrow on a very long walk all day.'

She did not answer. Perhaps he had sent her a note already, she thought, that woman who was dining across the other side of the tiny room with a man who looked like her grandfather.

'I'm going to start packing tomorrow,' she said when he had finished the sole, every mouthful fuelled by his unobstructed view of the black woman. The main course had passed in virtual silence.

'Packing? There's no need to start packing yet, darling, not till next week. You could stay longer. You could be a nuisance longer. What will I do when you aren't cluttering up the place, getting in my way? Stay a bit longer, Rosalind.' But he was still looking at the black woman eating her salami and olives with black bread and cottage cheese.

'What for, James?' But that remark was lost in a clatter of dishes as a waiter dropped a tray, and James leaned forward with a card in his hand and said to the woman dining with the old man, 'I couldn't help overhearing about your holiday in Athens. Perhaps I could give you the number of my travel agent for your next trip.' And the woman put the card in her handbag with such a practised twist of her wrist that Rosalind suddenly thought that she must be a tart, dining with an old and less active client, to get everything put away so swiftly.

'The poor girl has no conversation,' she said now on the telephone and continued to listen to the profundity of his silence, 'and you don't know how to get rid of her. It's like that time you met the black woman in that Greek restaurant in Camden Town and she made a nuisance of herself for days.'

'Oh,' said James, 'so you remember that, do you? You could've got rid of her yourself. Priscilla chucked her out in the end. Priscilla's got a lot of go.'

'She certainly has.' She could imagine how the air would have whistled through Priscilla's thin nostrils that day.

'Priscilla's furious you're here,' he used to say. 'I mean, she's not furious with you. How could you know anything about it? She's furious with me.' But he seemed pleased with that, delighted with his mischief, full of the idea of using her to entice Priscilla back to London.

Having a lovely time, she used to print carefully on postcards in the evening while James talked on the telephone. *The pictures in the Tate are wonderful. I particularly like the gallery with all the Gainsboroughs. I had dinner last night in a lovely little restaurant in Camden Town. They specialise in calamari. Love from Rosalind.* Then she used to drink, in one large gulp, the glass of wine James had already poured, her ferocious intent to insulate herself from all barbs and anguish taken care of in that one swift and practised movement.

'You drink too much, Rosie,' James said.

'I'll stop as soon as I get home. I agree with you.'

'If you agree with me so much, why go home? Why not stay?' He seemed reluctant to let her go. Like an impresario he wanted the whole orchestra, the complete gamut of music and discord of all kinds, was reluctant even to allow the smallest flute, the most insignificant piccolo to depart.

The parcel sitting on the hall table was as telling as the tap of a conductor's baton at the beginning of a major orchestral work, she thought. Soon James would start the concert, and they would all be expected to play. Lorraine with her infinity of pubic hair on a large pelvis could be, say, a mythical cello. Margaret in Adelaide, the university lecturer with thick and mobile lips, might do for a trumpet, Priscilla in Wiltshire could be allocated star billing in the major movement of a concerto and Rosalind herself, the court fool and jester, must skip, whistle and shake a tambourine. The lovely Phyllis, large and magnificent and still perhaps loitering in James's house on the Welsh border, could bang a large drum from time to time.

'I don't want to see you, James,' she had said on the telephone.

'Rosalind, you're not going to spoil everything, are you? You're a rotten little cow. I've got it all worked out.'

'I'm sure you have, James, but I'm staying home.' She waited for a moment. 'Thank you.' That *politesse* again, she thought, as much a physical disadvantage as a withered foot or an ear not exactly formed. She hung up. The stillness at the other end of the line was as absolute as that in her garden on the morning of Christmas Day, the parcel still unopened and possessing the bright and alluring streak of those excessive stamps.

As she took her first step up the hall, past the portraits and the remnants of the Rockingham, there was a fusilade of barking from the hounds of the lost lane. Her front windows provided a brief view of policemen, with tracker dogs straining at leashes, making their way towards the rough fall of land behind the grey house. Two squad cars followed, and the cavalcade disappeared behind a grove of scrubby trees where the body of an old lady wearing a pink nightie had been discovered a week and a half before James's parcel came. She had wandered away from a home for the infirm and died quietly, without a protest or contradiction that anyone in the street heard, under the tallest and greenest of the saplings. The local dogs followed this silent passage of invaders, their baying fading away into the gully.

In the morning the newspaper, which Rosalind bought as a treat, provided the story of a video shop heist only three blocks away. The robbers, wearing balaclavas and black raincoats, had held up the owner with sawn-off shotguns and then made off in a stolen car with $50,000. The car itself, a red Toyota of recent make and good appearance, had been stolen three days before from a suburb near Dinah's place. There, life was usually respectable and quiet with ladies whose husbands loved them, or at least bought them reasonably valuable presents to hide their lack of affection, and who drove smart red cars with sheepskin upholstery and a racing stripe, in black, down the sides. In such a car the robbers had made their getaway and abandoned it not half a dozen paces from Rosalind's rose garden. The story gave specific details, so Rosalind, newspaper in hand, wandered down to the bottom of her section and slipped through the hedge. On the road were chalked marks in a rectangle, and she supposed these showed the exact position of the car for the police photographer.

As for the robbers, the story said their scent had been lost in the trees on the edge of the gully, and Rosalind thought they must merely have gone home. In the infestation of little cottages and houses in varying stages of dereliction, they could probably be found now sitting on the sofa watching television and eating baked beans while they lay low for a few days.

The lanes held many secrets, including why the old lady had wished to wait for death under a tree and why Rosalind lived there in a cottage with a green roof, did not open parcels or letters that came in the mail sometimes, and bought a newspaper only occasionally. She did not doubt that her own disturbance over the arrival of James had filtered out and affected those as far from original innocence as she was. The police said the car must have been hidden somewhere in the intervening days between its theft and use as a getaway, but a hundred cars could be hidden in the anonymity of the area's pathways. These also gave shelter to thieves, scatterlings of all kinds who fled from debt, failure or their own stupidity, and innocents whose brains were seamed with betrayal by those who professed false love. In such a place, one car and a few robbers could disappear in an instant.

'Where do you live now, Rosalind?' people sometimes asked.

'Not in a place that's very easy to describe,' she would say. 'It's difficult to say how to get there.' The road to it, she thought now, had been puzzling and saddening.

'Where do you think you're going in life, Rosie?' James had asked. 'I just can't believe anyone could possibly get to your age and be so innocent.'

'Oh, yes, James? And what age is that? And how innocent

is that?' And she had set off, coughing and with that pain in her chest, on a journey across the world again, to her burgled house and the sharp assessing glances of the land agents who came to price it the day she came out of hospital. She was ready to go, she thought. Fit enough to leave. Wanted to leave it behind. At bay and gone to ground like an animal that is sick, she lived now amongst the fleet of foot, the sleight of hand and those who were suddenly richer by $50,000.

6

ON THE DAY the three buds on 'Peace' opened, Rosalind also began to open the parcel. It was some time in the hiatus between Christmas and New Year, after Benjamin's visit. Shops were still closed, houses shut up while people were away on holiday. The day was very hot and still, and early in the afternoon the silence in the limpid lanes became profound. Everyone had gone away, Rosalind thought, or had gone to sleep or died, and in this deathly hush she began to unwrap the gift.

The paper was yellow, a jaundiced shade, and had been measured to fit the contents perfectly. There were faint pencil lines to guide James's scissors. The pieces of Sellotape were all exactly parallel and the same length. She pulled them off the paper and placed them in the wastepaper bin, side by side. It was like a surgical operation and must follow established procedure to avoid septicaemia of the spirit and haemorrhage of honour. It was, she thought, a beautiful little parcel, and wondered why James had taken such care. Perhaps Priscilla had gone off again with Crookbain and all the others on a holiday somewhere.

'Isn't James a bastard?' Priscilla had snorted into the telephone the year of the dreadful winter. 'Fancy telling you I'd gone off with someone and he never saw me. It was just a holiday. Several of us went. I mean we had to have at least six to pay for the house, and we were only away a fortnight. Cruikshank? Gone off with someone called Cruikshank? I think he must have meant Crookbain — that's Crookbain with a double *o*. He's my accountant, and his wife came too, and her mother. Her mother's Amelia Lyons, the concert pianist, or she was. She's nearly eighty. Oh, isn't James terrible?'

Perhaps, thought Rosalind now, Priscilla had gone away to the same cottage in the Loire Valley and James had begun to speak again in his glittering vernacular of deceit, illusion and fabulous forgery to gild her absence.

'I could kill James,' Priscilla had said, and there had been more snorting. Her nostrils sounded very fine and thin that day.

The parcel contained three things. There was a card in a large white envelope with a deckled flap, a letter written on pale blue paper (fountain pen, not biro) and a book.

She explored the card first. The envelope that held it was of the finest quality, watermarked, and bore a large sticker of Santa Claus pointing over his left shoulder as though showing the way to all luxuries, charms, indulgences and carousals. Santa Claus the tempter. Her name, with embellishments, was written across the envelope. *The Lady Rosalind*. Inscribed by the master of cajolery. Nothing James did was without meaning, so she clattered up through the cottage to find the magnifying glass. The sticker of Father Christmas was not a sticker at all. The glass showed that James must have sat at his desk far above the High Road with his scissors and he had cut out a little picture from some old Christmas paper or a card from a season long gone, and he had glued it on the envelope. His care had been meticulous and dedicated, she thought, and wondered about the reason for this.

Alone in her cottage on that hot and sunny afternoon, she thought Priscilla might have gone away on holiday for four weeks this time. Perhaps she had gone as far as Italy. Perhaps she had fallen in love with Crookbain, with his double *o* and possibly much else, and they had run away together notwithstanding his wife and her mother, the concert pianist.

The flap of the envelope had been sealed with a kiss. James had been busy with his fountain pen again, and a cross had been drawn across the seal, yet another little task after the embellished script of her name. *The Lady Rosalind*. Perhaps, she thought, James only ever wanted what he could not have. Anything she did, therefore, would have been a mistake. If she had said, 'This is private property. The gate is this way,' when she first met him that would have been an equal, if different, error from the one committed. He might have sent flowers, posted cards written in that exquisite script and she would have smiled as women do when they think somebody likes them. 'I found a very handsome man in my garden one day,' she might have said to her friends, 'and he keeps sending me things. Look what he's sent me now.' That would have been as much a waste as when she actually journeyed out into James's territory and thus ensured her own castigation by contempt. The difference between the errors was like that between physiotherapy and actual surgery. Both were painful and expensive and took a lot of time.

Far away, down the valley behind the cottage, someone had started up a motor mower. The ebb and flow of that distant and pleasant sound was like the throbbing of blood in her ears. But even that agreeable noise, almost hypnotic in its regularity, presaged the death of grass, she thought. And the distant swish of traffic on the motorway might also reinforce rigor mortis and destruction as vehicles bore down on the already bleaching corpses of hedgehogs flattened earlier. All pleasantries seemed to hide abominations of some kind. *The Lady Rosalind*. What idea of gain or conscience had provoked that?

'Over the weekend I've been talking to Priscilla about you,' James had said. 'Priscilla doesn't think you should get spoilt while you're here.'

'Oh yes, James?' It was odd, she thought, that much of the dialogue of tawdriness was heralded by the words *I see, Ha, ha, ha* and *Oh*. Like little bricks they shielded their deliverers from shots that November.

'Yes, actually Priscilla thinks I should make it quite plain to you that the kitchen's mine. I don't want you in the kitchen, Rosie. You're so clumsy.' And she was, she thought. Sadness had made her ungainly as she turned away from mayhem and walked into doors or stoves. 'When I get up in the morning, Rosie, the kitchen's all mine. As long as you understand that. The kitchen, and the bathroom as well.'

'If you give me my things I'll go to a hotel, James.'

'Don't be so silly, Rosie. Why go to all that expense? Just as long as you understand the kitchen's mine till I don't want it any more. That seems reasonable enough. You can go in then and get yourself an apple or whatever you want to eat.'

There was silence then.

'Priscilla thinks it sounds very reasonable.'

'Oh yes, James?' There was another of those *ohs* again, she had thought.

The envelope was sealed at the back so she inserted a knife to lift it cleanly, shattering the drawn kiss. Only James could master glue so well.

'And have you been using my glue?' he used to say. 'I've told you not to touch anything on my desk. Someone's touched the glue and it wasn't me. Look at this, Rosie, the top's off.'

'I did use your glue earlier.' By that time the brother had rung twice from Hereford and the letter had come from Phyllis, or Félice as she was correctly called, and there was an obscure pleasure in copping the flak. And there were only three days to get through till she went home.

'How long ago was that? How long has the top been off my glue? I'll have to throw the whole thing away.' The pot hit the wastepaper bin. It might have been the head of a small child or a dog that had misbehaved. 'What time was it?'

'I didn't look at my watch.'

'You didn't look at your watch?'

'No, I didn't look at my watch. Where I come from, if we find the lid off the glue we just calmly screw it back on again, particularly just paste like that stuff, and we don't look at the time when we use glue because the time's of no importance.'

He opened his wallet and crammed some coins from it into her hand.

'Just go away, Rosie. Get out. Go to the stationer's and buy yourself some glue. Just don't touch my glue.'

She turned before she went out the front door, putting the money on the bookcase.

'James? I forgot to put the lid on the glue because I was listening to a bird singing in that tree outside. Birds don't seem to sing very much in London,' she said, but by now James was talking to someone on the telephone, perhaps

Priscilla. 'I wanted to hear the song of the bird,' she said, and went out on to that barren landing, where the linoleum was the colour of liver, to wait for the lift.

That evening she sat in the blue chair in the farthest corner of James's little sitting-room and wrote a few last postcards to her friends. James, she thought, had taught her well in the arts of rearrangement of simple truths, obfuscation and vanishing. Her postcards were exemplary examples of this:

By the time you get this, I'll be home again, but it is not such a silly action as it would seem. Probably I'll be very busy for the first few weeks and might not get in touch for a while, so this will reassure you that all is well. I went to the Tate again today to say goodbye to the Gainsborough portrait on this card. It is my favourite, but I think the dancing girl on it has such sad eyes. London has become very cold, but it is winter now.

With such messages she hoped to buy herself a little respite from their curiosity, time to fluff up her hair from the lankness of infelicity and wash melancholy away.

Inside the envelope that had been sealed with a kiss was a Christmas card of extreme refinement. Rosalind, with the card in her hand, went out of the back doors, across the little sunlit yard and sat on the steps leading to the lawn. The cat came from its nest under the bougainvillaea to sit beside her, sniffing the card. Then it looked away. Beyond the steps the roses were in full bloom and rampant salvias threw themselves over the grass in a form of horticultural kindness, like a loving arm over that little shoulder of land. It was an affectionate landscape, she thought, a place in which it might be possible to be lost gracefully for ever.

On the front of the card was a picture of a banquet being prepared in a baronial hall. Vassals, all of whom looked happy and unmenaced, were hastening about with dishes of food that included pheasants served splendidly with all their feathers intact. Everyone looked serene. Nobody was anxious or afraid. A little dog, a King Charles spaniel, sat at the foot of a throne awaiting its master. The master's velvet cloak, a tasteful beige, lay thrown over a wooden seat. A happy old man was leaning on the throne mixing what looked like fruit salad in a big glass bowl. Both items were unprocurable in mediaeval times thought Rosalind, but the festive season brought on incongruous behaviour in nearly everyone, including the characters on cards and the people who sent them. *To My Darling Rosalind, With Much Love From James*. That was the message inside, also in Gothic script (fountain pen).

She examined the picture again. No one was afraid of the master of that household. All the activity was caused by love, not fear. The dog sat beside the throne, the servants hurried around with logs for the fire, the suit of armour loomed over the scene from a dais and nothing attracted fear or horror from anyone.

In delicate shades of ochre, cinnamon, fawn and bronze with flashes of subdued scarlet, the little card flickered in her hands, promising charm and goodwill as fictitious as the scene. *To My Darling Rosalind*. James, she thought, was heading out of London for some reason, to distant theatres of mayhem, canard, cacophony and belittlement and was assembling his cast of bewildered players in which the court jester, or knave, recipient of all jibes and maledictions, was essential. *The Lady Rosalind*.

'You really don't have to go, Rosie.' They stood in that little dog-leg hall for a moment before she went out of his front door for the last time. 'It'll seem odd round here, Rosie, without you.' She waited, the suitcase in her hand and trying not to cough. 'I get a bit tetchy sometimes, but I've always been like that. Mother says I was like it as a child.' She waited for him to stop talking. 'I'm not malicious, Rosie. I have my explosions and they're over the next minute. I don't bear malice. I get it all off my chest and then it's over as far as I'm concerned. You could stay if you liked. I could get you a little desk. You could write your poems. I'd clear a space under the window for you, Rosie. No? No luck for James? No soup? No more of Rosie's soup for James?'

I must not cough, she had thought. The coughing was becoming a problem.

'Priscilla thinks you're a nice girl. I've shown her your

photograph, and she's taken quite a fancy to you, Rosie. Priscilla loves three in a bed. That's how she and madam up in the place in Hereford fell out. Got too friendly, naughty little things, and then fell out over me. Priscilla says that, if you stay, you can come down to Wiltshire at weekends instead of staying here by yourself. You'd be most welcome, Rosie. Don't fancy three in a bed? Won't stay?' Already she was turning away, towards the door. 'But Rosie, I'll be here all by myself if you go. I hate being by myself.'

Like a caliph with no courtiers to provide his image, he might, then, look in the mirror and see nothing, she thought, but that idea started her coughing again.

'Oh, God, Rosie, one thing I won't miss about you is that bloody coughing, but you've been quite useful to me in various ways. I can get my money out of the house in Hereford — madam's brother's going to buy me out so I'll leave her in peace. They've all gone religious up there. And Priscilla's in a happier frame of mind. Priscilla's much easier to get on with these days, Rosie, thanks to you.'

'Thanks to you.' The telephone had begun to ring in the cottage, so she went across the old bricks again to answer it. Possibly it might be Dinah wanting to say thank you for the Christmas present.

'Darling? Is that your pretty voice?' It was James again, and she wondered what threat of illness, death or litigation had provoked this sudden and unaccustomed fondness and attention. 'Darling, I haven't got much time. I've just slipped away for a moment.' The voice became a whisper. 'Priscilla's had someone here to dinner. They've gone upstairs for a moment. Have you read my letter yet?' It was in her hand, with the card.

'No.'

'I was sure you'd have read it by now.' There was that old impatience. 'So you won't know about my arrangements.'

'No.' She stood looking out at the garden. Later a bunch of those pink roses could be picked. And the garden seat needed staining again with teak oil.

'You don't even seem to be paying attention, Rosie. Will you please listen. I'm coming down your way and I want to get everything set up before I leave. The weather here's bloody awful and I've had a little windfall — dear old Mother. But never mind, she was very old, in a nursing home for years. One could hardly regret it at that age. But it means I can travel, so I'm setting off, Rosie, to see my —'

'Worldwide theatre,' said Rosalind.

'Worldwide theatre? Rosie, I don't understand what you're talking about. If it wasn't for your beautiful little untouched bum I'd be inclined to leave you out of my plans. If you'd just listen. I'm setting off to see the very few girlfriends I've got left. I've only got five now, no, I tell a lie. Four. Moira died last year. Cancer. It was terrible, Rosie, but I won't bore you with the details.

'She's got an identical twin, a lovely girl, but sadly I haven't been able to make contact with her. She lives on a farm up in Northumberland somewhere. Wrote to her asking if she wanted a rest from the ducks and cows and whatever. Thought she might like to come to London, but no answer. But never mind about all that, Rosie.' It seemed impossible to quench the spate. 'I'm spending the last fortnight in January in Adelaide with Margaret. She's another naughty little thing who likes three in a bed, but she's got a friend there who's a good little sport, so that's Australia under control. There's only you, Rosie, being rotten about it all. You're the fly in the ointment. You're only two miles from Lorraine's place, and if I could just get you two girls all set up —'

'Didn't you tell me once that Margaret's a university lecturer, James?' Tacking violently, like a yachtsman, away from the main course of conversation, she innocently struck blood.

'Did I tell you that, darling?' James's laughter was a fleeting beggary of sound. 'Well, she's a schoolteacher actually, but she's quite a clever girl. There again, she's not actually a girl, but she's kept her figure. Got big boobs, all that.' The silence lengthened. 'She's got holidays in January so she's free then.'

'I see.' There was another of those little conversational bricks to join all the other *Ohs* and *Ha, ha, has* and the *Well, wells*. 'What age children does she teach?' It was just idle talk, but there was blood again.

'They're not actually schoolchildren. Not yet. She teaches them before they go to school.'

'You mean kindergarten, James.'

'Something like that. I think it's called a nursery school. What are you laughing for, Rosie?'

'And what about Priscilla?' she said. 'I seem to recall you told me she was the headmistress of a girls' school.'

'They're taking boys now,' he said.

'And what age do they cater for?'

'Oh, you know, Rosie — look, of what interest is all this? I rang you to tell you about my arrangements. If you must know about Priscilla's school they take the three to five age group.'

'You mean that's a nursery school as well? And what about Félice and her career in hotel management?'

'Rosie, they aren't called waitresses any more. It's a very upmarket restaurant, and they're called epicurean executives. I gather Phyllis is superb at it. We're still good friends even though she's gone religious.'

Upon swathes of kindergarten teachers, juvenile of mind and accustomed to building towers of wooden blocks that were then knocked over into suspicious puddles, James must have descended like an untrained teddy bear. And waitresses.

'I don't know what you're screeching like that for, Rosie. It sounds terrible. I don't know how I'm going to put up with you, but I keep thinking about your bum, Rosie. It's so neat, and I've never known anyone with each buttock so separate, like two peaches. But it's lucky I've got Lorraine, she's a big girl, and I can divide my time between the two of you. Oh, hello, darling,' he said. There was the sound of a door opening and footsteps on parquet. 'Been upstairs, have you? Everything all right?' and he hung up in Rosalind's ear.

Out in the garden, beyond the shabby french doors, a golden fern flung up fronds so bright they seemed like a promise of virtue, and a yellow daisy had come into flower, the blooms spangling a shady corner like the bullion of an *ancien régime*.

'What is your garden like,' people sometimes said. 'It's all round the back, isn't it? All hidden? We've been past, but we couldn't see a thing.'

'My garden is wild,' Rosalind would say, 'and sweet and beautiful,' and she went out to it now, to the roses, and the rosemary and the rue and Queen Anne's lace and foxgloves rampant near the hedge.

In James's manipulation of named beads on his abacus she would be missing in her own piece of human subtraction, and the sound of this arithmetic echoing in her ears was like that made by the thrashing of a bitter harvest after a sad, bad summer. The rest of the parcel could wait for another day, and she went, instead, out to the flowers.

7

IN LONDON THERE were no plants. James's flat was devoid of growth, except for mould under the sink. The telephone there was the only horticultural item and it bloomed with spite and bad news, blossomed with contention. Far above the High Road, like an aerial deadly nightshade, it flowered with noise on the last Sunday she was there. It was late in the afternoon, nearly evening really, and the gloom had begun to descend. The Sunday traffic was not as heavy as usual. Snow had kept people off the roads. Over the road lights were on in the front rooms of three Victorian terrace houses. They sat oddly in that part of the street amongst the high-rise apartment blocks.

A straggling tree, embattled by constant wind around that corner, had strapped itself to one window cornice with ivy growing from a terracotta window-box. As Rosalind picked up the telephone, she saw a man in a dark suit walk across that bay window with a glass of something, wine perhaps, in his hand, and he was laughing. Happy. Perhaps those people were cooking dinner, the warm smell of roasted meat filtering through that little house. Upstairs a woman was combing her hair at a mirror in a bedroom window. Happy again.

'Hello?' said Rosalind, and it seemed like a sigh. There was silence. 'Hello?' James was away at Priscilla's place till Tuesday.

'Why don't you go away?' It was a man's voice. 'Why don't you take yourself off to where you come from? South Africa, isn't it? Well, go back there.'

'Have you, perhaps, got the wrong number?' Her politeness again, a bitter thing to bear.

'I don't know your name and I'm not interested in it, anyway. I'm Félice's brother, and I'm very concerned about her position in all this.'

'Félice? I feel sure you've got the wrong number.'

'I feel sure I haven't got the wrong number. I'm Félice's brother. My sister Félice lives with bloody James in that house of his in Hereford. Well, actually it isn't James's house. It's as much my sister's house as it is James's house, not to put too fine a point on it.'

'I see,' she had said. Another *I see*. 'You mean Phyllis.'

'Félice,' he said. 'My sister Félice.' There was a pause. 'I've got no axe to grind with you personally,' he said. 'I don't even know who you are, and I don't care.'

'No,' said Rosalind.

'I just want you out.' There was another pause. 'I've got my sister to think of.'

'Yes?'

'And her children.'

'Oh!' said Rosalind. 'Has she got some children?'

'By her previous marriage.' His voice grated over the line. 'The girl's very musical — plays the flute beautifully. We have hopes — well, never mind. The fact is that they're all so upset that it's even affecting the children. Now Natasha can't even do her music practice properly, and the boy's all upset. He didn't go to school two days this week, and his mother found him hiding in the attic. And it's all your fault. My sister came all the way down from Aberdeen, gave up all her friends and her family on this whim. We told her. I didn't mince my words, if I may say so. But she was set on it.' There was another lengthy silence. 'Her divorce came through three months ago and there's never been so much as a whisper of marriage. Her patience has run out,' he said, 'and I blame you entirely.'

'Marriage?' Rosalind was watching the man in the bay window. He had sat down in a blue armchair. The room looked pretty, filled with a soft light from lamps. The woman had come downstairs with her hair combed and was now lighting candles on the table. Definitely dinner, thought Rosalind. And probably delicious. Dinner, anyway.

'My sister understood that they just had this arrangement, as it were, till she was free to re-marry and then he'd do the decent. We are', said the man, 'a very religious family. My sister's very deeply disturbed at the moral and ethical implications of all this. And there's the effect on the children, as I said. They go', he said, 'to a cathedral school.'

Rosalind waited. There seemed to be nothing to say.

'Now, why don't you pack yourself up and go back to South Africa —'

'I don't come from South Africa.'

'I thought you came from Johannesburg. I was told you flew in here a fortnight ago from Johannesburg.'

'I did fly in from Johannesburg a fortnight ago, but I don't come from there. I come from' — and here she hesitated — 'somewhere else. And how have you found all this out?' The coldness her own voice could suddenly contain was a surprise.

'I'm a lawyer. We have our ways of finding things out. Now, lady —'

'My name is Rosalind.'

'Your name is of no interest to us. We just want you out. Not to put too fine a point on it again. I want to be reasonable, but you're in our way. We want you out. Nobody could say I'm not a reasonable man, but I've got my sister to consider. I've salvaged what I can for her from the marriage and it's all in the house in Hereford. I think myself, if I were to be asked, she'd have been better to stick to old Douglas, notwithstanding his manifold faults. He wasn't a bad fellow, not really. Drank a bit. Smoked a bit. Bit of a bore. Not much conversation. But, I mean, there he was.'

'Yes,' said Rosalind.

'And', he said, 'there you are, which brings me back to the point of this call. Please go away. I've got nothing against you, but my sister's very upset to find you're there, in James's flat, in her place.'

'I thought this was mostly Priscilla's place.'

'Priscilla? How does she come into it?' he asked. 'That was all washed up long ago. She went off with someone called Cricklebank or something. Some name like that. Her accountant, actually.'

'No, she didn't. She just went on a holiday with various people to share the cost of a cottage in the Loire Valley and they had to have at least six to make it economically viable. Her accountant went, and his wife, and her mother.' The silence was infinite. 'Her mother's a concert pianist, or she was. She's about eighty, I think, and her name's Something Lyons. I can't quite remember. I'm not good with names. But the accountant's name is Crookbain, with a double *o*. I do remember that.'

There was a hush that might have been daunting.

'Are you sure this is right? May I ask how you know all this?'

'I'm positive. I often talk to Priscilla on the telephone, and she told me herself. I've never met her, but we talk on the telephone. She lives in Wiltshire now because her aunt left her a cottage there, and a dog called Ollie —'

'Oh, for heaven's sake,' said the little man. She thought he would be a small man. He sounded small.

'— and she lives there, but James goes down every weekend to see her. He goes down on a Friday and comes back on Tuesday, sometimes Sunday till Wednesday. Depending.'

'Oh, God.'

'Regular as clockwork,' said Rosalind. From far away, from his end of the line, she heard the beginning of hysteria and lamentation.

'Oh, God,' he said. 'I'll have to go. It's my sister. She's very upset. I've managed to keep her quiet till now — oh, dear. Natasha, Natasha, come quickly. Oh, God. It's all your fault.' He hung up.

The telephone rang again immediately.

'I've been trying to get through to you for ages.' Priscilla's nasal voice was instantly recognisable. 'Whatever have you been doing, Rosalind? Can you give me your recipe for French onion soup? I'm bloody sick of James. All I ever hear from him, day in and day out, is how you cook soup and how you stay out of the way and don't bother him when he's working. Well, how can I help it if the dog barks and the telephone rings and my friends call in to see me? Is that my fault? If he says, "Oh, Rosalind, why aren't you here to make me some nice soup," again I'm going to go screaming mad, Rosalind, really I am.' The oration had ended. Rosalind listened to silence. Of course, she thought. In James's invented world of mirror images everything was duplicated elsewhere.

'Have you got any recipe books, Priscilla?' She spoke slowly, as if to a child who was not all there, or to herself.

'I've got a few, I think.' Priscilla didn't sound like much of a cook, thought Rosalind. 'My aunt had some. I think they're in the dresser drawer.'

'Have you ever made soup before?' Rosalind proceeded with caution.

'Mostly I just open a tin. I mean, I haven't got time, have I? I just whizz off to the supermarket and get things, but they haven't got onion soup in a tin, and I don't know what to do, Rosalind. They've got cock-a-leekie, but he doesn't fancy that, and oxtail, but he doesn't want that. All I hear all the time is, "Oh, Rosalind, why aren't you here to make me some French onion soup?" I'm brassed off, I can tell you.'

'Look, it's perfectly easy,' Rosalind had said. 'Just find any recipe, and I do mean any recipe, for onion soup in one of your aunt's books, there's sure to be one somewhere. Look it up in the index, and if you can't find anything ring me back and I'll tell you over the telephone how to make onion soup.' She waited. 'I'd put anything in his soup if I were you. The last lot I made I put some carrots in. I found a whole lot all withered in the vegetable basket.' She waited, standing on one leg like a disorganised heron in sudden embarrassment at this revelation of her own carefulness. 'So, strictly speaking' — and she wondered if this was a phrase that should ever be used for James and his ménage — 'it wasn't really onion soup at all. It was just sort of anything.'

'Aren't you bloody marvellous,' said Priscilla.

'I don't think so. James spends all his time here shouting, "Oh, Priscilla, why did you go away and leave me".'

'Does he?' She sounded pleased. 'Isn't James a bastard?'

'Isn't he.' They rang off and Priscilla rang back within a minute, the usual routine.

'I've decided to open the cock-a-leekie,' she said, 'and I'll mix it with the oxtail and put in some dried onion, and I'll just hope for the best. James is a bit much really. Has he really been saying, "Oh, Priscilla, why did you go away and leave me?" '

'Yes.'

'Isn't he awful?'

'Yes, isn't he awful.' Rosalind waited for a moment. 'Can I ask you something, Priscilla? Did you tell James I couldn't go in the kitchen? And the bathroom?'

'No.'

'I didn't think you did.'

'James can be awful if he wants to be.'

'I know.' Rosalind waited again. 'I got a phone call this evening from an awful man. He said he was Phyllis's brother' — it was difficult to know whether to call her Phyllis or Félice — 'and he was worried about her money. And she's not actually called Phyllis at all, she's called Félice.'

'What a mad name,' said Priscilla. 'And they're all Scots to the bone. What was the brother ringing you for? I never even knew she had a brother, the fat cow.'

'He's a lawyer, and he rang me to tell me to go away. He said I'm ruining things for his sister now she's got her divorce. It seems', said Rosalind, 'that she got a divorce from her husband who was called Douglas and he was quite hopeless but not such a bad chap, according to this brother, and she's been expecting to marry James. She owns half that house, according to this brother, and they're all so upset that the son went and hid in the attic for two days and the daughter can't play the flute.'

'And he rang you to tell you all that?' The air was whistling through Priscilla's narrow nostrils again. 'What a nerve some people do have. And fancy old Phyllis owning half that house. James didn't tell me that. He said it was his.'

'Yes,' said Rosalind and wondered how one small affirmative word could possibly sound like a stone. Over the road the couple was sitting at the candlelit table and had begun dinner. 'He told me' — and she spoke tentatively now, like a person who has just learned a new language — 'that you were a very high-ranking headmistress of a notable school.'

'He told me you were a world-famous novelist here to sign a film contract, under a *nom de plume*.' The shrieks of laughter started the dog barking. 'Down, Ollie, down. Down, I say.'

'Oh, God,' said Rosalind. 'I used to write poetry and it used to be in the odd magazine, just sometimes. Not often. But I haven't had anything published for a long time, for a couple of years. I mean, I know perfectly well my work isn't wanted any more. I've been told so very clearly.'

And she thought again of that last letter from her publisher.

Rosalind, your work in this day and age has missed the bus. 'The Rose', I am fully aware, attracted considerable literary attention a decade ago, but times have changed, Rosalind. There is no demand for this sort of thing today. 'The Geranium' is a spirited and talented work, but it has no application to today's world. What do you want us to do with it?

Please send it back to me, she wrote in reply, each word carefully formed in black ink on blanched paper, clear and sharp.

'Did that brother chappie really ring up to tell you to go away?' That was Priscilla again. 'Ollie, get into your basket like a good boy. Did he really tell you to go away?' She did not wait for an answer. 'You're going at the end of the week, anyway. What's he on about. And James is terrible. I could eat him alive.' Shrieking at the dog again, she rang off.

8

'I'VE BEEN THINKING about your cousin Mark,' says Rosalind to Dinah. There is another orchestral concert tonight, but it is Mozart. Each note will be like an icy drop of water on a flushed forehead, thinks Rosalind. It will be a pleasant evening, one of many in the concert season for the Christmas holidays. She orders the lamb again in their usual restaurant.

'Your favourite,' says the waiter. By now he knows them by sight. *You two ladies*, he calls them.

'Not really,' says Rosalind, 'but I always seem to order it somehow.' There is no somehow about it. The lamb is the cheapest thing offering.

'My cousin Mark?' says Dinah. She is ordering fillet steak.

'Yes, your cousin Mark.' Rosalind decides to be bold now.

'How funny you should ask,' says Dinah. 'I got a card from him just the other day. He doesn't always send me one. You never know', she said, 'with Mark.'

Indeed not, thinks Rosalind, sitting very still, waiting.

'He manages a supermarket where he lives,' says Dinah, 'and he's decided to stand for the council. His wife', she says, 'is musical.'

'Well, well,' says Rosalind. Here is another *Well, well* to add to all the other *Ohs* and *Ha, ha, has* that form the solid wall of conversational stones and bricks, some of them thrown, in the story of James. How strange it is, she thinks, that much of what she imagines turns out to be true. Perhaps, when Mark has been on the council for a term or two, he will stand for mayor.

'He says that if he gets on the council he might stand for mayor one day in the not too distant future. He says they need new blood.' Dinah is still reading the menu, and the sinister implications of all this leave Rosalind speechless for a moment. 'I might have dessert,' says Dinah, 'if I've got room.'

'Does he still know any of his old —' What could they be called? 'Associates,' says Rosalind after a delay.

'Why do you ask?' Dinah is justifiably cautious, thinks Rosalind. Her occupation has trained her in the art of concealment.

'If someone wanted to get someone else's kneecaps shot off, or perhaps just one kneecap grazed by a bullet — not exactly shot completely off, more a warning if you see what I mean — would he know people who might help?'

Dinah continues to read the menu.

'I'd better see how big the main course is', she says, 'before I decide. I might just have some Irish coffee. What were you saying, Rosalind?'

Rosie explains it all again.

'Or even just one smallish bullet, low calibre,' she says, 'right through someone's foot. Just something painful and inconvenient for quite a long time. Not fatal. Just something to make someone sit down for a long time with their foot up. Something to stop someone moving about much. But not fatal.'

'No,' says Dinah. 'Definitely not fatal.' She seems to be considering this, and also the menu. 'The lemon cake sounds nice,' she says. 'I'd better leave deciding till later.' She puts the menu down. 'Well, Rosalind, as I understand it, they don't start off with the feet or kneecaps. Those come later, but don't quote me. Usually they start off by crushing your letter-box. You hear this terrible noise in the night and when you go outside your letter-box is all broken.'

'Well, well,' says Rosalind. Another brick or two. 'But what happens if the person hasn't got a letter-box?' The porter in James's block of flats used to deliver the mail through a slit in the front door. There were no letter-boxes.

'Then they crush the back of the person's car, if he's got one,' says Dinah. She is warming up to it now. 'And it goes on from there.'

'I see,' says Rosalind. James will probably stay with Lorraine and her pubic hair, she thinks.

'But if the person was, say, in another country and using

someone else's car and staying in their house, what would happen then?' Poor Lorraine, she thinks.

Dinah's beef has arrived and she begins to eat.

'This is even better than usual tonight, Rosalind. You really ought to try the steak sometime.'

'I will,' says Rosalind, waiting. Dinah takes a few more mouthfuls.

'They'd still crush the host's letter-box as a warning to the person staying there,' says Dinah, who takes some broccoli from the dish of vegetables. 'I do hope yours is coming soon, Rosalind.' She turns round and stares at the waiter who goes through the swing doors into the kitchen. 'I hope you don't mind me going ahead, but I want to have my dinner while it's hot.' The waiter reappears, with a plate of food.

'Of course,' says Rosalind. The lamb has arrived and looks no better or worse than usual. 'Thank you,' she says.

'What's your lamb like, Rosalind?' The waiter retreats.

'It appears to be fine,' says Rosalind, still waiting. 'But what about the letter-box and the car?'

'They wouldn't care whose car it was,' says Dinah. 'As long as the person had been seen in it, even just as a passenger, it could still meet with a nasty accident. Sometimes,' she says, 'they throw a Molotov cocktail as a starter, though, before they get on to letter-boxes and cars. They might throw a Molotov cocktail into the garden so it sets fire to a tree.' She seems to be considering this. 'But I couldn't really say what they'd do, Rosalind, with any authority. What I'm talking now is just hearsay. I wrote my thesis on violence.'

'Of course,' says Rosalind again, as if she has understood all this from the very beginning. 'I don't know if there is a garden. I don't really know if there's a house.' Perhaps Lorraine just lives in a flat with paving and a carport in which she keeps old grocery cartons. Perhaps she does not have a car at all.

'If the person had a house they might throw another Molotov cocktail nearer the house —'

'It might be an apartment,' says Rosalind.

'— or apartment so that it singes one wall or burns part of a deck,' says Dinah. 'Do you want some of this broccoli,

Rosalind? There's plenty. They've done it with pine nuts.'

'Thank you,' says Rosalind. 'I might try some.'

'And how are you two ladies enjoying your dinner?' The waiter has suddenly appeared again, from behind a potted palm. Rosalind and Dinah exchange glances.

'It's fine,' they say, almost in unison.

'You seem to be enjoying yourselves. Nattering away.'

'Yes.' They speak exactly in unison now.

They have dined many times in that little restaurant and know that the waiter has a share in the business. He might, thus, be concerned about what goes on there.

'It's nice to see people laughing and having a good time,' he says.

Dinah takes charge.

'We were just talking about the weather,' she says.

'Yes, we were.' That is Rosalind.

'We went to school together. We've known each other since we were five. We're always talking.'

'And laughing.' Rosalind again. 'And it's all about nothing.'

'Well,' says the waiter (another little brick), 'it's nice to see you two ladies enjoying yourselves.'

While they wait for him to go, Dinah takes another stab at her steak and Rosalind eats some broccoli.

'Do you think he heard what we were saying?' she asks.

'I don't think so.' They both turn to look at the waiter, who is standing over by the bar. He catches their eyes and they both smile artlessly at him.

'I think he's suspicious,' says Rosalind.

'I don't think so,' says Dinah. They both look at the waiter again. 'I think it might be better if we don't catch his eye,' she says, so Rosalind moves her chair a little to the right. 'Anyway, Rosalind, you're just kidding me again, aren't you? Admit it.'

'I'm not sure I like this lamb.' Rosalind takes refuge in the food. 'I think I can see something like a knee floating round in the sauce.' Dinah puts her glasses on and stares at Rosalind's dinner. 'Don't be silly,' she says. 'It's just a knuckle or something. Eat it up, Rosalind, you have to pay for it.' Rosalind finishes the dinner.

'I wonder,' she says when the waiter has taken the plates away, 'how much it costs.'

Dinah has decided to order apple pie.

'Apple pie, with fresh whipped cream,' reads Dinah from the dessert menu, *'Four dollars ninety-five.'*

'I meant the kneecaps.'

'Aren't you having dessert, Rosalind? You really should eat more. You only picked at that lamb.'

'It was the knee,' says Rosalind.

'I'm sure it was a knuckle, Rosalind, but we won't argue about it.'

'I wonder how much the kneecaps would cost, though.' Rosalind is relentless.

Dinah sits back in her chair.

'I'm trying to remember. It's eight years since I wrote my thesis. My costings might be out of date, but as far as I recall, they cost about two thousand.'

'Two thousand dollars?'

'Yes,' says Dinah, 'and the other prices were on a descending scale from there. The letter-box was the cheapest. I think that worked out about five hundred. I can't quite remember. It might all be different now. I mean, you've got inflation to consider and all those things. And I wrote my thesis eight years ago. It's probably all out of date, my information.'

'I see,' says Rosalind. 'I might have to give up the idea. It's far too dear.'

Dinah's pie has arrived.

'This is very good,' she says. 'They've put cloves in with the apple. My mother used to do that. I haven't had apple pie with cloves since —'

Since her mother was killed in the air crash, thinks Rosalind.

'One mustn't be nostalgic,' says Rosalind, 'as you're always saying yourself, Dinah.' But she is still pursuing violence. 'If two kneecaps are, say, two thousand, one kneecap might be one thousand. A foot might be about the same. A toe might be a bit less.'

'A toe' — Dinah is speaking between mouthfuls again —

'is part of the foot, though. It might cost the same.'

'In that case,' says Rosalind, 'if you had to pay the money you might as well have the whole foot.'

Dinah finishes the pie, and the waiter returns to take the plate away.

'Is there anything more you two ladies would like?' he asks, and waits with a little pad and pencil in his hand.

'No, thank you,' says Rosalind. She is worried about the bill.

'I might just have coffee and a chocolate,' says Dinah. Dinah, thinks Rosalind, is a professional person and has a career. Her salary cheques are probably quite large.

'It's a funny thing about you,' Dinah says periodically. 'You were the cleverest one in the class and yet you — um —' She always stopped just there.

'And yet I accomplished the least? Passed the fewest exams? Amounted to very little? What are you saying, Dinah?'

'It's just a pity, that's all.' There is always a long silence after that. 'But, I mean, it's not as if you've really accomplished so very little. I mean, well I don't know what I mean.' Dinah has confused even herself. 'Anyway, Rosalind, I've seen your poetry in magazines.'

'Not for a long time.' Rosalind is unremittingly truthful.

Thank you for submitting your poem entitled 'The Geranium' for our autumn gala issue, the editor of a noted literary quarterly had written to her some time ago. *We regret, however, that although your use of the English language has not lost its magnificence and your descriptions of light and shade are, as always, incomparable, and your use of past and present interlock with great skill, this latest work has no application to modern life. It is, actually, a very chauvinist work, which we feel would deeply upset our feminist readers. But thank you for submitting it to us. Perhaps you might like to consider sending us more modern works at a later date. Yours sincerely, Blarty Blarty Blah.* Rosalind has forgotten the name.

'And you were happily married to Roger.' Dinah is recklessly steamrolling her way through Rosalind's attributes.

'And you've got the children to think of. And you're very good at growing roses. And your friends really like you.' The list is becoming audacious. 'And Roger's old colleagues must think kindly of you. Think of how many times you gave those huge dinner parties for the directors and did all the cooking yourself, Rosalind, and gave garden parties for their wives and everything.'

Rosalind puts one elbow on the table and uses a hand to hold her head, which is suddenly too heavy to support merely on her neck. Aha, she thinks. Aha. Only a few weeks ago she found an old letter in the desk.

Dear Mrs Wentworth,

It is with great sadness that the directors write to you with condolences after Roger's untimely death. He will be a great loss to us all. It is a great tragedy that a man who was of such value to the company should be cut down in his prime. If at any time you are in need of help, please call on us. Our financial advisers could help you with the administration of Roger's trust funds if you find yourself in financial need. Our company lawyer would be most happy to help if there are any difficulties. Do not hesitate, if you are troubled, to telephone the company's head office for an appointment. Yours sincerely, Blarty Blarty Blah.

Yet another name that Rosalind cannot remember.

The company offices were closed. And for sale. Rosalind has already walked there and thinks of this as she sits in the restaurant with Dinah.

'You're suddenly very quiet, Rosalind,' says Dinah.

'I'm just thinking about something. Just a matter of business,' says Rosalind. 'Nothing very important.'

For Sale, the notice said, planted in the middle of what used to be the managing director's carpark. *Auction of this prime commercial site 1 February. All enquiries to Hartlepool, Fosdyke and Grace. Viewing by arrangement.*

Rosalind views the building not by arrangement.

'What's happened here?' she shouts over a hedge to a panel-beater banging away at a Cortina on the next allotment. 'I mean, where's everybody gone?' The hedge is made up of scrubby hebes beyond their prime.

'Didn't you read about it in the papers?' He is a contemptuous man with a dirty face and cold pale eyes. 'Went bung, I forget when.' He continues banging at the car. There is no enlivening splendour of eloquence.

'But my husband used to work for them,' she yells over the sound of hammering. 'They said I could call on them if I needed help. He died, you see, my husband.'

'You'll be lucky.' He took a few more swipes at the Cortina. 'Ha, ha, ha.' There is another man going *Ha, ha, ha* at her, thinks Rosalind, but the sting of laughter is not exactly directed at her. He means *Ha, ha, ha* for the empty promises.

'I thought it was rather funny', she had shouted at him, 'when all I got was a disconnected signal when I rang.' The hammering continued. 'So I just walked here.' She was talking to herself now. 'I thought I'd made a mistake,' she had said. 'I thought the wires were crossed. I don't know what I thought,' she said and set off for the cottage again. The offer of help from the company was just a verisimilitude of affection, as unthinkingly false as James's protestations.

'Rosalind? Is that you, darling?' He used to remember her name then. 'Rosalind, you're so beautiful. Everything here's gone wrong. Priscilla's gone away and left me. She's gone right out of London, won't ever come back, but things haven't been any good for a long time.' Perhaps, she thought now, Priscilla had had to have her tonsils out or had a throat infection that lingered. Perhaps she was having comprehensive dental work done. Perhaps anything. 'Come to London, Rosie. I'm so lonely. I love you, Rosalind. Meet me in Johannesburg, Rosie, and then I'll bring you back to London.'

'All your friends love you,' says Dinah now in the restaurant. 'Think of the interesting times you've had. Think how you've travelled. A lot of people haven't ever gone anywhere. I mean, you've even been to Africa. Imagine that.'

Yes, thinks Rosalind. Imagine that. Imagine arriving in Johannesburg in all that heat after being in transit for thirty-six hours, and within half an hour of getting there being pinned by the throat to the wall of a hotel's marble bathroom with James, possessor of a poisonous whisper, saying, 'You're obviously as much use to me, Rosie, as a chocolate teapot. You're a very boring person from a very boring country where all the habits are boring. Let me tell you a little joke, Rosamund. How does an Englishman hold his liquor? By the ears, Rosie, by the ears. Think about it, Rosie, and tell me what you think. Come along now, answer me.'

But it is not possible to answer, thinks Rosalind, if a person is half strangled against a wall.

'You've had some very interesting experiences,' says Dinah.

'Yes.' This is the exact truth, so Rosalind feels able to admit it by answering squarely.

'Such a lot of people haven't ever done anything or been anywhere, Rosalind.'

It might have been better never to have gone anywhere or done anything herself, thinks Rosalind.

'Yes,' she says. It seems a safe answer.

'And anyway,' says Dinah, 'you really ought to have wider interests, Rosalind, and get your mind off imaginary violence. What, for instance, do you think of the chances for peace after the world talks at Camp David? It was all in the paper this morning. I hope you're reading the paper, Rosalind. It's a very psychologically healthy thing to do.'

Rosalind thinks for a moment or two about the battle she is facing herself. James is set to arrive in the country sometime soon and interest rates at the bank have dropped another two per cent.

'Speaking from my own experience,' she says, 'I don't hold out much hope.' She does not say she has ceased to get the newspaper regularly because it is too expensive. She reads the headlines over other people's shoulders on the bus.

'I don't hold out much hope either,' says Dinah. 'How interesting that, for once, our views coincide. I think they're just playing around, actually. I think they've just got their toe in the door of real peace and no one wants to commit themselves to anything.'

'Talking of toes,' — Rosalind turns her back on the waiter — 'I definitely think that if you had to pay the same for a toe and a foot you might as well have the whole foot.'

'Rosalind.' Dinah puts her coffee cup down. 'I've told you

before — you'll just have to stop this. Last time we had dinner here you told me a story about being a tart. Now, Rosalind, that was a story wasn't it?'

Rosalind tosses up the difficulties of arguing about this.

'Yes,' she says. The easy way out.

'And this is a similar story about shooting someone's foot, isn't it Rosalind? Admittance, Rosalind, is part of the cure.'

'Yes,' says Rosalind. The easy way out again. She has not slept well lately and feels very tired.

'I think we should hurry,' says Dinah. 'We've only got nine minutes to get into the hall and find our seats and everything.' They pay their separate bills and the waiter opens the door into the street for them.

'We'll hope to see you two ladies again,' he says.

'It really makes a difference, doesn't it, if you don't have the extras?' says Dinah. They are crossing the road now to the concert hall. 'Rosalind, wait for me. I'm getting left behind. I noticed your bill was so much smaller than mine, and it's because you don't have the garlic bread, wine or any dessert or salad or anything. You don't even have coffee. It really does keep the bill down, doesn't it?'

'It does.' Rosalind is striding along, curiously light-headed.

'Rosalind, please wait for me.' Dinah is running behind her. 'Rosie, you're not going to go all nostalgic again, are you? You look very sad.'

'I'm okay.' Rosalind slows down. 'It was just that I found the prices you quoted rather shocking. I hoped for less.'

'Oh, I don't know.' Dinah is very laconic. 'The mains were up a bit from last time we went there, but I thought four dollars ninety-five for the apple pie was reasonable enough. It was a big piece,' she says, 'with cream.'

Dinah finds the tickets in her handbag and they both go up the stairs to the concert chamber. There is a large crowd and Dinah spends her time saying hello to people, none of whom look actually happy. They look ageless, preoccupied, abstracted, expressionless or merely dull. Nobody looks happy or animated.

'Have you noticed', Rosalind whispers as they go slowly up the last flight of stairs, 'that most of these people don't look cheerful?'

'Sssh, Rosalind. They might hear you.' Dinah leans closer. 'I know quite a lot of them professionally. Do be quiet, Rosalind.'

'Are they patients or doctors?'

'Sssh . . .'

There is an usher on duty tonight and he shows them to their seats.

'There you are,' he says, 'you two ladies, number eighteen and number nineteen, just beside the lady in the pink coat. Thank you so very much.'

'Have you noticed', says Rosalind when they are seated, 'how many people call us "you two ladies"?'

'Rosalind, we are two ladies.' Dinah is saying hello to a few more people. 'Hello, Alice and Bill, how are the children? Hello, Elspeth, hasn't it been a lovely day?' Rosalind is gazing at the ceiling and thinks she can hear rain starting. 'Hello, Jane, yes, here I am again. Hello, Mrs Jarrold, yes, Mozart, always a pleasure.'

'Don't you know a lot of people,' says Rosalind.

'Hello, Marion and James.' Dinah is waving at some other people now. The final name is a disturbing reminder.

'You don't mind if I go away at weekends, do you?' James had said in London. 'You'll be here for two weekends, but Priscilla's asked me down there. You can keep yourself occupied, can't you? I mean, you've been here for two days now, you'll know your way around London. You've got friends, haven't you, that you can go to see?'

'I might walk over to Kenwood.'

'Kenwood?' He was already getting a suitcase down from the top of the wardrobe. 'That boring place. Don't they have boring concerts there? I've never been there. No, I tell a lie. I took Mother there once on her birthday for afternoon tea.' He put a suit into a large plastic bag and hung it on the bedroom door. 'Priscilla wants me to meet the vicar. He's a boring little fart, but the wife's very lively. Priscilla's quite fallen for her. Move, move. Now, what ties? Just pop out of my way, will you, darling? Just move a little bit more to the right, and a little bit more to the right and a little bit more. Oh, good. Ha, ha, ha. Now you're right out the door.' That was when the thought first came to her that the world was full of men going *Ha, ha, ha* at her.

I want to go home, she wrote on a piece of paper and put it in the wastepaper bin. Neat and orderly Rosalind. Her heuristic efforts at happiness, she thought, had been just as ineffectual as her note now in the rubbish. They had merely resulted in the exposure of lubricity, a prurient and stanchless surfeit of exalted distress, some of it enacted at The Ritz.

'Now, I've brought you to The Ritz, Rosie, and that's it.' That was the previous day. 'Priscilla wants me to go and stay in Wiltshire so I'm going to have a lot of things on my plate.'

'Thank you, James. It really doesn't matter.' Civilised Rosalind. She looked across acres of pink carpet, great flights of stairs leading up to more warmth and music. 'The orchestra sounds nice, James. Isn't the carpet pretty?' Civilised Rosalind again. The people having afternoon tea alone looked happiest, she thought.

'What? Oh, I hate pink. I'm going to find a drink, Rosie. Ooo, look at those lovely little bums.' People were dancing. 'Get yourself some tea or something. Don't just stand there looking stupid, do something. No, don't do anything. You haven't got your glasses have you? You'll just blunder into something and make a silly arse of yourself.' Unease and infelicity had made her clumsy. 'Here you are, nuisance. Put my eyes on.' He put his reading glasses upside down on her nose. 'Ha, ha, ha. God, you look frightful, Rosie.' In the insubstantial pageant of venery her bewilderment was always, those days, like an edentate and presbyopic creature that had her by the throat.

'Please give me my tickets and my passport back, James, so I can go,' she used to say in the evenings.

'Don't be stupid. It's not long till you go, anyway. Why go to the expense of a hotel when you can stay here?' A million reasons, she would think.

'Please be assured', she had said to Félice's brother on the telephone, 'I'd leave if I could, but he's taken away all my travel documents. He's locked them in his safe, and he won't give them to me.' That was the brother's second call.

'One of his favourite tricks.' The little man gave a chuckle that could have been horrible. 'I'm a lawyer, so I'd advise you to go straight to the police station at Muswell Hill and make a complaint.' He waited. 'And won't the *News of the World* just love that.' He rang off, laughing, 'He's quite well known, you know, or perhaps you didn't.'

'Please give me my tickets and my passport, James.' She had one more try. 'Félice's brother says if you won't give them to me I should go to the police station at Muswell Hill and lay a complaint.'

'Do that, darling.' James looked up, though, from his work. She noticed that. 'They love me. The *News of the World*'ll just love it. It's a while since I've been in the papers. Didn't I ever tell you the funny story of how I once made *The Times* no less? And I don't know what you're worrying about. I've taken you to The Ritz, haven't I? And I took you to the Burlington Arcade, all the way across London in the peak hour. Just to see some silly art exhibition. What more do you want? I bought you a gold bracelet, didn't I?'

'Gold plated,' said Rosalind, turning away. 'Just gold plated, James, and very thin.'

'Oh, Priscilla.' James sighed, a huge heave of his chest. 'Why, oh, why did you go away and leave me?'

'Rosie?' says Dinah now. 'Are you all right? You look miles away. You're very quiet. I think the conductor's coming out. Yes, there he is. Come on, Rosalind. Clap.'

Tap, tap, tap. The conductor signals the beginning of the work. He is just like James, Rosalind thinks, with his sudden attention in the mail, his parcel and its enclosed card and letter, his postcard, his telephone calls. James is orchestrating his journey to the Southern Hemisphere, assembling his violins and his cornets and flutes for a major and tricky symphony of greeting and abandonment, cultivation and harvest, attention and neglect, persuasion and abuse. But when it is performed, thinks Rosalind, there will be one empty seat on James's stage of chicanery, a minor movement never completed, a player named Rosalind absent.

'Are you going on holiday or anything, Rosalind?' asks

Dinah after the concert.

'No,' says Rosalind. 'I'm just going to stay quietly at home. Staying home and being rotten is all I'm going to do.'

'You're being a real pain, Rosie,' James had said on the telephone. 'I've got it all planned. All the other girls couldn't have been nicer about it. There's only you, Rosie, being rotten, and I haven't given up hope yet of assailing your unassailed —'

'Thank you, James. I think that's enough.'

'Really, Rosie, you're rotten.'

'What did you say, Rosalind?' Rosalind's mind returns to the concert and Dinah is speaking again. 'Hello again, Jane. Yes, indeed, a lovely evening. What was that you were saying, Rosie, about being rotten? That's a word I haven't heard used for years.'

'I really didn't say anything,' says Rosalind. It might all be a bit much for Dinah. 'I just said I was going to stay quietly at home by myself. It will', she said, 'be lovely.'

'You're rotten, Rosie,' James had said earlier in the evening. 'Your very negative attitude's ruining everything.'

'James, I've got to go out now.'

'You're rotte—' but she had hung up then. He would look in his little black book, which was actually quite large, and there would be other names to consider. Any diverse instrument would do for his orchestrated finales, as long as it played.

'And before we both go home,' says Dinah as they climb into their respective cars, which are parked side by side in the concert theatre's carpark, 'just remember, Rosalind, to try to think positively and get away from thoughts of violence. Think of cheerful things, Rosalind. Think of the people you've met and the wonderful places you've been. Think', says Dinah, 'of Africa.'

9

'THINK OF AFRICA,' Dinah had said. 'Think of Africa.'

Don't think of Africa, thought Rosalind.

The African rains had come and ceased just as suddenly minutes before the aeroplane landed, so, when Rosalind walked down those pitted metal stairs to the tarmac, part of Zimbabwe lay before her as if washed for her coming.

A fractious baby wailed as all the passengers queued for Customs and Immigration, and they were watched by soldiers in a long and ragged row. Rosalind held out her hand to the baby who grasped it in small hot fingers, possibly feverish, and the crying ceased with the introduction of this miniscule entertainment.

'You're very entertaining,' Dinah would say now. 'I mean, not when you're tired, but at your best, Rosalind, you can be quite entertaining if you want to be.' But James had not been entertained for any more than half an hour, she thought sometimes in her moods of self-mockery.

'And what are you smiling at?' Dinah used to say.

'Nothing.'

The baby's mother, who was plump and looked very tired, held a little boy by the hand, and his ashen face and silence hinted at the length of the journey, the time in the sky when the sun had been followed but never caught and it had been blinding day for nearly twice as long as usual. The benediction of twilight had never come down upon them till they all stood in that queue.

'I'm so tired I could die,' said the mother of those children, so Rosalind took the other hand of the little boy. Together they went through Customs, past more soldiers with bigger guns, as if they might be a devoted little imaginary family made up of total strangers. Outside the airport buildings, which were of incomparable simplicity, taxis waited and their drivers shouted for customers, this noise becoming a final bewilderment.

But in the morning the dawn came sweet and dim as a memory, skirting the trees around Rosalind's hotel, lingering in small undulations in the surrounding countryside. Rosalind, watching the innocence of this, began to forget the previous evening.

Big, black birds like a variety of crow gave harsh and eager cries that, she decided, were kind and friendly. They marched in rough formations over the lawns of the hotel, like children looking for sixpences, their long, curved beaks giving an impression of smiling benignity. It was then, laughing, that she opened the window with a sense of absurd optimism. The journey was nearly over. The proximity of her destination, only the breadth of her hand on the map, made it feel like next door.

Three African men in striped shirts were walking along a dirt road behind the hotel as she shut the window again, cutting off the sound of those mellifluous voices as they called to each other, nearly chanting in the very early morning.

When the sun rose fully, luminous and shocking-pink against the outlines of houses and a market that was already stirring, she went down ten floors in a brown marble lift to pay the bill for a fitful night's sleep. The foyer was brown marble as well, and the room in which breakfast was served had a brown marble floor, and the bathroom of that later hotel in Johannesburg was also brown marble, so she often thought afterwards that brown marble, the colour of dried blood, was an augury of ill fortune.

'Do not be alarmed,' said the driver of that morning's taxi as they inched through an army convoy on the way to the airport again. 'It is quiet today.' She sat very still and silent, like a child told to be good, as he got them through the traffic. They passed schoolchildren walking along the dusty roads, the girls with their hair stiffly plaited and tied with ribbons, and groups of soldiers waiting for army trucks to pick them up before driving away to the hills that lay to the west. Later she used to think, in more moods of self-mockery, that the whole journey had been riddled with children and she had been as juvenile as any of them to imagine, irresistibly, that she might be loved. Her face was that of an adult and yet had odd gaps in expression, she thought, because parts of the brain behind it were missing. Parts pertaining to deviance, lubricity and violence were, simply, not there. But after the business of the bathroom, her reflection was something she avoided.

'Come on, Rosie. It's delicious. Protein, Rosie. Good for you. Priscilla loves it.'

'Why', she had said, 'are you talking about Priscilla in the present tense? I thought you told me she'd gone.'

'Never mind about that now, Rosie. Come and have a little entrée before lunch,' and she saw in the mirror how her face changed then and the kohl around her eyes made her look, suddenly, like a little carnival pierrot. 'What do you think I brought you here for, Rosie?' The hands had gone round her throat, pinning her to the brown wall that was the colour of old blood. 'Answer me, Rosie,' but it had not been possible to do that, and even if it had been, the words would have been unsuitably and childishly ridiculous.

However, in the very early morning, hours before all that, she saw great cumulus clouds filling a wide and luminous sky, an area so vast that it seemed those heavens and that vapour were the only things of any importance and the land beneath was only a saucer to hold it all up.

'Go slowly, please,' she said to that morning's taxi driver, 'so I can see everything.'

Haberdashers were rolling up canvas blinds in shop windows to show children's dresses covered with crisp lace, and at the Red Lily Panel-beaters two men, suitably, were beating a red car with hammers. Far away, as the taxi inched past another army convoy, she saw the colonnades of a school. It stood on the opposite side of a generous hollow where the mist still lingered. A nun was ringing a bell while women with very small children made their way towards that sound. Fat babies slept on their mothers' backs, tied there with blankets or bath towels knotted in all four corners, colourful and lovely.

The hotel, though, had been amorphously bland. It could

have been anywhere. Her suite had a brown marble bathroom, like a prophecy but she did not know that then, and water was available from only one tap. When it at last emerged it came with a shriek from the pipes, and was also brown.

Driving through the dust and the soldiers to the airport, she understood clearly that all these things were at once suitable and logical. So, sitting back in the taxi then, hand relaxing on the little suitcase, she watched the passing view of children, mothers and babies wrapped in innocent bath towels, and also soldiers waiting with guns.

The previous evening there had been only darkness with the odd glimmer of a lantern sometimes, always in the distance and faint as the eyes of the dying. Twilight had been fleeting. The boy who took her up in the lift to her room pulled back the drapes to show her the view of Africa by night, and there was nothing to see but darkness. As soon as he went away again, with one of those peculiarly stained and crumpled dollar bills she had obtained at the airport's bank, she drew the curtains again. There was, simply, nothing to see.

Please state clearly what money in all currencies and travellers' cheques you have with you. Fill in all details accurately on the attached form. This will be checked against expenditure upon departure. Any shortfall between actual funds and the amount stated must be covered by receipts from hotels or commercial establishments. The penalty for trafficking in money is imprisonment.

That was what the form, distributed on the aeroplane prior to arrival, had said.

In the hotel room, after those lavish curtains were drawn to keep the night out and the boy had gone away with the battered dollar bill in his hand, she sat down in an armchair that had legs carved like those on a beast. *I have given*, she wrote on the form for the airport tomorrow, *one dollar to a steward in my hotel*. And then, after lengthy thought for by this time she was past making decisions, she wrote the name of the hotel.

In the morning she awakened at dawn and was still wearing her blue silk dressing-gown. During the night a vaguely recalled nightmare had made her cry out, the sound of her own screams still echoing in her ears as she stirred for a moment and saw on her travelling clock that it was two o'clock. At dawn, when she padded over to the windows to pull the curtains, she found she had pushed one foot through that blue robe and the Paisley silk hung now in tatters.

Later, in those mocking moods, she thought there had been many signs along the way to hint at disaster. A canny landsman would have recognised these portents of a bad season, but she had dismissed the nightmares and disquiet as stupidity. It was only much later, in the cottage in the lane, that she would look herself straight in the eyes in her mirror and became tolerant of her fallacious belief of love and the way it had caused her to journey forth to have grace plucked away.

It came back, though. As she lived for longer and longer in the little cottage near the trees where the old lady decided to die, it came back. It returned slowly as she worked in the garden and made the roses bloom, and found a little cat that was dying of neglect and made it well again. She might have become a sullied banshee, unknown but with a healing touch, amidst the grime of recollection. Grace and honour came back as she began to stand a little straighter, got out her rings and her pearls to wear again, made innocent plans for the months ahead like growing white primulas. Until the parcel came, that is. Until the parcel arrived, grace and honour had come again.

'The vicar's wife's all smiles and nothing else,' James had said in London. 'Priscilla's sounded her out and it's no go there. I told her it was a waste of a glass of good sherry. But Priscilla's had a better idea. Why don't you stay, Rosie, and you can come down to Wiltshire at weekends? Three in a bed's wonderful fun. Priscilla gets wonderful videos. There's no stopping her, naughty little thing.'

'No, thank you, James.'

'You're a bore, aren't you, Rosalind?'

'Yes, James.' It was passive resistance, quiet insubordination. There were only three more days to get through.

'I wish you'd stop coughing, Rosie.'

'I wish I could too.'

Now, in the garden, the little cat ran out from the honeysuckle hedge to greet her and bounced out from behind daisy bushes to smack her foot with one paw, but it always kept its claws in because it loved her as sweetly as she loved it. So there was honour and grace on her own property. Rosalind did not ever go away now, could not tear herself away from the little house. Never took a holiday.

'Are you on holiday?' the receptionist had asked in that hotel in Zimbabwe.

'Are you on holiday?' the tired mother of the children had said while they waited at the airport.

'We're supposed to be on holiday,' James used to say later. 'This is Rosie, by the way. She comes from a very boring place, don't you, darling? No, I don't think I've drunk too much. I've taught Rosie a little joke. Come along, darling. Say your little piece. How does an Englishman hold his liquor? Oh, dear, getting up and going away are we? Got the huff? I had my birthday the day I arrived here, but now I'm aged a hundred. It's boredom that's done it.'

'Are you on holiday?' an official at the airport asked as he stamped her forms and told her not to lose them.

'I'm in transit,' she had told them all. 'I'm just passing through. I'm going to meet someone, a friend, somewhere else.'

At the airport in the morning she climbed the wide stairs that led to the concrete plinth, and stood there for a long time looking out over the brown grassland with its smattering of thorn trees. More soldiers came out of the building, climbed into trucks that took the road to those western hills, and when the last of them had gone she went inside because it might be less crowded now and therefore more bearable. With the small suitcase placed at her feet, with one foot actually resting on it, she filled out another form about the reasons for her stay and departure and watched, nearly mesmerised by her own completely controlled alarm, as another soldier read it slowly. Then he stamped it.

Are you on business, the form asked, *or on holiday? Are you a resident of any African country going home? Are you going to meet friends?* So she ticked the last category, but crossed the 's' off the final word to be entirely accurate.

Total truthfulness seemed to be required, and the penalty for anything else was a disquietening proposition she preferred not to probe. Like the night before, when she had thought lengthily about the exact nature of the dollar she had given the boy, she now thought steadfastly about that question, placed an 'a' with an arrow pointing to it on the form so it now read, *Are you going to meet a friend?* Then changed her mind completely and asked the soldier to return the form and while he watched her she crossed out the whole question, writing above it in very small, neat letters, *Are you going to meet somebody?* And she ticked this gladly.

The soldiers had made an avenue of all the suitcases to form a path out to the aeroplane, and she wandered quietly along this little road, thinking of the formation as a sudden sweet aberration to temper her fright.

Her feet in those neat, beige shoes took the steep metal ladder to the aeroplane with care, for she was remembering now legends about people who died the day before their birthday, lost the winning ticket before the prize was awarded, expired just before the cure was found. So she took the steps with ferocious and scholarly attention, hoping faithfully not to break her leg or neck as the last few hundred miles of the journey lay before her.

'Did you identify your case so they could put it on board?' asked the old lady in the seat beside hers as she sat down and heard the engines start. 'You have to point out your bags, my dear, or they won't put them on board. It's because of bombs,' said the old lady, 'and things.' Enigmatic as a toad on a rock, she watched the hostess open the door to the ladder as Rosalind ran down the aisle.

The little suitcase was put into the hold by a soldier with yellow eyes, and Rosalind said, 'Very well. That will do very well, thank you,' though there was no real gratitude there.

The guns and the soldiers and the strangeness of it all had made her nearly bellicose.

The air hostess brought coffee to the passengers when the aeroplane took off. She had hair that was stiffly plaited and bound around her head. She might have been one of those children on the road earlier, except she was bigger and older but had the same air of withdrawal and watchfulness. The coffee was cold and unpleasant and mostly spilt as the aeroplane climbed suddenly.

'I wonder what all that's about,' said Rosalind to the old lady sitting beside her, and she, without interruption or acknowledgement of this, continued to show Rosalind photographs of grandchildren. They came in varying sizes and were engaged in disparate activities from cycling vigorously (the older ones) to crying (the babies). 'Perhaps,' said Rosalind, 'it's best not to know the reasons. It might be kinder not to know, do you think?'

'It's always the same,' said the grandmother. She was putting the pictures away now. 'I come here every year to see my daughter. You never know what's going on. They said in the town yesterday that there's a big push going on, in the hills.' She pointed out of the window then to other hills and distant slag heaps, skyscrapers far away. 'Look,' she said, 'we're nearly there. Johannesburg, my dear.'

She waited until she was last to leave the aircraft, like a child again, one who leaves a parcel till later as a treat to be savoured. There was nobody to meet her.

She went through Customs again and Immigration, filled out all the forms and ticked the boxes thereupon. *How long do you plan to stay here?* A month. *Where will you be staying?* At various hotels. *Is your accommodation booked?* Yes. *Why have you come here?* To meet someone. *Will you be attending any political meetings?* No. *Do you plan to visit any African townships such as Soweto or Alexandra?* I don't think so. I don't know. *What cities and towns do you plan to visit?* Johannesburg, Port Elizabeth, Plettenberg Bay, Cape Town. *Are you an active member of any political party?* No. I am not a joining-in kind of person at all.

Then she stood there, bereft amongst other people's glad

greetings for each other and did not know what to do. That was when a hand fell on her shoulder and she turned wildly and sadly because it would be another soldier or official with a form to be filled out and she suddenly nearly cried at this endless repetition of fright.

'Hello, Rosalind.' It was James. He left that one hand on her shoulder, took her suitcase in his other hand with a courtesy she never saw again and they went out into the sunshine to a taxi.

'Look at the zebras, Rosie,' he said as they drove past the zoo. 'It's a lovely sunny day, feel the heat. Look at the giraffes. We'll come back here one day, Rosie, for a picnic.' But they never did.

'Quite a walker, aren't you,' James used to say later, 'for someone who's as much use as a chocolate teapot? Off again, are you?'

'Yes, James.' That was when that killing and stunning passivity had been learnt so well.

'Well, off you go then, and don't get eaten by anything.'

The streets around the hotel in Johannesburg were filled with dark crowds and the people stood aside to let her pass on her wanderings. It was an area that specialised in shoe shops and they sold beaded sandals and other footwear made of plaited leather with tassels, not quite shoes and yet not sandals either. Something in between had been invented in those grim streets, and Rosalind bought two pairs one day in shades of green and terracotta with brown beads that looked like agate.

'Those are African sandals,' James said. 'European women don't wear sandals like that, Rosie. Where did you get them? Where have you been, Rosie?' When she pointed out to the wide hinterland of debasement beyond the hotel's luxuries, he said, 'Rosie, you're only supposed to go down that one street right in front of the main entrance. They told you that at Reception. The other streets aren't safe, don't you understand?'

'The streets seem okay, James. If people look at me I just say hello to them.'

'You can't do that here.'

'I have.' Hello, she would say to people lounging in doorways, standing on street corners. Hello. And they looked at her with their yellow eyes, and she looked at them with her faded eyes and they all recognised, she thought, that they were similar members of a lost legion who searched for something that was not available. Freedom, respect, *égalité*, love. It was all the same in the streets where the shoe shops had brothels above and everyone wore sandals of plaited buckskin.

'Well, you've got that very dark hair, perhaps they think you're Coloured,' and he turned back to his work at the desk.

In Plettenberg Bay the streets were just suburban roads, far away from Johannesburg with the tarts on the inner-city balconies, and she walked down those paths with a greater loneliness for they were mostly empty. A beach stretching for miles lay beneath cliffs that edged the hotel grounds, and the sea there was warm and gentle; it held her kindly when she swam in the shallow water and tumbled her over and over in small waves.

Opposite the hotel, at the very bottom of the street, was a house called *Four Winds*. It had a crooked fence of wooden palings, chest-high and stained an immaculate bottle-green, which, she thought, showed a certain sanguinity of temperament by the owner. Decay was refurbished there. At the beginning of every day an old lady came out of the house and opened the double gates that led to the street, and each evening she closed them again. It was a ritual that did not seem to alter or show any sign of ever having done so. The house had been elegant and still possessed a shabby chic with its peeling yellow plasterwork on the balconies of the upper floor and a broken cane garden swing, with frilled cushions, on the veranda. On her daily walks Rosalind saw all this.

Apart from opening and closing the gates, the old lady remained out of sight, except for brief appearances with a watering-can out on the patio and only in the evening when the gates were locked.

Michaelmas daisies grew in rough swathes beyond the gates, and there were old white roses, gone wild, covered with aromatic blooms that smelt of incense. Amongst these, with her watering-can, the old lady moved with grace bringing sustenance for the plants. There was never a sign of anyone else. She was alone, except for an old Labrador dog with a broad square muzzle and a studded collar with a name tag. He used to bark at Rosalind, but without conviction, and then wagged his stumpy tail, but always from a little distance so she could not read his name. It might have been Brutus, she thought, or a bold name of that sort, but he had grown old under the weight of it. In the overgrown garden he and the lady existed honourably and with grace; and after seeing all this, Rosalind would go down to the sea again because it was clean and beautiful. It might wash away her thoughts, which were graceless and shaming, and might replace them with the example of the lady with her plants in the house called *Four Winds*.

'Think of Africa,' Dinah had said. 'Think of Africa.'

10

'I'LL HAVE TO go, James. There's someone knocking at my door.'

'Last time I rang you said you had to go out, Rosie. If you knew how difficult it was for me to get to a telephone you'd be a bit more understanding. You're just wasting yourself, Rosie. You've got that marvellous little untouched —' She hangs up.

'Sorry to keep you waiting,' she says when she opens the front door. It is Benjamin again. 'I was just talking on the telephone.'

'I could have waited.'

'Certainly not. It doesn't matter, anyway.' And it doesn't. It doesn't matter at all.

He steps through that narrow front door, its wooden panels stripped of paint and polished to a peachy bloom. Fashions in architecture are coming slowly to the neighbourhood. The proprietor of the superette up on the corner says, for instance, that the peculiar assortment of beams and boards left lying beside a bulldozer on a piece of wasteland behind Rosalind's cottage will one day be a three-level townhouse designed by a noted architect for a doctor. For a lady doctor, he says, with one child and no husband. The child is a boy, he says, so there is faint approval there, and a shimmer of envy goes through the saris of his three unmarried daughters who help in the shop.

'Anyway, come through, Ben.' Benjamin follows Rosalind down the narrow hall that goes straight through the middle of the house, swift and sure as a knife in the heart.

'You've got the place looking very nice, Rosalind. Just look at those flowers.' She has picked a bunch of pink roses. 'Last week you had yellow daisies in that vase.'

'Thank you, Benjamin.' They are always very civilised. 'Come and sit down. Shall I make you a cup of tea?' He seems to like tea.

'That'd be very nice, Rosalind.' Civilised again.

They head for the parlour. In the big house, the one on the hill, the front door was very wide, commodious enough for two people to step through side by side. The entrance hall was like a room, spacious enough for a sofa where people sometimes sat and read.

But here, in the Lilliputian cottage like a little doll's house, Benjamin and Rosalind walk in single file down that narrow hall that is like a knife in the heart. It is presented as a tiny gallery with old portraits hanging on the right-hand wall, and one painting that cannot be placed anywhere leaning artfully against a door and held there by a copper watering-can exactly opposite the Gothic cabinet. In such a way Rosalind hopes to arrange all homeless possessions, including herself, in a geometric manner and thus create order out of chaos.

'It's a shame not to display this where it can be seen from a distance.' Benjamin has stopped halfway down the hall, and Rosalind, far ahead in the parlour, has to go back and find him. He is standing in front of the cabinet and has one hand on its pediment. 'You really need a big room to show this off, Rosalind.'

'I haven't got a big room, Benjamin. This is the only place it would go.'

'Mmm.' He caresses the finial on the pediment as if it might be a rosebud. 'Just let me have a quick, little tour, Rosalind.' He flits in and out of rooms for a minute or two and then returns. The cottage has only five rooms, and Benjamin has explored them all now. 'I must say you've got a talent for arrangement,' he says, 'but there's nowhere else you could put the cabinet. I can see that now.' His hand returns to the apex of the pediment. 'You're a very lovely woman, Rosalind, standing there just like that.'

'I could sell the sofa,' says Rosalind to change the subject, and they set off on another tour of the house. There is much perambulation this afternoon. Benjamin is not yet anchored by his usual cup of tea and seems in an exploratory mood, ranging round the cottage with an air of purpose that is almost frightening.

'I don't think you'd want to do that, would you Rosalind?' His hand slips inside her camisole again. 'If you didn't have a sofa where would you sit on my knee, for instance?'

'I'll put the kettle on,' says Rosalind, changing the subject again. 'I just thought that if I sold the sofa I might be able to put the cabinet along that wall.' Rosalind begins to bustle about her kitchen.

'Don't be in such a hurry, Rosalind. I really came to give you this.' He has been carrying what looks like a plastic bag — perhaps some shopping, she has thought — and now hands it to her. 'Just be careful opening it. I don't want you to break it,' he says. 'It's Ming, Rosalind. It's part of my Ming collection.'

Nothing today is as it seems, thinks Rosalind. James has telephoned to tell her something unprintable. Benjamin thinks the telephone call he interrupted was probably pleasant. The plastic bag is not shopping at all, but a present. And the present is not actually a gift, in the correct sense. It has not been purchased especially for her, to be given at the proper moment (say, Christmas). It is part of Benjamin's own collection, and the plastic wrappings are those used by companies who pack household goods for storage. Benjamin, Rosalind thinks, must have made a special journey to one of his warehouses where all the things are stored, ratting round amongst the packing cases to find a suitable little something. And it is late January, far from Christmas.

The piece of Ming is not large, but its smudged inky blue peonies and the reign mark on the bottom, scratched there by an ancient hand, have all the charm of a wise cobalt eye in the face of the universe.

'Just be careful, Rosalind, how you handle it,' says Benjamin. He is hovering over her. 'Don't break it now, will you, dear?'

'How lovely,' says Rosalind. 'How beautiful. Of course I won't break it. Why would I break it when it's all you've ever given me, apart from a roast of beef?'

'I'm sorry about that, Rosalind,' — he coughs and shuffles — 'I get very busy and I forget about things. I should have given you something for Christmas, but things have been very stressful lately. I've had a lot of travelling to do,' he says, 'and I've been trying to get everything sorted out. I've been getting myself together. January's been a real pain. I'm looking forward to February. I'm really sorry I forgot Christmas.'

'It's quite all right.' He has embarrassed Rosalind now. 'I think I'll just put this' — she is holding the piece of Ming, the little tea bowl, closely to her chest as if it might be torn out of her hands any minute — 'here, on this table. Do you think that might be nice?' They both stand back.

'Lovely, Rosalind. Very suitable. I must say you always get things arranged in your own unique way. There's order in your clutter,' he says. 'You've got a very nice atmosphere here, Rosalind.'

'I'll just put the kettle on.' He seems to be stepping closer.

'Leave the kettle for a moment.' Benjamin is looking very pensive. 'Come here, Rosalind.'

'No.'

'Well, I'll come over there then.'

Rosalind is busy clearing a few things off the table.

'This piece of Ming needs to be on its own, I think. It's so lovely.' She is changing the subject once more.

'Just leave that for a moment, please, Rosalind.' He takes four steps to traverse the room, a kind of walking calculus.

'Yes?'

'Just let me get a little bit closer, please, Rosalind.'

'Yes, Benjamin?' It is possible to look straight into his pale blue eyes now and they are flecked with brown, like birds' eggs. His arms slowly encircle her waist.

'You've got a very beautiful ribcage, Rosalind.'

'Please let me go.'

'Just stand there quietly, Rosalind. Now, that's not so bad is it?'

'I suppose it isn't,' says Rosalind, grudging as an old schoolmistress.

'Rosalind, I've been thinking about what you said the other day.'

'And what did I say the other day?' Rosalind knows

perfectly well what she said, and hopes he has forgotten.

'You know what you said, Rosalind, about the five hundred dollars.'

'Oh, that,' says Rosalind.

'Don't just say, "Oh, that," like that, Rosalind. You said —'

'Yes, I know what I said.'

'Well, Rosalind?' The little tea bowl seems to tremble on the table.

'Well, I don't know,' says Rosalind. 'It was a silly thing to say. I'd be too shy.'

'You're not shy, Rosalind.' His cheek is against hers now and it feels very smooth, faintly scented. Rosalind breathes in deeply. 'That's right, Rosalind. Take a deep breath. There's plenty of time.' Fahrenheit, she thinks, by Christian Dior. Has there been a massive liquidation of an up-market chemist lately? Or a fire in a block of luxury boutiques? 'I don't think you're shy, Rosalind. Reticent, yes. Difficult, yes. Temperamental, yes. Shy, no.'

'Yes, I am. I'm very shy.' And she thinks about James and that hand round her neck and how the marble wall had felt very cold. 'You're a very boring person, Rosie, from a very boring country where all the people are boring and even the cars and the way people drive them is boring. Get out of my way.' 'And I'm very boring,' she says. 'I'm a very boring person. My whole life's been very boring and I only know how to do very boring things,' and a tear creeps and seeps down Rosalind's cheek like the coming of a pox.

'Rosalind, you're a funny girl. What are you crying for?'

'Everything,' says Rosalind and goes away into the kitchen to put the kettle on. 'What china would you like me to use today?' The question is a form of idleness and embarrassment. She does not know what to do or say.

'Perhaps I could look in the cupboard and choose.' Benjamin, careful as a banker, has followed. 'I think the pink,' he says. 'I had the blue last time, your lovely willow, Rosalind. I might have the pink.'

Animation has left Rosalind. All she can do is loiter near the kettle. There have been so many phone calls in the middle of the night, so many nagging references to her bum, that she is like a defeated army that has left the battlefield rather than lower its flag.

Rosalind has become, in the last few days, nearly sullen, almost unnerved. And the latest bank statement which says she has $11.23 in her cheque account has not helped. Interest rates have also gone down another three points in the last week.

'Definitely,' says Benjamin. 'I'd like the pink, with rosebuds. I'm very fond of your rosebuds, Rosalind. Shall I get out the cups, Rosalind?' He is very bland about it all. 'Shall I help?'

'You can if you like.' This remark is a sign of defeat. Benjamin is invading her cupboards, inspecting the porcelain, handling the merchandise, touching her rosebuds. She looks away, out into the garden, which looks splendid in a miniature way. The flowering cherry is now covered with leaves of tender green that show no nibbling by insects or bashing by rough weather. The roses are flowering. A bunch of creamy-yellow ones could be picked later from the old climber, thinks Rosalind. The little garden out the back of the cottage is an arcane and miniature wilderness.

'Quite a nice little area you've got out there, Rosalind,' says Benjamin. 'Must be worth a bit, all that privacy right in the middle of the city. You could take a little deck chair out there' — the birds' egg eyes narrow now and the look is speculative — 'and you could sunbathe, Rosalind. Naked. You could sunbathe naked. Your kettle's taking ages to boil, isn't it? Shall I make the tea? Shall I carry the tray? Where would you like to have it?'

'I don't know what you're laughing at,' says Rosalind. 'We always have a cup of tea in the parlour. The parlour's the nicest room.' She follows Benjamin up her own hall now, like a visitor, and he leads the way as if the house is his.

'I must say you keep everything very nice, Rosalind. You're very tidy. Even your roses haven't got greenfly. Everything's immaculate, inside and out.'

'Have you got a garden?' Rosalind has no idea where he lives, has never been to his house. He lives with Roberta who is nearly a lawyer, according to what he said on his last visit, and she is not any sort of housekeeper. Rosalind knows no more.

'I haven't had a garden up till now. I'm very busy, Rosalind. I'd like to have a garden, but there's time to consider.' Ah, yes, thinks Rosalind. Time. It passes in the cottage with an inexorable grace. She gets up in the morning and feeds the little cat, which then goes out on to the veranda to lie in the sun. Rosalind does all the chores, then goes outside to the beneficence and refuge of the roses. Rosalind works at passing time because it is not punctuated by much except the visits of Benjamin, sporadic at their best and usually presaged by distressing domestic upheavals with the unknown Roberta. And there are concerts with dinner beforehand with Dinah. And worries about money figure in it, too. Her time is punctuated by worries about funds. Interest rates keep falling.

'You're very fond of roses, aren't you?' says Benjamin. 'Now, this is very nice.' He polishes his horn-rimmed reading glasses and stands looking at a small oil painting of flowers. The painted roses are dying, and Rosalind, looking at herself reflected vaguely in the doors of the old bookcase, decides she might be dying as well. Like a furled neat rose that never reaches full bloom then wilts and drops in the space of a day, that is how it will be, thinks Rosalind. 'Do you understand what I mean, Rosie?' James's sibilant whisper echoes in her ears again. 'How does an Englishman hold his liquor? By the ears, Rosie, by the ears. Don't you understand what I'm saying?' And she had begun to die by millimetres then. 'Come along, Rosie.' She would watch the people James had just introduced her to as they shuffled a little, made excuses to depart. 'Must rush. Catch up with you later, James and um . . .' Her name was seldom used. 'Nice to have met you. Perhaps we might see you some other time.'

'You look a bit tired,' says Benjamin. 'The holidays are very tiring.' He puts his glasses on the end of his nose and stares at the picture of roses. 'I like this little picture,' he says. 'If you ever wanted to sell it, Rosalind, you've got a buyer here. I'd like to hang it in one of the bedrooms. Have I told you I've moved into my house? Thank you, dear, yes I do have milk.' There has not been a break between any of these remarks. Rosalind has begun to pour the tea.

If Benjamin has just moved into his own house, she wonders, where has he been living? There is Roberta and her housekeeping, or the lack of it, and there is the subject of gardening, and the lack of it again, and there is Roberta's career (ditto), but where has all this taken place? She continues to pour the tea, circumspect, self-contained, reticent as a little doctor.

'And I've left Roberta,' says Benjamin as he takes his cup. 'This is a very pretty teaset, Rosalind.' Once again, there is no break between remarks. 'Victorian, I'd say. A very pretty little set, and of quite some value,' and he raises one of his pale and languid hands to cup her breast as she bends over the teatray.

'For heaven's sake, have a cake,' says Rosalind. But they are almond tarts with a cherry surmounting yellow sponge. Even the sweetmeats are ranged against her, thinks Rosalind, and watches Benjamin bite the cherry off one.

'I think you're blushing, Rosalind.'

'No, I'm not. I'm too old to blush.' So, thinks Rosalind, he has left Roberta. Throwing china was a mistake, but the cut on his head has healed nicely.

'Rosalind, you're looking very fixedly at me again.'

'I was just looking at your head, Ben. I remembered you had a cut on your head.'

'Oh, that.' Now it is Benjamin's turn to say, *Oh, that*. 'Healed up really well, Rosalind, had the stitches out last week.'

Rosalind takes her own teacup and sits over the other side of the room. He always proceeds better in conversation if he is unprompted, so she lets the silence lengthen and amidst the somnolence of the disenchanted lanes they drink tea and Benjamin eats the cakes.

'These are very nice little tarts, Rosalind. I think this is my fourth. Did you make them yourself? You're a good girl, Rosalind, aren't you?' Munch, munch, munch. He eats another two cakes.

'Yes,' he says at last, 'I've finally left Roberta.'

The parlour is a pristine, little room and the high windows, only two of them but their size is generous, are uncurtained. There is a Spartan simplicity about the architecture that makes the interior look like a hospital, a healing place for weary jugglers and necromancers at the magical apex of a triangle of rough streets. It is a place for confidences.

'Would you like another cup of tea?' asks Rosalind. Medicine. 'Would you like another cake?' A pill.

'I might.' He holds out his cup and saucer. 'I didn't have any breakfast, Rosalind. It's been very upsetting. It all — yes, I will have another cake, thank you — blew up in my face, Rosalind.' He snaps his fingers. 'Just like that.'

'And how did you feel about that, Benjamin?' That is what Dinah would say, thinks Rosalind.

'How did I feel about it, Rosalind? My feelings were mixed, definitely mixed. I've been living over at her place,' he says, 'but I've decided to move into my own house now, Rosalind. You ought to see the mess. I can't find a thing. I've got packing cases everywhere. Yes, thank you — I might have a drop of milk. You're a kind girl, Rosalind, and I didn't come over here to bother you with my problems. I just popped over to give you the piece of Ming, and to ask you about what you said.'

'What I said?' Rosalind knows what she said, but retreats behind her teacup with an air of abstraction.

'You know what you said.' Benjamin bites the cherry off another little tartlet. 'I seem to be making a meal of these.'

Rosalind thinks of the interest rates at the bank. They have gone down again, and more falls are expected soon. The gas bill, the electricity bill, the bill for rates, the account for the water rates and a Visa account for $140 have all arrived tied into a pestilential bundle by that misguided postman. He is the one who whistled *Hello, Dolly* the day James's parcel arrived, thinks Rosalind, and adds this to his list of minor crimes.

'Anyway, Rosalind, what've you been doing with yourself today? You're looking very nice.'

'If somewhat tired,' says Rosalind. Perhaps writing out that list of accounts to be paid (by what means?) has brought a healthy flush to her cheeks. She has written it out in longhand, with no numbers, so it reads like a prose narrative and not arithmetic.

Rates: one hundred and fifty-eight dollars; electricity: twenty-five dollars and thirteen cents with discount for prompt payment; gas: thirty-eight dollars and forty-seven cents, ditto; telephone bill: forty-seven dollars and eighty-five cents; repairs to turquoise necklace, still not collected due to lack of funds: fifteen dollars; water rates: forty-five dollars; a total of three hundred and twenty-nine dollars and forty-five cents.

Her bank statement clearly says that there are eleven dollars and a few cents in her cheque account.

'I suppose you've been working in the garden,' says Benjamin and goes to the window to look out at the roses. The cat is staring in the window from its perch on the outside sill. 'Hello, Tiddles,' says Benjamin as the cat runs away. Tiddles is not the cat's name and it gives him a sharp glance before it disappears behind a salvia bush. 'Shy little thing, isn't it?' says Benjamin. 'You've done a grand job there, Rosalind. You saved the cat's life. You're a very kind girl. Yes, thank you' — the dialogue once more proceeds without a break — 'I'll have another cup of tea, these are small cups, Rosalind. And I'll have another of these lovely little cakes.' He bites the cherry off again.

I've forgotten the Visa account, thinks Rosalind. Another one hundred and forty dollars added to three hundred and twenty-nine dollars and forty-five cents comes to —

'Rosalind, you look so far away. What on earth were you thinking about?'

'Just some arithmetic,' says Rosalind. Four hundred and sixty-nine dollars and forty-five cents. That is the total, she thinks, and the difficulty is insoluble.

'Ah,' says Benjamin, 'talking of arithmetic, what about the business of the five hundred dollars? And don't just say "Oh, that" again.'

'I was only joking.'

'You're a very boring person, Rosie.' There is that poisonous whisper again. 'I can't believe anyone could get to your age, Rosie, and be so ignorant. Surely you must have known what I like? People talk, Rosie. Other people listen. Surely you must have heard.'

'I don't think you were joking, Rosalind.' Benjamin puts his cup back on the saucer with a leisurely deliberation. He looks as if he is going to spend time on this. 'You're a businesswoman, Rosalind. You've been in business. You had that little art gallery. You did quite well, I seem to remember. You must understand the law on contracts. You must know all about offer and acceptance.'

'It was a long time ago. It must be four years ago, at least that.' It all comes into her mind then, the life in the little gallery with its walls painted a mellow Chinese red to show off the pictures and how she worked there in the mornings with her old friend Pamela. Pamela. And what happened to Pamela? Pamela went off to Sydney to marry a man called Peter Something. Rosalind has forgotten his surname. She is not good with names. Peter Something turned out to be a very nice man who made Pamela very happy and they opened another little art gallery in some suburb of Sydney. They send her a Christmas card every year with all this continuing news, plus pictures of their children. Thomas aged two and Mary aged three. 'It used to be quite interesting,' says Rosalind now. 'It used to be good fun.'

'Business is good fun, Rosalind,' says Benjamin, 'if you obey all the proper rules. And we have here a situation where one party has made an offer and someone else has accepted it, so we've got a proper deal.'

'It doesn't sound like a very proper deal to me,' says Rosalind watching Benjamin take another tart.

'I must have eaten about six of these,' says Benjamin, biting the cherry off again. 'They're really delicious. We've got a proper deal all right, Rosalind. It's just a matter of time and place.'

'Time and place?' Rosalind is feeling claustrophobic now.

'Don't look so horrified, Rosalind. It was you who said in the beginning —'

'I know what I said. Just let me think for a moment.'

'Certainly, Rosalind.' He is biting into the yellow sponge now. 'Take your time. There's no hurry.'

'There'd be some extras fees,' says Rosalind, 'over and above your basic five hundred.' He is known as a careful negotiator in business. Perhaps, she thinks, this will put him off.

'You didn't say anything about extra fees when it was first mentioned.'

'That was because we were just beginning these negotiations,' says Rosalind. 'Now that we've begun what you might call a dialogue,' — Dinah would be pleased with all this terminology, thinks Rosalind — 'we might as well both fully understand the situation. The other fees would encompass, say, wear and tear, general refurbishment . . . even baby oil's quite expensive these days, Benjamin, and I'd have to rub my arms and legs with oil, and I'd need to paint my toenails pink and all my nail varnish is gucky, Benjamin. Even in a sale the best kinds cost at least five ninety-five for a little bottle. And', says Rosalind, 'they don't last long. And there'd be electricity —'

'I didn't have in mind using electricity.'

'I have to have electricity on at the house in case you want to use lights. I might need to boil the kettle for one of these cups of tea you're always having.'

'Rosalind, I've never heard you talk like this.'

'And there'd be a carpet fee for when you walk on my rugs and wear them out.'

'Rosalind, they're worn out already.'

'That's the patina of age' — she is very dignified now — 'and you have to pay for it.'

'I see.' Benjamin pours himself another cup of tea. He is slowly invading the territory and making proprietorial gestures towards herself, her teapot, her china and other things. 'So how much would all these extra fees come to, Rosalind?'

'I think you'd be talking in the vicinity of another two hundred. Two to two-fifty might cover it.'

'Is there room for negotiation on this, Rosalind?'

'Possibly. That's why I said two-fifty.'

'So are we talking two hundred here, Rosalind?'

'Something like that. And there might be other minor fees for other small extras like hanging up your clothes because I hate clothes strewn around, and there'd be a tea fee and a biscuit fee.'

'I didn't have tea and biscuits in mind.'

'But I'd have to have enough tea and enough biscuits in case you wanted some.'

'Well, Rosalind,' Benjamin sighs, 'how much are we talking now for all these other little fees. All these little extras on top of the extras.' He sounds reproachful.

'Say, another fifty,' says Rosalind, 'with a discount of five dollars for prompt payment, in cash. And there'd also be a basic cover charge, like they have in restaurants, because I'm actually a poet, or I was, and my poetry has been in magazines.' There is a long silence. 'In the better magazines, but not for quite a while,' — a slight effort at conciliation there — 'but you still have to pay an extra fee for having the attention of —' For having the attention of what sort of person? 'For having the attention of someone notable,' she says.

'And how much is this extra fee,' says Benjamin, 'this cover charge for a poet?'

'Eleven dollars and twenty-three cents.' A Freudian slip. This is the amount her cheque book contains, but the sum is so specialised and peculiar that it silences Benjamin.

'I see,' he says and eats another cake. 'I'd prefer to round it up to fifteen dollars, Rosalind. The arithmetic would be much easier.'

'That's very kind of you.'

'Not at all, Rosalind. Now, to introduce a hypothetical situation: if I were to provide the premises what would the cost be then?'

'That's a very hard-hitting question,' says Rosalind. 'If you were to provide the premises then all you'd pay would be your basic five hundred, plus the notability fee, plus an allowance for my travelling time, and you'd also have to pay another extra fee, a deprivation fee because I'd be deprived of my basic fees at my place. But with a discount for cash and a slight incentive bonus we'd be talking somewhere in the vicinity of seven hundred.'

There is another long silence.

'Tell me something, Rosalind,' says Benjamin. 'Do you like me?'

'Yes, of course I like you.'

'Well, why do I have to pay?'

'You have to pay so you'll value me. If you got me free you might not.' And there are all the bills to pay.

'I'd value you, Rosalind. I think you're quite a lovely woman. I think you're very kind.' The cat is staring in the window again. 'Look at little Tiddles there. You saved its life, and that's just one thing, Rosalind. I have quite a high opinion of you. We've known each other a long time. I definitely value you highly.'

'But how do I know I can rely on that? I mean, you might just suddenly start being rude to me, or offhand or anything.' And she thinks of James in London saying, 'Just a little bit more to the right and a little bit more and a little bit more, ha, ha, ha, nuisance, now you're right out of the door.' She thinks of that. 'It's all very well saying you value a person, but do you really? And if you've paid, then the person does know that you valued them that much at that moment.' Another long silence. 'And they can go and pay all their bills and buy groceries.'

'I see,' says Benjamin, and his eyes are very pale blue and half closed, looking past her or through her. She is not sure which. And that thin smile has gone. 'Very well, Rosalind. I'll supply the premises and you can have your little foible indulged about the five hundred plus all the other little fees including your notability fee —'

'I am a bit notable,' says Rosalind, 'or I used to be. My long poem, "The Rose", attracted quite a lot of critical acclaim; mind you, that was nearly ten years ago. I was quite well reviewed then, before the market changed. My open verse used to be considered quite unusual —'

'I'm sure it was, Rosalind.'

'— and once I got a fee, in three figures, to appear at an arts festival. I read from my work, Benjamin, at the Town Hall, and I had the whole place in the palm of my hand.

You could have heard a pin drop.'

'I'll certainly have to pay for that,' says Benjamin.

'To be quite fair to you,' says Rosalind, 'since then it's been a bit downhill. My latest long poem, "The Geranium", isn't going to be published. My publisher wrote to me and said that my use of the English language hadn't lost its majesty and my exploration of time and place showed my usual remarkable skill. But this is a permissive age we live in, that's what he said, and no one wants a long poem called "The Geranium" these days. He said I'd missed the bus.'

'I wonder what he meant by that.' Benjamin eats another tart. 'Never mind, Rosalind, perhaps you might like to read a bit of it to me sometime.' The clock on the mantelpiece strikes five. 'Good God, is that the time?' He is taking his mobile telephone out of a large pocket in his jacket. 'Just excuse me for a moment. I have to give someone a call. And, by the way,' — he is waiting for someone to answer — 'Rosalind, is that clock of yours all right? Isn't that the one you paid sixty-five dollars to have overhauled? I'm not quite sure I like the sound of that — oh, hello, John,' he says. 'Yes, I know I said I'd ring earlier, but I got caught up in another little deal.' He places a hand on Rosalind's knee. 'Just a tiny reminder, John. The cheque's due today. Of course, of course, and none taken I do assure you. Let's not worry the postman.' He pulls a face at Rosalind. 'I'll get Wally and some of the boys to come round and collect it from you. Shall we say half an hour? Good doing business with you, too.' He puts down the aerial and prepares to leave.

'Thank you for the cups of tea,' he says, 'and the tarts. Very nice, Rosalind. Now, about these arrangements. Shall we say I'll come this evening at eight o'clock and I'll take you to view my premises? I've got the decorators in at the moment. They've got paint and ladders everywhere, but the boys got me a sofa out of storage and a few bits and pieces to keep me going till I get the place right. See what you think, Rosalind. I must say you're looking very bonny, not like the time I found you sitting on the stairs in your other house. You gave me a fright, Rosalind, but it's quite a long time since that hap—'

'Two years,' says Rosalind, and wonders if she has spoken too quickly or in a voice that is too loud.

'As long ago as that? It seems like yesterday. Anyway, eight o'clock, Rosalind. I'll see you then. Be careful of the Ming.'

11

THE TREES AROUND the big house, the one on the hill where the Gothic cabinet showed itself off in a large room, were dense and fine. From the street it was possible to see as far as the first bend in the drive, and then everything was lost in the undergrowth. On each side of the gate was a magnolia tree, and when Rosalind came home from London they were in full new leaf, so bright and green and beautiful that each tree looked as if it had been painted. Another magnolia tree, a different variety with brown papery leaves and blooms that smelt of lemon, lurked in a thicket of rhododendrons as the drive's first bend hid the view of the house. Above this small forest reared four high brick chimneys with ornamental tops. Anyone passing in the street could also see just one gable of the roof, but only from a particular angle between a coprosma higher than a man and covered with a red creeping geranium and a Swedish birch, which had grown tall and straight to penetrate the lower canopy of underbrush. That was all anyone could see from the wooden gate.

When Rosalind opened it to let herself into her own property, like a thief at twilight, she saw that someone in a car must have mounted the pavement sometime during her absence. Several boards in the gate were broken, others grazed. The paint, a Victorian bottle green, had looked as if it would last for ever six weeks ago, but now seemed long overdue for another coat in that uneasy dusk.

It was dusk when Rosalind finally came home, dusk when the final taxi driver left her at her own gate and wanted to walk down the drive with her to carry the little suitcase. But she waved him away. 'No, thank you, no, no.' And she went in the gate alone, to face her house by herself, like a small animal from *The Wind in the Willows* that creeps back to its lair from the marshes.

There must have been heavy rain in her absence, she thought. Many days of rain. The gravel of the drive had formed into eddies. In some places it was ankle-high, in others the track was down to bare earth where pieces of rubbish had stuck in the mud. There were sweet papers and ice-cream wrappers from the shop on the corner. Someone had thrown beer cans over the fence. Several lay on the lawns, amongst the dandelions.

An empty green wine bottle from a cheap, late-pick Riesling had fallen off the letter-box to smash on the concrete edging that defined the main path. The lawns had been mown, she thought, so the contractor must have come. On the front approach to the house the soil was good and rich and the grass grew luxuriantly there. On the northern side of the house, struck by sea winds, the lawn never did so well and out there she could see the stripes of reasonably recent mowing. In more eddies of rubbish on the front porch lay piles of dead leaves and large pieces of tree branches, so she thought there must have been a storm, or storms, to bring all that down. Storms, she thought. There must have been more than one to make all that mess.

In the last of the twilight she passed all this like a dreamer, coughing, a gentle lunatic come back to old haunts. The coughing was much worse now, and so was the pain in her chest, together with an odd sense of isolation from the world. Sounds seemed to come from far away, but they always did in the big house. It was, simply, so far from the street. From a long way off she heard traffic, the cries of children, a man shouting at his dog, the dog barking. Then she put the key in the old lock of the front door and went inside.

It was always a dark house. The upper floor was filled with light, but that was nearer the sky and the sun shone in there, through those pretty little windows. Downstairs, where the walls were panelled, a great wide stairway went up three bends past a dim window taller than two men. Its red and blue panes cast an ecclesiastical light that was noble, but also sombre. Downstairs was always dark. That night, as darkness fell, the shadows were profound. Only somebody who knew the place could have walked into it with such insane assurance, such a fevered anxiety to be home and with the door slammed against the world. But after thinking for a moment or two, she went back and propped it open, just an inch or two, with an old iron doorstop shaped like a basket of flowers, another dupe for the unwary. Flowers that were not flowers, baskets made of iron, pleasures that were not pleasures, friends who were not friends, and love that was not.

The old credenza at the foot of the stairs was covered with dust. There was a smell of damp and lack of use. Far away a door was banging. The house might have been closed up for years instead of just six weeks. From far away again she heard the banging of that door. A wind had sprung up and was whistling round the eaves. An antique doll with a very white china face — an ill doll, thought Rosalind now — had fallen over in her miniature chair. The doll always sat on a little wooden chair on the credenza and wore a black lace dress with a pillbox hat of black silk, a young-faced widow doll, and she had fallen over sideways, that doll. So Rosalind stopped to straighten her up, sat her on the chair in an attitude of ease and pinned the pillbox hat into that fine hair at exactly the right angle. Marigold, she thought as she began to climb the stairs. The doll was called Marigold. And that boy in Zimbabwe wore a pillbox hat like that, that boy in green trousers and bare feet who carried a blackboard upon which her name was written, and misspelt. The hotel must have sent him, she thought now, to make sure she was put in the right taxi at the airport, and she remembered striding away towards a car that bore the hotel's name, walking with the courage of complete uncertainty and the knowledge that this must be apparent to nobody. But that strength, those strides, had gone now. She was too breathless to move any more than one step before resting. The fits of shivering were much worse.

The staircase rose through the full height of the house and its carved wooden balustrade formed a gallery at the top. The daylight and the moonlight were sweet and sharp there. It was a good place to hang pictures. Some of these portraits now glimmered in the narrow hall of the cottage. Some had been stolen.

Twelve wide and shallow steps led to the first landing, and she made it there, coughing, and stood resting with the suitcase on the carpet beside her. The old runner that ribboned up to the bedrooms was in muted shades of pink and blue, a promise of daisies and roses in that mellow pattern.

It was a prediction of the cottage garden that awaited her much later, but she did not know that then, knew nothing at all except that she was at home and must climb the stairs. There were thirty-five stairs to the next landing, the longest flight of all, and this went past the old window with its blue panes like a night sky and the red ones that were like blood. Its sill was as wide as a seat. The children, before they grew up and went away, often sat there and dangled their legs out on to the fire escape. The lower part of the window opened and made a sweet breeze through the house in the summer. Rosalind hoisted herself on to that sill, let the suitcase fall from her hand to clatter down the stairs again as she lay beneath the window. A few of the panes were made of clear glass, and through these she saw the moon rise to cast stripes down the stairs, across the entrance hall and on to those puzzling blanks on the walls and floor where there had been pictures and furniture and a large Chinese vase that held the umbrellas. Outside she could see the vegetable garden where the spinach had gone extravagantly to seed, and sometimes there was a glimpse of the house next door and its kitchen windows. There a boxy, little woman with short arms bashed an evening meal into some sort of shape amidst clouds of steam and with a cigarette stuck in one corner of her mouth. A man with a yellow face that was creased from frowning came and ate what she had put on a plate. They were not far away, but Rosalind's hand never went to the window catch, she did not call out or wave, had not even managed to get as far as the kitchen in her own house. The switchboard was there, for the lights. Her house, as it had been for the six preceding weeks, remained in darkness, the only alteration to its state was that Rosalind had come back and now lay along a window-sill.

'Didn't you think of calling your neighbours?' the doctor said later at the hospital. The doctor who had come when Roger died said much the same thing. 'Have you got any neighbours you could call? Could anyone come and stay with you?' And she said, both times, 'Oh, the neighbours are very unfriendly. They don't even say hello. I've got some nice people on the other side, but they're always away. They're hardly ever there.' In the hospital she turned slowly over in the bed, turned her face to the wall.

'How long have you been there by yourself?' that hospital doctor wanted to know. 'When did your husband die?

'Do you have any next of kin we can notify? Is there anyone who could come and see you? Are you really sure you don't know the neighbours?'

The neighbours, that boxy, little woman and the thin man, put their dishes in the dishwasher after they had eaten the mess on the plates. Rosalind observed them intermittently during her night on the window-sill and never thought they were real, did not imagine they were people who could be called upon, signalled to. She thought of them as a picture show, and as she woke and slept she saw them turn on their gas heater, then they watched television, and the next time she awakened the moon was high in the sky and their house was in darkness. The boxy, little woman who mashed potatoes while she had a cigarette stuck in one corner of her mouth and the thin man who dredged the dinner into his mouth had gone to bed.

'How long had you been there?' the doctor wanted to know. 'Had you just arrived home?'

'Yes,' she said. 'I'd just arrived home,' and did not answer the other questions. And it was not untrue. People who had travelled for a long time often said for weeks that they had just arrived home. 'We haven't managed to clean up the garden yet,' she had heard people say. 'We've just got home. We've only been back from Scandinavia for three weeks.' Or back from anywhere. It was all the same, so a night hardly counted, she thought. A night was an instant. It was a leaf's fall, a dream.

'And what about next of kin?'

'My children live in New York,' she said. 'They're both lawyers. They really couldn't do anything from that distance. It's probably best not to worry them.' Already she was rehearsing in her own mind what she would say to them when next she wrote. *Just a note, my dears, to let you know your old mother* — and she would say this, she thought, as an ironical put-down for herself, to make the journey seem like that taken by a venerable and ancient beast — *is safely home again. Came back with a chill but am better now. I used to see the old colonel in London, that friend of your father's, and sometimes he would take me for a walk in Hyde Park. It was very nice.* It was my only pleasure, she thought now. *Please don't worry about me.* That would make it all seem above reproach.

They would write back, when they had time, and would say, *What's this about being an old mother? Don't you remember the time we were all walking down the street and someone thought one of us had a new girlfriend? Don't you remember that?* They were lawyers, she thought, and knew how to court pride and vanity. It would be impossible to tell her own children that she was more of a child than they had ever been, that in the end she had hoisted herself up on to their old eyrie to watch the advancing and retreating shapes of the ugly neighbours as if they might be passing mummers or a myth of the mind. That she had thought her wish to be loved was sufficient for such a thing to be so.

In the depths of the night the old house lay within shadows. A wind sprang up and far away, somewhere else in the house, that door began to bang again. Rosalind awoke and lay on the sill watching the house next door. A cat came through the open front door downstairs and stood staring at the doll, then washed its face before going out again.

Morning came sweet and dim as a memory, just like it had in Zimbabwe, but here the mist lingered only on the old vegetable patch and clung to the hedge on the western boundary. The people next door came slapping out to their kitchen in woollen dressing-gowns and slippers. The early mornings were always cold in that part of the street because the land was high, on a promontory, and caught the wind. The boxy woman and the miserable man ate something in bowls that they poured, steaming, from a saucepan. Porridge, thought Rosalind. Breakfast.

'How long is it since you ate properly? When did you last have a proper meal?' the doctor wanted to know. 'When did you last eat?'

'I had some soup coming home. They kept bringing trays of food, you know how they do on those aeroplanes, but I only wanted the soup.'

'And what did you have before that?' He was writing something on a card.

She thought for a long time.

'The bread and butter was nice. I used to go to Muswell Hill and get bread and butter in a teashop there. It had green and white gingham tablecloths. Priscilla told me about it.'

'I see.'

'And sometimes I used to go to another teashop opposite the tube station when I got back in the evening. It was so dark it seemed like evening, but it might have only been four o'clock. I can't remember. There was a teashop there called The Hollywood,' — and from somewhere she rustled up a rusty half-laugh — 'and I used to get a cup of tea there and a piece of fruit cake.'

'A piece of cake, and was that all?'

'It was a big piece,' said Rosalind.

'Didn't you want to eat?'

'It was a bit difficult', she said, 'with James's kitchen. I felt very tired. I felt very sad. I couldn't really be bothered thinking about food.'

'I see.' There it was again, thought Rosalind. *I see.* That, and *Ha, ha, ha* had been the language of the past few weeks. 'What I think we'll do with you, Mrs Wentworth,' — the doctor had finished writing now — 'is keep you here till the end of the week. You're responding well to treatment. The old pneumonia bug goes out the window these days I can tell you, with all the modern drugs. And you've got a few bumps and bruises but nothing broken, luckily. It could have been a lot worse. You'll notice you've got a couple of little stitches in your hand. We'll take those out the day after tomorrow. Do you remember cutting yourself?'

'It was the key,' said Rosalind. 'I held on to the key to the house all the way from Los Angeles. My hand felt sticky. I had the key all ready for the door. I wanted my own house.'

'Of course,' he said. 'Of course.' And that was another of those phrases. *I see, Ha, ha, ha, Of course.* The whole thing was built on those.

'I think on Saturday we'll send you down to the private hospital, that one past the shopping centre. I suppose you've got health insurance, have you? Oh, good. We'll just pop you in there for a few days and get you eating again and so on. If you had anyone at home you could go home on Saturday, but I think not, not as things are.'

'There's only a china doll there,' said Rosalind, and she managed that rusty laugh again. He looked very young, the doctor, and it would be a pity to tell him about doom in the heart, blight on the brain, an abandonment of will, the awakening of a dreamer.

'This name you mentioned.' He was reading the card. 'Priscilla. Is that your daughter?'

'No,' said Rosalind. 'She's not anyone of any importance. I hardly know her.'

'I see.' There it was again. 'And James? James isn't your son?'

'No. James is of no importance either.'

'I see. Well, what I suggest is that you have another little sleep before lunch, when you can have some soup.' He had gone away then, whistling, down the corridor.

She had heard a man whistling when morning came after her night on the window-sill. There was the click of the gate and the sound of footsteps crunching on that untidy gravel. A man was whistling the 'Flower Song' from *Carmen.*

Rosalind's knowledge of the sights and sounds of the old house was encyclopaedic. She had lived there for a long time. The man, whoever he was, stopped whistling and began to call 'Hello! Hello!' as he passed the old stone birdbath four paces from the front door.

'Hello! Anyone home?' The voice sounded familiar. The door opened wider as the iron basket of flowers fell over. 'Rosalind? Are you back? Hello! I think you might have got home yesterday. Oh, there you are.'

Far away, down in the entrance hall, she saw Benjamin advancing from a hundred miles away. He looked very small, so she opened and closed her eyes several times to get him the right size.

'Rosalind? I got your postcard and it said you were coming home yesterday.

'Rosalind? What are you doing up there? Rosalind, are you all right?' He stretched out his hand and the weight of it on her shoulder was too heavy to bear. 'Rosalind, answer me.' She tumbled forward as he shook her, fell slowly off the sill and dreamt it was the block of flats in London and she was falling down the liftwell, followed by James's virulent whisper. 'You're a dead loss, Rosie. Stay out of my way or wake your ideas up, one or the other. It's protein, Rosie. It's good for you. It's supposed to taste faintly fishy, like caviare.'

12

'GOOD EVENING, ROSALIND.' It is Benjamin at the front door again as eight o'clock peals from the old clock in the hall. For once it has got the time right. Ben is oddly formal in manner and dress. He is wearing a grey suit with an even paler shirt and a maroon silk tie in a Paisley pattern. 'Are you ready?'

'I'm not sure,' says Rosalind. She eyes the splendid tie, the pearly shirt, the suit with hand-stitched lapels. 'I haven't ever seen you wearing a suit before. I've just got the same clothes on that I had on before.'

'They look fine, Rosalind. Are you ready?'

'But I've had a bath,' she says.

'Oh good. Well,' — another brick — 'are you ready, then?'

'Would you like a cup of tea?' Rosalind feels strangely reluctant to leave the safety of her own cottage and the little cat darts out of the door for a moment to whack Benjamin on the foot with one paw.

'Hello, Tiddles,' says Benjamin. He is obviously trying to be pleasant, thinks Rosalind, but this is not a pleasantry from the cat. It is a sign of war. 'Um . . . tea . . .' he says.

Rosalind is proud of her tea and wants, secretly, to get his opinion about it. To a large packet of ordinary tea *(Woolworths Own Brand, Special This Week, More In Yellow Bins At The Back Of The Shop, Enter Our Lucky Number Competition)* she has added a small box of Lapsang Souchong. She has tipped all this into the largest mixing bowl to blend her own unique brand of tea, as the sun slants across the old garden and the cat plays with a leaf under a yellow rosebud on 'Peace'. And the telephone rang then, like a factory bell.

'Hello, Rosalind, what are you doing? It's Dinah here.'

'I'm blending tea,' she had said. 'I'm making my own brand of tea. I'm mixing it myself.'

'Oh, Rosalind, don't you lead an interesting life?'

'No, it's very dull. It's full of stress and worry.'

'Oh, Rosalind.'

The tea has, when she samples it herself, an interesting and indefinable quality, a singular charm which hints at rarity and great expense, perhaps even a journey to the East, specialised shopping in arcane byways known only by the *cognoscente.* The tea-blending is a great success.

'I've got some very special tea,' says Rosalind now on her own doorstep while the cat bashes Benjamin's foot again.

'Playful little thing, isn't it?' says Benjamin while the cat bares its teeth.

'I've got a very special blend,' says Rosalind. It might be best to ignore the cat. 'Are you sure you don't want to try it?' The new tea blend seemed to swell with stirring and has filled three large Twinings tea tins. The quantity her blending has produced is gratifying and extraordinary. Roger brought the tins of tea home a long time ago, and Dinah would say now, 'Rosalind, are you going all nostalgic again?' Rosalind remembers giving them a cursory glance when he put them down on the kitchen table. 'What've you been buying now?' she had asked, accustomed then to generosity, and went on unpacking pâté and smoked-eel fillets and crackers and camembert and a whole fillet of beef from the supermarket. It is not nostalgia though, thinks Rosalind now. It is hunger. But the new brand of tea, put into these old tins, which have been empty for years, masquerades gladly and splendidly as Russian Caravan Tea, Fine Assam and Best Ceylon. Interest rates have dropped another one per cent, but the fictional luxuriance of her tea-blending takes away the curse of this.

'It's really lovely tea,' says Rosalind, enticing as a hotel-keeper. 'Are you sure I can't make you a cup of my special new tea, Benjamin?'

'I don't think so, Rosalind. I won't come in.' He looks at his watch.

'Is there some sort of hurry?'

'Not really, dear, but we might as well get on our way.'

He is a clipped, neat, dapper man and his black shoes twinkle down the front steps. 'Here you are, Rosalind.' He opens the door of the car for her. The cat pushes its head through a gap in the trellis fence. 'Goodbye, Tiddles,' says Benjamin, and pats the cat while it stares at Rosalind. Its eyes are full of accusations, and the set of its head hints at illness and sudden collapse.

'Oh, dear,' says Rosalind. 'She's used to coming inside to watch television in the evening.'

'Tonight,' says Benjamin as he thrusts the gear lever into first, 'it can watch the garden.'

'She likes *Coronation Street*,' says Rosalind.

'So does my mother, but you can miss a few episodes and pick the story up just like that.' He snaps his fingers while doing a racing turn out of Rosalind's street and turns on to the main road just past the kindergarten fence. Here an immortal piece of graffiti has appeared in the past few days. *PLAY DOUGH SUX.*

'Isn't that funny?' says Rosalind pointing at the writing as Benjamin accelerates.

'Disgraceful,' says Benjamin.

'And there's another quite witty bit up here, Benjamin.' Rosalind is pointing out of the window. 'Just slow down a bit. There you are.' They are speeding past a long tin fence now and upon it is written, *BAN BENEFIT CUTS, HOW WILL WE AFFORD PAINT?* 'You've missed it, Ben. Do you always drive so fast?'

'Always, Rosalind.' He does another racing turn at the first set of traffic lights.

'I'm still quite worried about the cat,' says Rosalind as they spin on to the motorway.

'Don't worry about it, Rosalind. It's only an animal. It can surely keep itself amused for an evening out in the garden. You have to inspect my premises, you've said so yourself. The only time I have to show you my house is in the evening, so Tiddles will just have to do without you for once.'

'I suppose so.' She tightens her seat belt. 'Do you always pass so many cars, Benjamin, so fast?' She glimpses, briefly, a large red truck, a Porsche and four members of Black Power on motorbikes following a bus full of old ladies, many of whom are asleep with their heads nodding against the windows. Or perhaps, thinks Rosalind, they have died after the excitement of going out for the day.

'Always,' says Benjamin again, and they shoot past three or four interchanges and off-ramps before Rosalind is able to speak.

'I see they've found that head,' Benjamin says as they rocket down the motorway. 'You know, that woman near you who had her head chopped off. By that maniac. They've found her head.' He passes two pantechnicons on the inside and filters back to the fast lane. 'Haven't you read about that, Rosalind?'

'I don't get the paper every day,' says Rosalind.

'Well, anyway, they've found the head and they've got the chap who did it, so you're okay, Rosalind. He'd put the head in someone's rubbish bin.'

'I use rubbish bags,' says Rosalind, ashen.

'Well, that's all right, Rosalind,' he says, nudging the car over to the left-hand lane.

'I don't even know where I'm going,' says Rosalind. 'I don't even know where you live, Benjamin.'

'Nearly there.' He almost sings this as he skims on to a loop road. This suburb looks very like Dinah's. The streets are wide and clean and some of them are cobbled. There are avenues of silver birches and oaks and small flowerbeds in the middle of the roads where polyanthus jostle with ageratums and marigolds of the better sort, a dwarf variety with bronze foliage and flowers that are nearly brown. There is no orange here, nothing glares in the realm of colour. The private gardens stretch away in pristine splendour towards distant and large houses that are smothered in roses and other flowering creepers, which, she imagines, might be remarkable for their scent as well as beauty.

'I'm not sure I've ever been over this way before,' says Rosalind. 'It looks very nice. I don't suppose anyone gets their head cut off here, do they, Benjamin?'

'Don't you believe it, dear.' He changes down to second gear at high speed while the tyres smoke. 'See that house there?'

'Benjamin, please keep two hands on the wheel.'

'Chap in there, back in '74, '75, chopped up his mother-in-law and fed her to the Dobermanns. And see this place here? I'll just slow down, Rosalind, so you can see in. See that veranda there with all those beams? After the big crash some chap that lived there strung his wife up after he belted her over the head with something and then he strung her father up. He was out of his tree, poor old chap. In a wheelchair. Just like Roberta's mother, but she isn't in a wheelchair. The son-in-law lost a bomb that day and he went home and had them all swinging. Then he shot himself and they knew he was mad because he shot the wheelchair.'

Rosalind is silenced. There is no remark adequate for all this.

'So you can see, Rosalind, we all have our moments,' says Benjamin and swerves from one avenue into another even wider, and from there he skims into a third that ravishes a hilltop with bigger oaks, better views and great swathes of stone fences, wooden trellises higher than a man, wrought iron security fencing in a Spanish pattern with discreet security telephones at gates, which, apart from being very ornamental, are obviously extremely strong and could be electrified.

'She had money,' he says. 'The old girl that got fed to the dogs, that's why he did it. That one over your way, Rosalind, I wouldn't worry about that if I were you, dear. It was just a crime of passion. She annoyed him. Nothing to do with you, Rosalind. Could have happened anywhere.'

'Benjamin, Benjamin' — she clutches his arm — 'watch out for the boy on the bike.'

He ignores this outcry.

'Anyway, Rosalind, what do you think of it?'

Rosalind looks around at the pristine roads, the unmarked pavements, fences empty of messages for the world.

'I find it a bit odd,' she says. 'I mean, it's a very empty landscape, isn't it, Benjamin? Where is your verbalisation of problems here, Ben? How do people state their pain? How do they communicate their thoughts?' She screams suddenly. 'I'm sorry, I thought you were going to hit that truck.'

'Of course I wasn't going to hit that truck, Rosalind.' He

makes a rude sign at its driver. 'As for your verbalised landscape. People pay good money over here to stop all that. They don't send their children to the Montessori school over this way, Rosalind, to have *PLAY DOUGH SUX* written up on the walls.'

'I suppose not,' says Rosalind. 'But it doesn't seem very vibrant, Benjamin. Where are all the people? And where are all the dogs?' Rosalind's street is full of dogs, the brindled and motley clutch of hounds that includes two boxer crosses over the road, a doleful old beagle with big teeth, several others of mixed and mysterious breed and a gang of golden Labradors.

'There's a person,' says Benjamin as he nearly hits an old lady with blue hair and a pink tracksuit. She is being dragged across the road by a giant black poodle, clipped like topiary. 'And there's a dog for you, Rosalind, as you're obviously a dog lover, dear.'

'I didn't mean that sort of dog,' says Rosalind. 'I meant kind of wild dogs that live in gangs on the white line in the middle of the road.'

'I don't think we have any of those here.' He does another racing turn, this time into a private cul-de-sac. 'This is my drive, Rosalind, and here we are.' He draws up beside a large white house with a veranda that goes on forever. A miniature wooded landscape stretches away into the dusk with casual plantings of either dark blue or white polyanthus under beech trees. Several sets of french doors lead on to the terrace and they all have long shutters painted a glistening shade of magnolia.

'I must say your paint's in good order,' says Rosalind. This is a subject close to her thoughts at the moment because the cottage is peeling badly and the effect is not pristine or even elegant.

'Really?' says Benjamin. 'Is it?' His interest is only vague. 'It should look good, Rosalind, the amount it cost. I told you, dear, I've had the decorators in. Now,' — he opens the door of the car for her — 'we'll just pop you out and you can have a look at the whole place. You can have your inspection, Rosalind. Rosalind? Where are you going?' She has run away, across the lawn.

'Isn't the grass beautiful, Benjamin? And aren't you lucky not to have any bare patches? Half of my lawn's died over the summer, it's been so hot.'

'Rosalind, come back. Where are you going, dear? Come back.' Rosalind skips over the lawn again. 'I must say, dear,' he says, 'you're very fit and lithe. You've got a very sinuous walk.'

'Do you ever go for a walk through those trees? How does everything stay so green?' Rosalind does not wait for an answer. 'Isn't it beautiful?'

Benjamin presses a button beside one wooden shutter and water erupts in little fountains everywhere.

'My underground watering system,' he says. 'Reaches every corner. There's the secret, Rosalind, if you want to keep your garden green. You should think about it.'

'Oh, I will, Ben.' But she has stopped skipping now.

'But you mustn't get wet, Rosalind.' He presses the button again and the displays cease. 'Come inside.' They step over the terrace, which is made of quarry tiles devoid of moss and dust. Even the terracotta pots of geraniums and more polyanthus look as if they have been put there three seconds ago.

'Don't you get moss and dirt here, Benjamin?' The cleanliness is almost horrifying. Does anyone, in fact, live here? Does life actually exist in these environs? Has anyone ever slept or wept or eaten or behaved badly here? Has anyone spilt the beans, either real or imagined, within these walls? 'Does anyone actually live here, Benjamin?' Rosalind steps slowly forward as if at an exhibition.

'Of course people live here, Rosalind.' Benjamin is holding one of the french doors open. 'I live here some of the time. I'm away a lot of course. And Max lives here. That's his cottage away through the trees.' He points to where a light glimmers in the undergrowth. 'Max is the gardener. He does things round the place. I suppose he sweeps the terrace. Don't you have someone to sweep your terrace, Rosalind?'

'Yes,' says Rosalind. She sweeps it herself.

'Well, there you are, Rosalind. Now, come on in, this is

the sitting-room. Mind the ladders. I told them to tidy things up a bit for you.' The ladders are all lying on their sides in neat vee shapes. The pots of paint are in a tidy phalanx on a large square of canvas. There is another pile of pieces of canvas folded in four. The brushes have all been cleaned and lie in a row to dry, immaculate and nearly fluffy, on an old newspaper.

'Those look very good quality brushes,' says Rosalind.

'What?' Benjamin is several paces ahead now. 'I suppose they are, I don't know, really. Anyway, come this way, Rosalind. Come and have a look at it all. Now, what do you think?'

'It's very lovely.' And it is. It is all painted a shade of palest ivory and the spaces are enormous. Rosalind advances, reverent as a pilgrim. The thorough cleanliness of everything, the mastery of the painting, give an atmosphere as ruthless as the murder of the woman who had her head cut off.

Benjamin is over the other side of the room.

'Now, Rosalind, do you see this long wall here? This is the sort of wall you really need for that Gothic cabinet of yours. If you had a wall like this you could stand off and really see your cabinet properly.' Rosalind is marching off in the opposite direction.

'I haven't got a wall like that so it's no use talking about it, Benjamin. What a lovely fireplace.'

'Oh, that. I'm having all that ripped out.'

'What a waste. You're a very wasteful man, aren't you? All it needs is whitewashing. Just whitewash those awful liver-coloured bricks and leave that nice old stone mantelpiece just the way it is. Chuck a bit of old silver up there. Something sculptural if you've got it. Say, three or four little open salt cellars on hoof feet. You'd have a very austere appearance, but quite wonderful.'

'And a great saving, too,' says Benjamin. 'I'll think about that, Rosalind. Rosalind? Where are you?'

'What's all this?' Rosalind has advanced to the next room, which seems to be a gutted kitchen, and has gone out of the back door.

'Rosalind? What are you doing?'

Rosalind is swinging on the clothesline.

'What a lovely clothesline, Benjamin. I haven't seen a clothesline as lovely as this for a long time. My clothesline fell down and I never got another one.'

'Wherever do you hang your washing, dear?'

'Sometimes I hang smaller things on my flowering cherry tree,' says Rosalind. She is still swinging back and forth. 'And I've got an airing frame, one of those wire things. You can get a lot of washing on those,' she says, 'if you really have to. But this is wonderful, Benjamin. You've got six whole circles of wire. You could wash sheets and not fold them in four to hang them out. You could wash blankets. It's really wonderful.'

'Rosalind, it's just a clothesline. They're two a penny. Any handyman would put one up for you.'

'I suppose I just haven't got round to it,' says Rosalind and drops to the ground with an odd air of finality, like a clown with its smile painted on. There is yet another silence.

There are many lulls of this sort in Rosalind's conversations, or her lack of them, and they all have a significance, though only Rosalind knows this. That nobody has sensed the profundities of these gaps is a signal, she thinks, that nobody loves her.

'Anyway,' she says, 'I think you've got a really beautiful clothesline and a really beautifully paved yard, Ben. If the wind sprang up and blew your washing off the line it might not even get dirty.'

'It's very ordinary.' Benjamin is loitering on the top step of the little flight that leads down to the yard. 'If you got a new clothesline, Rosalind, you could get paving put down. Might cost you a couple of grand altogether. Not a problem, dear. It's not even a skilled job. Anyone could do it for you.'

'Oh, could they? Thank you, Benjamin.' She uses his full name now, like a stick. 'Thank you very much for your advice. I'll certainly remember it.' Surely, she thinks, this is also the time of year when she has to pay the insurance premium on her house and contents? Another four or five hundred dollars or even more. Sweet heaven, she thinks. And where is it coming from? She walks blindly away in the nearest direction, through a slight gap in a camellia hedge.

'Rosalind, what are you doing now?' Benjamin's voice follows her. 'My God, you're a difficult woman to control. Rosalind, come back. That's not my place in there.' Rosalind is striding across a tennis court now. 'Rosalind, that's next door. That's a nunnery, dear.'

'What?' Rosalind turns round. It is now nearly dark, long past dusk. And it is silent. There is the sound of cars from far away. Some children, out playing late, are laughing across the road. A dog barks, a deep, throaty, healthy sound that indicates proper training, good meals of balanced Fido and vitamin pills crushed into his milk. A bell rings inside the nunnery and this reminds Rosalind of the telephone. It is a while, hours, since James telephoned. He must be immured in the pleasures of Adelaide and Margaret, who is probably a big and accommodating girl of uncertain age and even more uncertain tastes. She, too, may have abundant pubic hair in which he is enmeshed like a drowned sailor in seaweed. It may, or may not, poke through her dresses.

'Come back, Rosalind.' Benjamin has appeared in the hedge's gap. 'That's the nunnery. What have you gone in there for, dear?' But it is too late. The front door opens and a nun comes out with a broom in her hand.

'Oh, hello, Benjamin,' she calls. She has a jolly voice like Dinah's, or like that of an old Girl Guide without guile. 'And how are you this fine night?'

'Good evening,' says Rosalind and sets off across the tennis court with her hand outstretched, like an invited visitor, someone who should be there. 'You must forgive me. I was admiring Ben's clothesline and I wandered through that gap in the hedge.'

'Hello, Sister Barbara.' Benjamin is shouting as he pushes himself through the gap now. 'I hope Max was a help.'

The nun has a sweet, round face like a lucky child's, or that of a fortunate dog. It is unremittingly plain, but good. She takes Rosalind's hand, which is cold and trembles a little, but this will not be noticed. Rosalind knows this. Her horrors are usually unnoticed and here is another one. In debt with a declining income, ageing and unwanted, thinks Rosalind, she is found wandering in the garden of a nunnery as darkness falls on an unknown suburb. How about that?

'My name', says Rosalind, 'is —' and stops there. Whatever is her name? Rosalind is not good with names. Her children called her Ma when they were being fond, Mother when they had been smacked. 'My Rose.' That is what Roger called her. 'Now Rosalind, you're not going all nostalgic again, are you?' The voice of Dinah. Roger's mother called her, well, never mind what Roger's mother called her. It doesn't matter now. 'Here's the nuisance again.' That was James.

The nun, calm and benign, is still waiting while Benjamin breaks through the hedge. 'My name', says the nun, 'is Sister Barbara.' She is like a prompt in a play. 'And we also have Sister Imelda here, and Sister Teresa and Sister Annette. And we've got an extra at the moment, Sister Victorine from Papua New Guinea.' And what, my dear, her eyes seem to say, is your name? What is your name?

'Rosalind. Come back.' Benjamin is through the hedge now and is coming across the tennis court himself. 'I don't know,' he says. 'Women!'

'My name', says Rosalind to the nun, 'is Mrs Rosalind Wentworth,' and so for one last time she summons up the melancholy myths of the past. The dinner parties she gave for the directors, the wives she gave garden parties for, the gala luncheons for heads of department upon retirement, the way Roger sat down at the big desk every Tuesday evening and wrote out cheques for all the bills, when money did not matter, and she went to the supermarket with that same cheque book and bought rotisserie chickens (size eight), wholemeal rolls, salmon quiche, asparagus, the large size in apricot yoghurt. Rosalind turns then, without another word, and goes off across the tennis court again — there is a lot of traffic over it tonight — and through the gap in the hedge, so the nun and Benjamin will not see the grip of her malaise.

'I hope Max did all that trimming properly,' says Benjamin. She can hear the voices clearly.

'Thank you, yes, he did indeed.' Is there a slight Irish

brogue there? thinks Rosalind. She sits down on Benjamin's back doorstep. 'Sister Imelda put you in her prayers. She was so pleased to get her view back.'

'He seems to have made a good job of the tennis court.'

'He has indeed.'

'If he's got time next week I'll send him in to cut the hedge.' This is a new view of Benjamin, Rosalind thinks. He is a benefactor for nuns and their garden.

'Thank you,' says Sister Barbara. The voices carry very clearly in the evening. 'God bless you, and God bless your friend.'

'Well, um, thank you.' Benjamin sounds discomforted, thinks Rosalind. 'I think she's just popped back home.' He returns through the gap in the hedge.

'Rosalind,' he says — she is still sitting on the back steps — 'you've ruined the hedge. Look at that hole. I don't know what Max is going to say. He likes to keep it looking all even and neat.'

'You can tell him', says Rosalind, rising to her feet, 'that I wrecked his hedge. And you can tell him — I don't know what you can tell him.' And she begins to cry very loudly, 'Boo, hoo, hoo.'

'Rosalind, be quiet. Rosalind, I don't know what's got into you. Women!' says Benjamin. 'Women!'

'Boo, hoo, hoo.'

'Rosalind, Sister Barbara might be listening.'

'I don't care who's listening. Boo, hoo, hoo.' There is a great relief in it all. Perhaps, thinks Rosalind, remembering the bill for the house insurance has been the final blow for her.

'Come inside, Rosalind, and I'll make you a cup of tea. This', says Benjamin, 'is an absolute disaster.'

'It is.' That is Rosalind again. 'And I'm sick of drinking tea.'

'I'll make you coffee then, or you can have a glass of wine.'

'I really don't drink any more, Benjamin. Boo, hoo, hoo.' And she thinks of James in London the year before last and how he used to say. 'Rosie, you drink too much.' 'I'll clean myself up when I get home, James. I won't need anaesthesia then.' And there is dear old Dinah who often says over dinner, 'Are you sure you won't let me give you a glass of my wine?' Dinah always buys a half-bottle of claret. 'Can't I tempt you, Rosalind?' 'No, thank you, Dinah.' 'I seem to remember you used to drink wine, didn't you, Rosalind?' 'Did I, Dinah? It's a long time ago.'

'Well, you'll have to have tea, then,' says Benjamin now. 'I really don't understand what all this is about.' He steers her through the back door and slams it. 'Thank God I've got you inside again. I don't know why you had to hike off and introduce yourself to Sister Barbara. I don't know why you did that.'

'I did it because I was in her garden and I'm a person, with a name, so I told her what it was. It was', says Rosalind, 'pride.'

'I see.' (Another brick.) 'Come on, Rosalind, and I'll show you the rest of the place. We might as well salvage what we can.' He has forgotten the tea, thinks Rosalind. 'Rosalind, will you please stop crying. I hate hearing women making that type of noise.'

'You haven't made my cup of tea.'

'I thought you said you were sick of tea.'

'I don't know what I said.'

'Women!' says Benjamin again. 'Come and see the entrance hall, Rosalind. I'll make you a cup of tea in a minute.' They tramp through the kitchen, which has been semi-gutted by the decorators, but there is a piece of board on the skeleton of a bench and upon this sits a new electric kettle. One cupboard door is open and inside is a tin of Twinings tea, Best China, which Rosalind feels sure is perfectly genuine and not a homemade concoction like her own. A jar stands beside the tin of tea and it contains three or four chocolate fingers, some pink iced wafers, one or two English digestives, a couple of little oatmeal offerings and several items wrapped in purple foil. Within the decimated framework are all the elements for comfortable living. 'Come through here, dear,' says Benjamin, and they continue the journey through the sitting-room. It is irregularly shaped, like a crooked letter 'L', and hidden round a corner is a white silk tweed sofa lurking amongst more pots of paint and ladders. Rosalind sits down.

'This is a lovely sofa, Benjamin.' She bounces up and down on the cushions. 'And these are all stuffed with feathers.' Rosalind is suddenly exhausted.

'Thank you, Rosalind. Just pop through here, will you, dear?' Benjamin is standing in another arched doorway. 'Now, Rosalind, here's my entrance hall.'

Rosalind follows, wiping her face on the hem of her long, black silk skirt. It is heavily gathered and contains metres of material so this is not such an embarrassing action as it might be. 'I must say you've got very nice legs,' he says. There has just been a flash of these as Rosalind wiped her eyes.

'You'll have to excuse me,' she says. 'I haven't got a hanky.'

'You only had to say, Rosalind,' — he hands her a polka-dotted, burgundy silk square — 'and I'd have given you mine.' So Rosalind wipes her face again.

'Thank you, Benjamin,' she says, holding out the handkerchief. 'Do you want this back?'

'No, thank you. I think you can keep it.'

'I see,' says Rosalind.

'Rosalind, I thought you'd stopped crying.' He is regarding her now with some doubt. 'Will your skirt be all right,' he wants to know, 'um, you know, after wiping, well, all that?'

'I suppose so,' says Rosalind. 'It's got moth holes, anyway.'

'Rosalind, if you ever, say, married someone very wealthy, would you throw away all your clothes and buy new ones, dear? You really wear the most extraordinary clothes.'

'I wear my clothes because I like them,' says Rosalind. 'Now, why don't you show me this entrance hall you keep going on about.' So they proceed through the house. The entrance hall is very Art Deco, even though Benjamin says the place is ancient. The inner hall is narrow and leads to four bedrooms, all of which have a wall devoted to storage. There are cupboards and wardrobes and special drawers for shirts and jerseys all hidden behind panelling. Life is organised here.

'Very nice,' says Rosalind. None of the bedrooms is furnished except for one, which contains a small truckle bed with green sheets and blankets in a blinding and clinical shade of malachite. This must be where Benjamin is camping for the moment.

'This is where I've been roosting, Rosalind,' says Benjamin as if he has heard this thought. 'I've got this walnut sleigh bed, its sort of Napoleonic if you like that type of thing, but it's in storage until the painting's finished. It's a very nice piece, Rosalind. Ormolu medallions, just very discreet, and amboyna wood inlays. Right up your street, Rosalind. Just the sort of thing you'd like, dear.'

'I couldn't possibly' — Rosalind is staring at the truckle bed — 'I mean, Benjamin . . .' What is there to say? 'And I didn't think it would be tonight,' she said. 'I thought I was just looking tonight.'

'Oh, you are, dear, you are,' says Benjamin. 'I never thought for one moment, I mean, not in that bed, Rosalind. When the decorators have finished, I'll send the boys over to the warehouse for the other bed and then —'

'Of course,' says Rosalind. 'But not green sheets, please. I'd have to have white, with lace.'

Benjamin is writing in a pocket diary. 'Bed linen, something pretty, white, with lace.'

'Or frills, or appliqué would be fine,' says Rosalind. 'I'm not that picky.'

'White,' intones Benjamin, bell-like whilst writing, 'with lace, or frills or appliqué. The lady isn't picky.' He stands thinking for a moment 'What about Battenberg lace, Rosalind?'

'Battenberg lace is very nice.'

'I've got a good line in at the moment. One of those arty shops over in the village went bust last week. I'll get the boys to bring over some samples, Rosalind, and you can see if it's what you want.'

'Thank you, Benjamin.'

'Not at all, Rosalind. My pleasure,' he says. 'Ha, ha, ha.' It is quite a while since he said *Ha, ha, ha,* thinks Rosalind. 'Well, on with the tour, Rosalind.' They go out into the hall again. 'And don't forget, dear,' he says, 'that there's a bathroom to go with each bedroom. You could take your pick.' He opens and closes doors quickly, flashes lamps on and off. There seem to be blue marble showers to go with possible blue bedrooms, ditto mushroom, but there are no marble bathrooms in brown. Rosalind notices this immediately. The only brown in the house is a gentle shade of umber, a soft ochre, on a huge rug in the sitting-room. It is handwoven, very soft and delicate underfoot and carries rune-like patterns that suggest magic. Rosalind is not fond of brown marble bathrooms, brown marble anything. 'You're as much use to me, Rosie, as a chocolate teapot,' James had said as he pinned her by the throat to the wall of a brown marble bathroom. 'I thought you knew about me, Rosie. Are you completely stupid?' And she had said yes, yes she was. Must be stupid to think anyone might love her.

'What do you think of it?' says Benjamin. They are walking up the inner hall now, towards the sitting-room.

'It's very lovely in its own way,' says Rosalind. 'If you had some Clarice Cliff you could put it in the entrance hall.'

'Sorry,' says Benjamin. 'No Clarice Cliff.'

'Oh, well,' says Rosalind. 'It doesn't matter. It was just a thought. Anyway, it's all quite lovely and I love that rug.' She points to the magical carpet with its mystic characters and elvish designs.

'Oh, that.' He kicks it with one toe. 'That's just some old Moroccan thing I bought once.'

'It's the most beautiful thing in the house.' Rosalind walks over the carpet as if it is medicine and will make her better, as if magic from its pattern will filter through the soles of her African sandals with their agate beads to make her malaise of memory go away.

'Do you think so, Rosalind? I'm pleased.'

It is now nearly eleven o'clock and the french doors show a garden beneath a full moon. Benjamin has turned on lamps in the house, but outside, when Rosalind cups her hands over the windowpanes and looks out, it is brighter than day. The moonlight shows every blade of grass, each flower, all the leaves on the trees.

'You should see how lovely it is outside.' Rosalind is still at the window and can see her own reflection in the glass. She is tall and slim, her black skirt flutters around her ankles and her toenails are painted pearly pink. 'And I've changed my mind a bit about that business,' she says. 'You know, what we were talking about before. I think I'll have to put my notability fee up, I'm sorry. I think I'm worth more.'

'I thought we were talking about the rug,' says Benjamin. 'You bewilder me, Rosalind, the way you hop about from one subject to another. And besides,' — he thinks for a moment — 'the terms have already been agreed.'

'In the normal run of business', says Rosalind, 'that would be so. But this is not the normal run of business so I can change it if I like, and my notability fee has gone up. I think I undervalued it. I think you should pay me at least fifty for my notability fee, and you haven't even made me that cup of tea.'

'Rosalind, I'll do that in a minute. Come here. Come a little bit closer. You've got a very lovely ribcage, Rosalind, just fleshed enough. You've got lovely skin tones, dear. Just hold up your arms for a minute, will you, while I get this little jersey off. First the left arm, now the right. Now, I'll undo the bows on these pretty little shoes.'

'Please make the tea, Ben.' Rosalind is standing, half-clothed now, on the magical runes of the rug. 'And you've messed up my hair.'

'Your hair's just fine, Rosalind. Just let me see how this skirt works. I see, more little bows.'

'Let me go, please Benjamin.' There is the formality of his full name.

'Won't do that, Rosalind. Just lift up that left foot, would you? Now the right. There we are.' He throws Rosalind's skirt into a corner.

'Please stop this, Benjamin. I'm a very boring person. I don't know what to do. This is a terrible mistake. Just let me go home. I'll get a taxi.' That poisonous whisper comes into her ear again. 'You're a very boring person, Rosie, from a very boring country. They stand on their heads to watch television where Rosie comes from. Rosie's the biggest disaster of my very disastrous career. I collected her from the airport on my fiftieth birthday and three days later she's bored me so much I'm now aged a hundred.'

'Rosalind,' says Benjamin now, 'you don't have to know

what to do. You don't have to do anything. Now, lift that right foot again, and the left. We'll just get these off, and I'll unhook this and I'll switch this off.' He throws some bits of black lace into the corner near the skirt and turns off the lamp.

'Ooo,' he says. 'Ooo, Rosalind.'

'I don't know what to do.'

'You don't have to do anything. I'll do everything that needs to be done. Not cold are you? Oh, good. Oh, yes, oh, yes. That's perfect.'

'Benjamin,' says Rosalind. 'This is hardly fair. You've taken all my clothes off and you've got all yours —'

'Stop talking, Rosalind. Oh, yes. Just like that. Oh, yes, oh, yes.'

13

ROSALIND SITS AT the big desk in her parlour the next morning. The day is fine with a promise of sun later, and children from further down the road are walking to school. So Rosalind imagines that, for them, she is the lady who has a white cat and who innocently sits at her desk in the bay window. The cat is sitting on the window-sill and watches as Rosalind writes out cheques and lifts one paw to bat the end of the pen in affectionate disrespect. Benjamin's cheque lies tucked inside the deposit section of the cheque book, the form filled out already, and now Rosalind is paying her bills and filling out her own ledger book.

Payment for services, she writes. *Basic fee $500. Notability fee $50. Travelling time $25. General automatic allowance (goodwill) to cover clothing, wear and tear, etcetera $125. Total = $700 (x 2).*

'Oh, Rosalind,' Benjamin had said. 'Oh, yes. Oh, Rosalind. Oh, yes. Oh, yes.' Then, in the moonlight, they had a picnic of tea and biscuits.

'Try one of these in the foil, Rosalind. They're very nice. Do you know what the time is?' He did not wait for an answer. 'It's after midnight, Rosalind. Have a look down the bottom of the jar, I think you'll find more of those ones you like down the bottom. More tea? Yum, yum,' — this last remark is a disturbing reminder of James — 'I love your little rosebuds, Rosalind. Just let me take that cup from you, dear. I'll make another pot later. Oh, Rosalind. Oh, God. Oh, yes.'

$700 x 2, writes Rosalind now, = *$1400*. Today she uses figures for the arithmetic because arithmetic is just arithmetic today, and everything adds up properly (or improperly, thinks Rosalind). The other day arithmetic had to be turned into prose, like a story, to make it readable, to turn it into a possible narrative and not calculus. But today arithmetic is just arithmetic, so Rosalind sits in the early morning sun

to write out her cheques. *Pay to City Gas, the sum of thirty-eight dollars and 47 cents.* Her pen neatly inscribes the correct letters and numbers on the line allocated for this, the jumble of letters of the alphabet and numbers a reminder that everything else is a mixture too. Good and bad. Nice and nasty. Friend and foe. Good intentions and bad intentions.

'Roberta's father's coming to see me next Friday,' Benjamin had said. 'The old boy's a lawyer.'

'Oh, yes?' The garden was then in shadow, the trees as dark as some thoughts, black as reproach.

'They're a bit concerned,' said Benjamin. 'Him and the mother, even though she's out of her tree. The old girl has her lucid moments even at this late stage.'

'Oh, yes?' If there is a prize for saying *Oh, yes?* with equilibrium and charm she will get it, thinks Rosalind.

'I've lived with her for nine years,' said Benjamin as if he has been told this, like a bill owing. 'Roberta.'

'There'd be a lot at stake,' said Rosalind looking out at that sweep of lawn, the raked drive, the pristine veranda upon which no leaf stirred, no detritus of garden or house lingering in the smallest nook and merest crack in the quarry tiles. 'People don't give up easily.' And the words fall like invisible bones or spoken graffiti in that mute and unverbalised landscape.

'She's wanting to move in, Roberta I mean.'

'She would be.' And she had got up then from the Moroccan rug. 'Just pass me my skirt, will you?' She did not use his name. 'Throw me my jersey. I'd better go home, I think.'

Pay to City Electricity, the sum of twenty-five dollars and 13 cents. Pay to Water Rates Department, the sum of forty-five dollars exactly. And so on. *Pay to J.B. Gray, Jeweller, the sum of fifteen dollars exactly.* Telephone bill: *forty-seven dollars and 85 cents.* House and contents insurance: *six hundred and forty-two dollars and 53 cents.* Car insurance: *two hundred and sixty-five dollars and 70 cents.* But there is plenty left over at the end of all this. When the cheque from Benjamin is credited to her account and after her own cheques have been drawn, there will still be a reasonable credit. So Rosalind writes out one last cheque, for cash, to pay for groceries. *Pay To Cash, the sum of one hundred and fifty dollars,* then writes out a shopping list. *Six tins of Gourmet cat food, mixed game flavour.* It is the cat's favourite and the cat, her companion *in extremis,* deserves this. *Wholemeal flour, cheese, eggs, six small tins of salmon, crackers, rosemary hair shampoo, soap powder, window cleaner, new dusters, toilet soap (Pears), baking powder, coffee, beeswax to polish dining-table, light bulbs, disinfectant, today's newspaper.*

The prosaic quality of the requirements is as endearing as the lower notes in a symphony for children. *Marmite,* she writes, *potting soil, onions, vegetelli, cooking oil, white wine vinegar.*

Then two letters have to be written. The first is to the manager of her bank.

Dear Sir,

Is it really true that the monthly interest payments on my trust funds have now dropped to such a low level that I cannot draw any money from this interest till at least every third month and possibly the fourth? I was told this by one of your tellers last week and I find it difficult to believe. The bank statement I requested at the time has not yet arrived, so I must make this enquiry. If it is not possible, under bank rulings, for me to draw any interest till it reaches a four-figure sum, would the bank please consider altering these regulations so that people such as myself, dependent upon these payments for their sustenance, could draw, say $500? This would mean that, although one's income had dropped dramatically, smaller sums would be available more often for ordinary household expenditure such as groceries. I would greatly appreciate it if you could give me a prompt answer to this question.

Yours faithfully, Rosalind Wentworth.

The second letter is more difficult to write.

Dear Malcolm, I remember you very well from your visits to our house, now sadly sold, when Roger was alive, and I wonder now if you could possibly help me with something. Rosalind has no hopes about this request, but everything must be tried. There are many questions on her mind. How long will this situation with Benjamin last? How long will it be before Roberta, backed up by her father who is a lawyer and her mother even though she is out of her tree (but mentally clinging to a branch when the occasion arises) goes to live at Benjamin's house? Or, at the very least, embarks on a complicated series of litigious moves to claim half his empire? Or even just the stove and the jar of biscuits? How much will she earn before Benjamin grows tired of her, if he is not tired of her already? Will the Napoleonic sleigh bed with its amboyna wood inlays and discreet ormolu medallions remain in storage? Is he, at this very moment, telling the boys — whoever the boys are — to sell all the Battenberg lace bed linen instead of keeping some for her delectation? What is going to happen? She continues the letter to Roger's old colleague. *I was a trained journalist, as you know.* He does not know this at all, thinks Rosalind, but he will now.

Although I realise that computers are endemic to newspaper operation these days and I am untrained in their use, I do have a great ability to learn and, indeed, the desire to do so. The thought has occurred to me that, possibly, you may have a position in your organisation for a sensible and capable person such as myself. I am in need of work and wondered if I could return to my old career. I used to specialise in the fields of art, literature and health, but would be willing to attempt anything.

Yours sincerely, Rosalind Wentworth.

P.S. Do you remember the time Roger brought you home from the office to wait for your plane and you both ate all those Easter buns I'd made? We used to have fun then, didn't we?

She wonders if this is going too far, but there is little to lose. It is mostly lost already.

The stockmarket crash took a lot, and the related drop in real estate values took more. Then there were dramatic falls in interest rates at the banks due to lower inflation. And James took a lot. Self-esteem, innocence, pride, charm, beauty, health. James took those. And now Benjamin has purchased flesh and flummery, duplicity, desperation, insurrection and insolvency because everything has to be paid for, if not by one person then by another. Justice does not come into it, thinks Rosalind, and just as she has paid dearly for James's casual and practised slaughter of tenderness so does Benjamin pay now for the dissembling of grace. 'This is Rosie. No, I haven't had too much to drink. This is Rosie, who's a very boring person. Rosie's been as much use to me as a chocolate teapot. Say yes, darling. Can't even speak? Struck dumb, are you? Rosie's from a very boring country where they watch television standing on their heads. Rosie won't eat. She doesn't know what's good for her, Rosie doesn't.' As long as somebody pays for that, thinks Rosalind, then it is a commercial transaction that is both complete and finished, the handing over of monies the final compensation.

It is too early to go to the bank yet, so Rosalind sits in the sun to read an old newspaper again. The idea of money and the ability to pay bills again, even briefly, gives the day a luxuriance.

If you are over forty, she reads, *you are over the hill and there is not much you can do about it.* This is a Press Association story from the capital so it comes with authority, like the trumpeting of a government. *A forty-eight-year-old woman* — Rosalind is not forty-eight but she shifts uneasily and almost blushes because she might be one day — *who applied for a job as a secretary was told: 'Sorry, love, we're not considering anyone over forty.' A fifty-four-year-old man, made redundant after company restructuring, reported he had applied for ninety jobs and had not been shortlisted for any, despite having a degree in mathematics and computing and considerable management experience.* This is not a cheerful story, so Rosalind turns the page. Her letter to Malcolm is waiting to be posted, as pale and small as a starving cheek, so she looks the other way and continues reading. *The laws on prostitution are not to be changed,* says a story at the bottom of page three. This also emanates from the capital, another blast. *It is still against the law to solicit for business in public places and to run a brothel using the endeavours of employees to provide an income for the keeper.* But, Rosalind thinks, she is not doing this. She is merely getting to know her old friend Benjamin better, and he is helping her with her groceries and a few other things.

The day is going to be warm and sunny and the weather draws Rosalind out, away from this coldness of thought. It takes half an hour to walk to the nearest branch of her bank — the car may not have enough petrol in its tank to get her there safely — and she leaves the cat sitting on the gatepost again. This post has also attracted local graffiti, but of the kindest and most loving sort, forgivable even. A child, in a careful but wandering hand, has written in thick black ink *KAT.* The cat must therefore be a small milestone in the neighbourhood, thinks Rosalind, and has left the word there. Perhaps *LADY* will appear on her window-sill one day.

At the bank she explains about the cheque from Benjamin.

'I've got this here,' she says and slides it over the counter. It would be best, she thinks, if it is not exactly mentioned. 'If I bank it in my cheque account today and also write out cheques today for accounts to be posted will it all work out all right? Will the money be acknowledged at the same time the cheques are drawn, do you think?' A profound doubt has come into her mind about everything.

'It'll be fine,' says the teller. He has a square face that looks kind. He looks like the sort of man who would have children and they would go out to the gate to meet him when he came home. A nice man. 'We know you, Mrs Wentworth,' he says and goes bang, bang with a rubber stamp, so the money is somehow in the cheque book. The numbers are true. After that she walks home again, past rows of houses that look locked and shuttered because everyone is at work or, if they are over forty, they are hiding round the back so no one knows this. She has money in her purse from the cheque for cash and goes home to fetch her car, which has been in the garage for weeks, hardly used. The last time Rosalind drove her car was to the Mozart concert and the petrol indicator was on *E* for empty all the way. It is still on *E* for empty today as she drives to the nearest petrol station.

'Give me twenty dollars' worth of Super, please,' says Rosalind, and leans against the back of the car with an air of laconic ease that is entirely assumed for the day. Even buying petrol is exciting, she thinks, if it is an unaccustomed pleasure.

'You're very cheerful today,' says Doreen, the girl who looks after the till. 'Haven't seen you for a while.'

'No, you haven't,' says Rosalind and offers no explanation for this. 'And yes, I'm very cheerful today.' Then she swoops off to the supermarket for the groceries, walking the aisles with a wire basket in her hands, marching into the now unfamiliar hinterland of pâté, cottage cheese and pita bread. Rosalind has been a grocery exile, an outcast amongst the bargain bins, plain packs and special offers for a long time. Butter. Gourmet cat food (mixed game flavour). Milk. Blue vein cheese. They all go into the basket. A piece of fillet steak. She loiters beside the meat refrigerator after this choice, then replaces the piece of steak. One larger piece of fillet steak. Yet again the cat comes into her mind. The cat is her devoted companion and so all treats must be shared. She and the cat will share the fillet steak for dinner.

The mail has arrived by the time she gets home with all the purchases. There are no bills, no Accounts Rendered, nothing but a letter from a distant publishing company and this brings good news.

Dear Rosalind Wentworth,

We are bringing out a volume of significant poetry, and wonder if you would sign the enclosed permission slip so that an excerpt from your poem 'The Rose' can be included. Our editor, Pearl Drummond, would like to incorporate stanzas 50-130. She has particularly stated that this portion of the work shows your extreme facility in the manipulation of diction and contrasts in tonal phenomena. Your open form approach to paradoxical activity was a milestone and shows the very unusual (for this country) influence of the French Symbolists. We very much look forward to hearing from you and would also like to know if you have any later, and possibly unpublished, work. This letter has been sent to your old publishers in the hope that it will be sent on as we appear to have lost your address. Incidentally, payment for the Drummond anthology will be at the rate of $75 per 100 words and you will also receive a complimentary copy of the book, which is to be called Glowing Lights Amongst The Stars *(hardback $52.95, paperback $29.95). We will send you an invitation to the champagne breakfast*

launch *of this notable volume.*
Yours sincerely, Blarty Blarty Blah.

This is a change, Rosalind thinks, from the correspondence she received at James's place the winter before last. *Dear Whoever You Are.* That was the note from Félice.

Please leave James alone. My divorce has come through and but for the mischief that you have caused I would now be married to James. I have also had the galling prospect of spending weekend after weekend alone in a house which has taken all my capital and more besides while James is kept in London by a person who I would describe as no better than she ought to be. Please go back to where you come from. Even my children are upset. One hid in the attic for two full days last week and my daughter, for whom we have great hopes of a musical career, cannot practise with the house in such a turmoil. She has a solo in the school Christmas concert, but has not been able to attend rehearsals (at the cathedral) due to the upset you have caused. My expenditure here has been considerable. I have had an extra bathroom put in upstairs, with matching bath and vanity, and I have also purchased a four-poster waterbed, in the queen size, so I am not anxious to let my investment slip away. Go back to where you come from. You are causing nothing but unhappiness for everyone. You are not welcome.
Blarty Blarty Blah.

The telephone rings and interrupts this train of thought.
'Oh, good.' It is Benjamin. 'You've been out, Rosalind. I rang earlier. It's a very welcome thing to hear your voice this fine morning. I just wondered if you were all right.'
'Yes, thank you.' They are always very polite. 'I'm fine, thanks. I just went to the supermarket very early, before it got too crowded.'
'Wise, Rosalind. Wise.' There is a long silence. 'Found everything all right at home, did you, when you got inside last night?'
'Yes, thank you Benjamin. Everything was fine.'
'Little cat waiting for you?' asks Benjamin. 'Nice, Rosalind, nice.'

'Do you know what time it is?' he had said when he made the second pot of tea. 'Just shuntle over a bit, will you Rosalind? That's lovely, dear. I've found you this dressing-gown of mine to put on. You might get cold. It's two in the morning,' he said. 'Gets a bit chilly in the early hours. We can't have you catching cold.'

Rosalind, wrapped in the robe, is unwrapping one of the biscuits wrapped in purple foil. Biscuits, women, it is all the same.

'I didn't know you could still get these,' she said. 'I think they're the ones I used to like years ago, when I was a little girl.'

'They're fairly common, I think.' Benjamin looks puzzled. 'You get them in the big boxes of biscuits, the gift packs.'

'I don't really buy biscuits that much.' Never, actually.

'Oh, well,' said Benjamin. 'Tuck in, Rosalind. More tea? Is that a bit strong for you?'

'It's fine, thank you.'

'I'll take you home in a minute, Rosalind.'

'I could get a taxi.' Perhaps it could be charged to her Visa card, thinks Rosalind, and by the time the bill comes she might have fallen under a bus.

'I don't think so, Rosalind. I wouldn't like you to go off in a taxi. And I've got this for you, dear.' He handed her a cheque, and tucked the robe more securely round her.

'Thank you.' She began to drink the tea. 'This is very nice tea. What sort is it?'

'Twinings, Rosalind. Like I'm always telling you, you must have the best.'

'I've got my own special blend at the moment.' Rosalind thought of her own tea-blending and how Dinah had said, 'Oh, Rosalind, you lead such an interesting life.'

'I'm a bit worried about that cheque, Rosalind — you'll put it away carefully, won't you, in your bag?'

'If you'd just hand it to me right now, I'll put it in my wallet straight away, Benjamin, thank you.'

'That's all right, Rosalind. Just our little agreement. We must keep to the terms of the contract.' He slipped one arm round her waist under the robe. 'Which I must say have proved immensely satisfactory up till now. It's very late, Rosalind. I suppose I'd better take you home.'

'I suppose you had.'

'Roberta isn't very good at — well, you know, Rosalind. She says it's because I won't marry her and it's made her so nervous and insecure that she can't fully — oh, well, I suppose it doesn't matter. It's a problem I'll have to face myself. My lawyer says an equitable settlement should shut her father up.'

They had spun back along the motorway in silence, back to the lost lanes where people's messages to the world were painted along fences and walls, past *PLAY DOUGH SUX* and all the other silently verbalised decrees.

'Oh, look.' Rosalind had pointed at the tin fence on the main road. 'There's a new message. *ROYALISTS ARE GROVELLERS*, and the lettering is exquisite. Benjamin, you drive so fast you've missed it.'

'My own father got an OBE for his services to the hardware industry,' said Benjamin. 'I wouldn't have called him a groveller, but when I think about it, he was a bully. Well, Rosalind, here we are. Safely home again, and your cat's waiting for you on the gatepost. I see the bastards have been at that as well.'

'I've rung about the bed linen,' says Benjamin now while Rosalind stands beside the telephone with the bag of groceries and the cat at her feet — it has smelt the fillet steak — and the letter from the publisher in her hand. 'I've got a choice here of three or four patterns in this Battenberg lace stuff. I've bought it all in as bankrupt stock. You've got no idea who's going to the wall these days, Rosalind, and it's every day, every morning. They're biting the dust, Rosalind.

'But I wondered, Rosalind, can I send one of the boys over now with some samples, and you can decide what you want? Then I can get the rest of the stuff out on the shelves by five. I can't start getting the money in till I get the stuff out, on sale.' Benjamin the businessman, the entrepreneur.

'Of course,' says Rosalind. She is into commerce herself now. 'You could choose it yourself, Benjamin. I don't mind.'

'No, Rosalind. We agreed you'd choose. I'll send old Wally

round in the van, but there's just one thing. I should warn you. Wally's a good lad, don't mistake me there, but he's a bit, well, you'll see for yourself. But there's nothing to worry about. At this hour of the day, Wally's fine. It's in the evening, when he's been smoking pot and drinking that he gets violent, but the counselling's helping. Well, Rosalind,' — there is no time to reply to all this — 'Wally'll be with you in a moment. Just choose whatever you like.' He hangs up.

The cat takes up its position on the gatepost marked *KAT,* and Rosalind waits in the bay window not yet marked *LADY,* and soon a yellow van noses down the street. The footsteps on her front veranda sound as if they belong to somebody very heavy, and the slam of her gate, resonating through the cottage, suggests a large arm and hand.

'Mrs Wineworf?' Wally blocks out the light at her front door, and the hinges creak in an uneasy sort of way as Rosalind opens it wider and wider to see all of Wally and his tattoos. 'Mrs Wineworf?' There is a liquor wholesaler called Wineworths and Rosalind suddenly thinks that Wally imagines she is in the wholesaling business as well.

'Yes?' He is far too big to contradict, and what does the name matter anyway, when the business is considered, thinks Rosalind.

'He', says Wally and gestures with one thumb over his shoulder, 'says this is for you, Mrs Wineworf.' He hands her a large parcel.

'You'd better come in, Wally,' says Rosalind, and he takes one large step, then another, and these two movements take him nearly as far as the kitchen. 'I have to choose something and then send you back with the rest, so you'll just have to wait.' Wally has a safety-pin through his left nostril and has the word *DEVIL* tattooed across his forehead.

'I won't delay you for long, though,' says Rosalind.

'S'alright,' says Wally. He points over his shoulder again with that thumb. 'He didn't say anyfing about anyfing going back.'

'I see,' says Rosalind, and yet again it strikes her that a lot of the dialogue is made up of *I see, Oh, Well* and things like that. She tumbles all the samples out on to the yellow silk, antique sofa, and its white china castors look suddenly like reproachful eyes. Oh, Rosalind, they seem to say, how could you do this when once you were a nice lady who wore beige satin, boxer-short knickers, trimmed with ecru lace and pantihose in the dainty shade of porcelain, and played mah-jong with other ladies who were equally protected and seemly, then went home in the evening to tell Roger the news of the day, which may include that the supermarket had burnt down, nothing more passionate than that? Rosalind? How can you do this?

'These are the ones I like,' she says, and her unerring hand goes straight to the ones with roses.

'Phone?' says Wally, and he lifts the receiver. 'That you?' Each finger has left a black mark on a number. 'I'm here. At Mrs Wineworf's. And she likes' — he waves at Rosalind, beckons, and she approaches with a pillowcase — 'your bee twenny-nine four nine ones.' He is reading a label stapled to one corner. 'It's your bee twenny-nine four nine ones you gotta watch out for there. Yup. Yup.' There seem to be instructions coming from the other end of the line. 'Right,' he says. 'Gotcha. Will do.'

'Don't you want these?' Rosalind trails up the hall after him, dragging the contents of the parcel. There must be four or five pairs of sheets and numerous pillowcases.

'Dunno,' says Wally. He is climbing into the van now. 'Feel free,' says Wally. 'He' — and there is that thumb again — 'never said nuffing about taking fings back. And I'm not going back anyway. I'm going out to the warehouse. I got lifting to do out there.' And he drives away tooting. 'It's been nice knowing you, Mrs Wineworf.'

The telephone is ringing once more.

'Rosalind?' It is Benjamin again. 'Did that big pain in the butt behave himself?'

'Yes, Benjamin. He's been and gone.'

'Oh, good.' *Oh, good* is one of the lines in the story too. And *Ha, ha, ha* is another, but there have not been many of those lately.

'He's a good lad,' says Benjamin. 'He's got slight difficulties, but he's good-hearted. He'd give you the shirt off his back.'

'Yes,' says Rosalind. She has the contents of the parcel spilling out from under one arm and makes this one word seem as long as a last breath.

'And you liked the B29s? Just checking, Rosalind.'

'The ones with roses.' She feels incapable of saying 'bed linen'.

'Your B29s — that's right. I'll get them packed up, dear, and the boys are working on the business of the sleigh bed. We've all been out there today, and it's not going to be too difficult. There's a lot of stuff stacked round it out at the warehouse, but once we get Wally there we'll be fine.' Wally could toss furniture round like corks, thinks Rosalind. 'I've had to send him over to the other warehouse now, but we'll get on to it first thing in the morning. Take care, Rosalind, and say hello to Tiddles for me.' He rings off.

Rosalind spends the rest of the day working in the garden. Oxalis, of a giant variety, has almost taken over the herb garden. Even rampant mint is wilting before its encroachments, and the thyme and sage have disappeared. A crop of red-stemmed spinach has outgrown its strength and must be dug out. The cottage and its little garden make up, in Rosalind's mind, a kind of small farm from which she harvests free crops, and everything, thus, must be carefully looked after. The parsley, sprinkled on omelettes, gives an illusion of greenery, and with broccoli selling at $4.99 a kilogram at the supermarket on special the value of her cash crops is incalculable. The spinach — only the ordinary white-stemmed variety is left now — after a bit of effort provides spinach quiche, which can pass as an immutable caprice not a necessity. The garden, in a very oriental way, saves Rosalind's face and fosters her masquerade of management as tellingly as the parsley poses as miniature broccoli.

Later in the day she reads the financial pages of the newspaper and learns that stocks improving outnumber stocks falling by more than two to one, and brokers publicly state that the market could edge a little higher next week. The small number of shares included in her trust funds may possibly pay a small dividend this year, or next year, so in the evening she and the cat share the piece of fillet steak with a sense of vague optimism. Things might be improving, and at least the rates on the cottage and the water rates and all the other bills have been paid. Thanks to Benjamin. And Rosalind thinks about this for a while. Thanks to her own activities with Benjamin; Rosalind the spinach-grower, the keeper of an excellent herb garden, protector of roses, saviour of white cats that are nearly dead and companion extraordinaire.

At midnight the telephone rings, muffled by the white towel, but still pealing through the night. It is James again.

'Hello, Rosie, woke you up, did I? Never mind. You can go back to sleep again. Couldn't ring you before now, darling. Sorry.' But the silence has been a benediction, thinks Rosalind. 'Looking forward to seeing you on the — Oh, God, I thought she was in the shower. Have you read my letter yet? Oh, hello, Margie darling. Out so soon? Just seeing if your telephone works. And it does. Cheerio,' he says into the telephone, and then Rosalind hears his voice more faintly, as if his face might now be turned away from the receiver. 'Just getting a weather report, darling. Come here and let me look at your gorgeous big — ' He hangs up in Rosalind's ear. She has not said a word.

The cat has not been disturbed by this interruption. It is still curled up beside Rosalind's pillow, and the other noises of the night are fleeting and far away, like music on a theme of withdrawal, because all the sounds diminish. Cars pass the cottage and go to other parts of the street. A train in the distance fades away to the north. The silence of the night is benign and beautiful.

But James is obviously drawing inexorably closer. Adelaide, compared to London, seems almost next door. The little white cat sleeps, nicely disguised by the lace pillows on the bed. It is an albino, bleached and parched already by its own genetic inheritance. No revelation of James and his activities can make it any paler, but Rosalind puts an arm around it and draws it up on to her shoulder for protection, not for the cat but for herself.

The bedroom has only one large window. A high narrow casement, it could have lit a stairwell in a larger house, though it is not nearly as lofty as the big window that brought light to the stairs in the big house on the hill. The glass is plain with no coloured panes. There is nothing cranberry pink or cobalt blue to detract from its austerity, and through its plainness that night comes the light of the moon. It holds the little room and its furnishings with a kind of affection, a sweetness from the sky, so that Rosalind falls asleep again amongst the lace and carved rosettes on the chests of drawers, between the high arched ends of the bed that protect her like a portcullis under the silvery light of the moon. A small oil painting of a child holding a doll hangs beside the bed, and she sleeps with the last waking sight of this in her mind, dreaming of pictures. Pictures bought and pictures sold, pictures swapped, dreams of the old life at the little gallery when once a broker in futures, when it was possible to believe they would all have a future, came in one day off the street to buy the entire stock. Pictures. And Dinah's voice follows her through the dreams, 'You've got so many pictures, Rosalind. So many pictures.' So many pictures, Rosalind. So many pictures.

14

'YOU'VE GOT SO many pictures, Rosalind.' The words echoed in her head the next morning. 'Rosalind, you've got pictures all over the place. Dust-catchers, Rosalind. Dust-catchers.' That's what Dinah always said.

The parlour, in the front of Rosalind's cottage, held the best of them. A lot had been sold, or stolen, already, and those remaining were the remnants of the collection. They marched up the walls, in ranks, four deep and hung with care they posed as something better, along with what was left of the furniture. The shades in the Chinese rug, previously refused by Benjamin, brought out the colour in the green silk chairs. The green silk itself was reflected in the old glass of a cabinet where the spines of leatherbound books, faded and mellow, glimmered like jade.

Beside the door to the parlour hung a series of small drawings by an artist nearly forgotten, but the simplicity of the work gave it an elegance that was nearly sculptural. Rosalind's notebook of clients was somewhere in the chest that had yielded up James's telephone number in an address book earlier in the month. And all the letters from James were there too, the ones that began *My Darling Rosalind.* She rifled through all this, past the derelictions of *It will be wonderful to see you in Johannes—.* It was a strange contradiction, she thought, that what she had once tossed aside without a thought — the notebook of clients' names from the old days at the gallery — was now of deep interest. *My Darling Rosalind* was kept as a punishment to be glanced at sideways, or not at all.

The telephone numbers and addresses in the notebook were long out of date. The stockmarket had crashed splendidly since then with other later dips in value that had prompted suicides and disgraces. The shrapnel, according to financial writers, was still flying. But the names, thought

Rosalind, the names might be a clue, and she thought of Dinah again, stalwartly munching through fillet steak, and saying, 'You'll just have to start writing poetry again, even if there's no money in it. Or you'll have to go into business. Rosalind, you'll have to do something.'

She sat cross-legged on the floor with the cat on her lap, searching the new telephone directory for names from the notebook. Middle Eastern Oil and Incidental was no longer listed anywhere. They had once bought a large McCahon for their boardroom. She remembered that nicely profitable day. Shwimmer Real Estate. Gone. They used to sell properties costing a million dollars and over, nothing less, but purchased only artworks in the medium price-range. They had bought a nice little Nairn once, when the price for Nairns was down a bit. A landscape with a river, trees and hills. She remembered that. It was a beautiful little picture. The man from Shwimmers had hardly looked up when she brought it into his office. He was red-faced, wore a dark suit that was too tight across the shoulders, and she had said, loitering in her quiet way, 'I really must insist that you look at this picture properly. These people, you know, might have broken their hearts painting these things. I couldn't really say with any authority, but this might have been the last thing he painted. It's certainly a later work, and very fine.'

'I'm expecting a client in a minute.' He had had a harsh voice, too. She remembered that as well. 'I've got paperwork to catch up on.' And his pen had gone scratch, scratch, scratch on some sharp and shiny paper.

'Your client must wait, then. I must insist that this picture is hung at a particular height. Would you be able to get me a hammer and a picture hook now? So that I could hang it for you, please?'

She watched him press some buttons on his desk.

'Debbie, is that you, dear?' He sounded bored. 'Debbie, have you got a tack hammer out there, dear, and the odd little nail or something. Mrs Thing from the Whatsit Gallery wants to hang the picky. Thank you, dear. I knew I could rely on you.' He turned to Rosalind again. 'Our Girl Friday,' he said. 'Couldn't move an inch without her.'

There was no sign of Shwimmers now in the new telephone book. Murray Engineering had bitten the dust too. Also Abbotts' Classical Cars. They dealt in Jaguars, Porsches, BMWs and similar makes, and their office had had handwoven carpets from Tibet. They had bought — and here Rosalind had to stop and think — they had bought a small Blomfield just before the crash, and then another, at a much reduced price, shortly afterwards. Winterburn, Heatley and Growcott, Barristers, Solicitors and Notary Public. Gone. They were in the upper bracket and bought a big Peele for the senior partner's office and smaller, but no less grand, works by Richardson, Perrett and Pruden for other rooms. Also gone.

On the fourteenth cross reference between the notebook and the telephone book she came upon Eric Kaufmann, investment analyst. Eric Kaufmann still existed, though in a new office. Cross references between her map and the address indicated that Eric Kaufmann had moved his premises from a glossy tower block in the main drag to an obscure sidestreet and was no longer working with Gilbert Vine. According to the notebook he had bought a big Smither for the boardroom in the months before the stockmarket plunged and had put in an order for something else that had to be large and colourful, artist unspecified. But nothing had come of this. The gallery closed and everything changed. Her partner had gone to Sydney. Rosalind had gone to London, had gone out of paintings, had gone wild.

'You're not going out again,' James would say. 'I haven't been outdoors for nine days. The wind's wild out there.'

'I'm just going to the Tate.' Already she would be at the door, the marvellous door that led to the landing and the lift and a chat with Mavis while she waited.

'Where's that girl that was here?' Mavis asked once. 'That one with the thin nose. Where's she gorn? Got rid of her, did he?' Ah, Rosalind had thought. Priscilla. That would be Priscilla. So she did have a thin, arched nose.

'She's gone away somewhere to live. She's got a cottage now.'

'Oh, some people do have all the luck, dear. Are you sure I can't fetch you a mini-cab?'

'No, thank you, Mavis, I'll be fine.'

'Going to the Tate, are you?' That would have been James. 'I've lived in London all my life and I've never been to the Tate.'

'The pictures are wonderful, James. It might do you good to see something beautiful and silent and that you can't have.' That was as much insolence as she permitted herself to use.

'If you've seen one you've seen them all. I don't understand how you can go there day after day. Most people would find it adequate to go once.'

She would be turning the handle of the door now, would have it half open and from the stairwell she could hear the sound of the caretaker mopping down in the entrance hall.

'I look at just one picture a day, James.' And already the door would be closing behind her then as the lie echoed up the dog-leg hall to James at his desk, for she always looked at two pictures. One to study in detail and then a lengthy rest in front of Gainsborough's *Giovanna Baccelli,* the dancing girl who lifted her skirts with such flippant frivolity and pointed her toes so sweetly, yet looked out at the world with sad eyes that might have belonged to a dying dog.

'Hello,' said Rosalind when the telephone was answered in the new offices of Eric Kaufmann. The receptionist sounded sensible and not young. 'This is Rosalind Wentworth speaking. I used to have the Pegasus Gallery, and Mr Kaufmann used to buy from me. He bought a large Smither' — and she jittered away from any mention of financial disasters — 'four years ago.'

'Oh, yes.' The receptionist suddenly became chatty. 'I've been wanting to take that home, but my husband won't let me.'

'Is that Mrs Kaufmann? I met you once, I think. Didn't Mr Kaufmann buy a Barraud drawing from me for your birthday?' She spoke slowly, afraid to go too far.

'He did.' Mrs Kaufmann was triumphant. 'And I've still got it.' That sounded as if a lot of stuff might have had to go, thought Rosalind. 'I just love it.' A nice lady.

'A windmill?' Rosalind was groping for a memory of it. 'Wasn't it a windmill?'

'Yes. How wonderful of you to remember.' There was more of Mrs Kaufmann's triumph. It was going to be easier than she thought it would be, thought Rosalind.

'Mrs Kaufmann, I'm starting up in business again, just in a small way and on my own. You and your husband were two of my most valued clients, but the whole emphasis of art purchases has changed in recent years and I'm changing the emphasis of my stock to match this.' Myths.

'Yes?' Mrs Kaufmann's reticence was sudden and disquietening.

'This is not the time, Mrs Kaufmann, to be buying major works and putting a lot of money into the marketplace, but I do believe, for thinking people, that one must continue to invest in a small way in a different type of work. And that is why I've contacted you.' Even Rosalind was daunted now by the Jamesian quality of her narrative. 'I'm dealing very discreetly with selected clients these days, and all I handle is' — and she cast wildly about in her own mind for some plausible word here, something to save her from conversational disaster — 'drawings.' Her eye had been caught by the little row of drawings in the parlour. 'And by a medium range of earlier artists, nothing earlier than, say, 1890, and going up to the 1920s.' There was a silence from the other end of the telephone. I have gone too far, thought Rosalind and felt she might weep at this. How many times had she thought, on varying subjects, 'Oh, I have gone too far?'

'Hang on a minute.' Mrs Kaufmann seemed to be recovering. 'I'll just go and ask Eric.' There was the sound of retreating footsteps.

'Mrs Wentworth?' Eric Kaufmann had come on to the line. 'My wife says you're back in business again, but I'm afraid we're not really in a position to buy.' He had been a nice man, she thought, and he sounded very firm.

'Of course not, Mr Kaufmann. Nobody's in a position to buy these days. I advise people not to buy, actually.'

'Do you?' He sounded mystified.

'This is not the time for big capital expenditure, Mr Kaufmann. I advise against it.' The whole thing was out of hand, thought Rosalind.

'That doesn't seem like very good business, Mrs Wentworth.' Mr Kaufmann sounded as if he was smiling.

'On the contrary, it's excellent business. I deal in drawings now, and possibly some etchings by the better earlier artists' — they cropped up fairly regularly in the ragtag and bobtail ends of smaller antique auctions and it may be possible to pick up one or two cheaply — 'and I advise my clients that this is the way to go. We've all had to retrench dramatically—'

'We have, Mrs Wentworth.'

'— but it's still possible to continue looking after the aesthetics of an investment portfolio by going quietly into smaller works, mainly drawings, by the very respectable stalwarts of the art world. I'm talking here specifically of, say, Alderton.'

'Alderton? I'm not sure I'm familiar with that name.'

'You wouldn't be. Alderton was a recluse. His life was secret and romantic in the extreme. Not much of his work survives, but for a small outlay you can continue to buy people like that, artists of that sort.' More myths.

'I see.' Mr Kaufmann sounded delicately but markedly interested now. 'Perhaps we could do with a couple of little somethings for the office. What do you think, Sheila?' There was a bit of mumbling from the other end, and Rosalind waited. 'Possibly,' he said, 'we might be able to do business. Are the drawings framed, by the way?'

'They're framed very nicely, but they're very small. I could put them in my attaché case.' This suddenly grand term could cover the small leather suitcase on top of her wardrobe in which she kept dress patterns, thought Rosalind. 'I trade now from my cottage. I live in a Victorian cottage — '

'How lovely.' A breathless Mrs Kaufmann was on the extension now. 'I've always wanted one of those.'

'Have you, Mrs Kaufmann? I use my cottage as my gallery now, but it might not be convenient for you to come here. I'm rather lost in a web of lanes, so I could come and see you, if that would be more convenient. We haven't mentioned price —' again she cast wildly about for a figure, or a remark, or anything. Sweet heaven, thought Rosalind.

'No, we haven't.' Mr Kaufmann was suddenly sepulchral. 'There's the question of price, Sheila.' There was more muttering and Rosalind heard a sibilant whisper from Mrs Kaufmann, 'Well, we can look, Eric.'

'On the question of price I keep everything well buttoned down. None of us has a lot of spare capital to throw about, and I can honestly tell you that I'm stocking nothing at the moment over two hundred.'

'Two hundred dollars? That sounds worthy of consideration anyway.' There were more murmurings from Mrs Kaufmann. 'Well, shall we say we'll meet here at' — and here Rosalind heard the noise of paper, sheets of paper being turned, perhaps in a desk diary — 'three o'clock tomorrow?'

'How lovely,' said Rosalind. 'I'll look forward to that,' and rang off.

Her telephone rang again almost immediately.

'Rosalind?' It was Benjamin. 'Rosalind, I've been trying to get through to you for ages, dear. Just a little bulletin about the bed.'

'Oh, yes?' said Rosalind, and thought there was another of those polite *Ohs* again, another brick for the wall against James.

'We've all been out here, Rosalind, working like Trojans. Got Wally here at the crack of dawn, and we've managed to get the bed out of the pile. Yes, Wally? What is it?' There was some whispering. 'Rosalind? Wally wants to speak to you.'

'Hello, Mrs Wineworf.'

'Hello, Wally.'

'S'alright about ya bee twenny-nines. We got all the bee twenny-nines all right, Mrs Wineworf.'

'Have you, Wally? Thank you very much.'

'Cat all right?'

'Yes, thank you, Wally. We're all fine here.'

'Righto then, Mrs Wineworf, I'll be seeing ya.'

'Okay then, Wally. Cheerio.'

'Rosalind?' Benjamin came back on the line. 'I don't know

what that boy thinks he's doing. Wally, go and put the kettle on, please. I'll have to get him out of my hair somehow, Rosalind.'

'Oh, old Wally's all right,' said Rosalind.

'I must say he's been much better lately. The counselling's made a difference, Rosalind, and the pills. But I haven't rung to be chattering about Wally, dear. I've rung about the bed, and by tomorrow night I think we'll have everything *in situ*. One or two of the bronze medallions have come loose in storage. These old sleigh beds are dynamite, Rosalind, and I do mean dynamite. They're very difficult to store. But we can get over all that. I've got good old Max coming tomorrow to go over it with a fine-tooth comb and he'll fix up anything that needs fixing. I think myself that one or two bits of the boxwood stringing need re-gluing, but there you are, Rosalind, that's storage for you.'

'Indeed,' said Rosalind. What else would there be to say, under the circumstances?

'And I've had to make sweeping decisions, Rosalind, about curtains. The bedroom can't be uncurtained.'

'I suppose not.' And it couldn't be, she thought, what with the french doors and the moonlight and the nuns next door.

'As you might remember, the whole place is done in just neutral tones — '

'Magnolia,' said Rosalind. Magnolia sounded better, again under the circumstances.

'Magnolia, then. I quickly chose a shade of cream for the curtains, Rosalind. Velvet. I hope that's all right. And they're going to be hanging from a wooden pole stained the same colour as the bed, and with wooden curtain rings the same. They're rushing it all through.'

'Very nice, thank you, Benjamin.'

'I hope you like them, Rosalind. I thought of ringing you, but then there was the question of time, and I decided to keep the whole room a decorative monochrome so that the only colour would come from your rosy little — Oh, God, I'll have to go, Rosalind.' There was a bit more murmuring from the other end of the line. 'Just put it down, Wally. Put the cup anywhere.' He sounded impatient. 'For heaven's sake, move some of those catalogues. Don't slop it everywhere. Oh, look what you've done now.' He rang off.

The telephone rang again immediately, as if trained to do so.

'Rosalind, you're always on the telephone.' It was Dinah. 'I've rung and rung and your line's always engaged. I'm at that café opposite the Town Hall, you know that one where they put up notices for jobs on the wall?'

'Yes?' What has Dinah come up with now?

'There's a job here, Rosalind, that might suit you. Somebody wants a tutor in English. It's only ten dollars an hour, but that's better than nothing. You could get extra pupils. You could end up with a school, Rosalind. You could have a school.' Dinah always was ambitious. 'Wait a minute, I'll put my glasses on. It's a Japanese name, Rosalind. It's someone Japanese wanting a tutor in conversational English. You'd be good at that.'

'Yes,' said Rosalind, wondering about the stultifying boredom of teaching 'Can you tell me where to buy ink?' and 'Where is the bus for the ice-cream parlour?' 'But just in the last couple of days I've decided to start dealing in pictures again, and I've actually made contact' — Dinah would love this phrase *made contact,* thought Rosalind — 'with a couple of clients I used to have. A lot have gone to the wall, of course. Great swathes of business firms seem to have been swept away since the crash, but I've made contact with two people who used to buy from me.'

'Oh.' Dinah's voice breathes respect. 'So you've made contact, have you?'

'Yes.'

'And how did you find that?'

'It was fine. Look, Dinah —'

'And how did they find it?'

'I think they thought it was fine, too. I have to go and see them tomorrow and show them some drawings I've got. Thanks for letting me know about the tutoring, but I'm not sure I could fit it in. I've actually got another job as well, just in the last few days, so I think I might be kept fairly occupied. Look, I'll have to go. I've got to sort out these pictures and do one or two other things.' Like painting her toenails pink. Like rubbing her knees with scented oil.

'And I'd better go back to the surgery. I've got someone coming to see me. I think Henry said I had to be back in an hour. I just nipped out to have a cup of coffee. Cheerio, Rosalind.'

'Bye, bye, Dinah.' So, thought Rosalind, that man who acts as Dinah's receptionist is called Henry, former violinist but now broken down (and being rebuilt) and owner of a formerly mammoth personality disorder (now diminishing).

'I don't believe', Dinah once said, 'in stereotypes to do with gender within the workforce, Rosalind. There's no reason, for instance, why you as an individual couldn't be a stevedore.'

'But I don't want to be a stevedore.'

'Or a linesman or a chauffeur or anything, and that is why I've taken on a man to be my receptionist so my patients can see, the moment they step in the door, that stereotypes are outlawed within the framework of a proper and modern society. And Henry's empathy with them is instant, Rosalind. Instant. Henry feels their pain, Rosalind. He knows their pain because their pain is his pain.'

'And how do you feel about that?'

'How do you mean, how do I feel about that?' Once again Dinah is not giving much away. 'Anyway, Rosalind, we'll have to hurry. It's only seven minutes till the concert starts. Isn't it exciting? It's going to be Mussorgsky's *Pictures At An Exhibition*.'

'Not that again.' Rosalind stands stock-still in the middle of the road. 'That's another one that sounds like your nerves all being pulled out by the roots.'

'Rosalind,' — Dinah is leading her over to the pavement — 'have you ever thought you might have an attitude problem? You just have to say the word and I could arrange for you to talk about it to someone.'

'I'll get back to you on that,' says Rosalind, trained now in psycho-babble after many pre-concert dinners.

15

DEAR MRS WENTWORTH — the mail has arrived — *Thank you for your letter of 20 January.* Rosalind stops reading. This reply is dated 2 February. James will be arriving soon, tomorrow perhaps, to stay with Lorraine and all that pubic hair. She continues reading.

Sadly, unemployment amongst journalists is now running at forty-seven per cent and, sadly again, many of these highly proficient people have university qualifications such as doctorates in behavioural sciences and are trained, also often to university level, in the computerisation of communications techniques. The current recession has dramatically cut into our expansion programme and our staff ratio has been cut by more than one-third during the past year owing to declining advertising revenue from the public and private sector. Thus, I am afraid we would not be able to offer you any employment and nor do I see any hope of this in the reasonably foreseeable future. Thank you, however, for your interest.

Yours faithfully, Blarty Blarty Blah.

Well, thinks Rosalind, that was a waste of good buns. There is a second letter, though. *Dear Mrs Wentworth* — this might be better news, thinks Rosalind.

May I congratulate you on your choice of our banking organisation for your monetary and investment needs. With regard to your letter of 20 January — another reminder of James's incipient arrival — *I am afraid I am unable to give you any affirmative assurance that bank rulings re withdrawals from certain investment accounts will be changed. According to guidelines laid down by the International Monetary Fund and the Geneva Consortium of International Bankers, interest on investment accounts such as the one you have can be paid out only when that* *interest reaches a four-figure sum. Thank you, anyway, for your enquiry. We are always very happy to answer any query. May I, however, respectfully point out that due to a computer error your latest bank statement is inaccurate. Your cheque account has an overdraft of $11.23, not a credit as incorrectly stated. Please accept our sincere apologies for this, and I am sure we can rely on you to rectify the matter as quickly as possible.*

Yours faithfully, Blarty Blarty Blah.

Benjamin's cheque will fix all that, thinks Rosalind. Even though the cheques for the bills will be drawn on the account in a day or so. There will still be a credit left.

The day is a misty one, with fine rain. February shows signs of being a mysterious month in every possible way, even geographically with the trees in the gully blotted out today by a mixture of fog and rain. Beneath the low cloud ceiling the smell of burnt bread from the bakery on the main road lingers, pungent as brimstone.

'Mrs Wineworf?' The telephone has rung again. 'Wally here. I'm over at the warehouse. He says,' — Rosalind can imagine how that thumb will be darting over the shoulder — 'he says to tell you we got the bed on the truck. I been here since seven, and the other boys, they didn't get here till eight, but we got it on the truck okay. He says to tell you.'

'Thank you, Wally.' What else is there to say? The whole of life has been spent saying *Thank you, This* or *Thank you, That, Well, Indeed, Ha,ha,ha, Of course.*

'Hang on, Mrs Wineworf.' There is the sound of yelling in the distance. 'He says he'll ring you later, Mrs Wineworf.' There is more yelling. 'He's got jammed in the truck behind the bed, but the boys are getting him out. Some bits have fallen off,' — it would be ridiculous, thinks Rosalind, to think of bits falling off Benjamin; Wally must mean some of the bronze medallions and the odd little inlay must have fallen off the actual bed — 'but I put them in a paper bag.'

So, thinks Rosalind when she hangs up, the bed has been uplifted from the pile of furniture and household goods in Benjamin's second warehouse and, although it is on a truck awaiting transport to Benjamin's bedroom, Benjamin himself is now trapped behind it. And there are no jobs at the newspaper, the bank has no intention of altering its stance on the payment of interest and the interest itself has dropped overnight by several points. As if to punctuate all this the telephone rings again.

'Hello, Rosie, I've come a day earlier than I said.' It is James.

There is a long silence.

'Hello, James.' Rosalind is as careful and judicious as the bank manager whose letter she has just received, as withdrawn as Malcolm, the gobbler of forgotten Easter buns.

'Rosie, I waited for you in Sydney and you didn't turn up. And now I've had to spend an hour on the telephone trying to get some sort of refund on the ticket I arranged for you.' There is another long silence. 'Now, is there some explanation of why you didn't come to Sydney, some explanation of why I sat in some bloody hotel waiting for you, Rosie, in vain? I waited for you, Rosamund, and you never turned up.'

'I didn't know I had to.' The clarity of this is appalling, and it makes the old clock in the hall quiver a reluctant chime, timely but wildly inaccurate. Thirteen o'clock. Rosalind counts the sounds.

'You didn't know you had to, Rosie?' There is that cutting voice again, that one that belongs to brown marble bathrooms. 'Are you completely stupid, Rosie? Are you completely without any form of brain?' 'Yes, James, I must be to think anyone would love me.' There is that voice again. 'But I explained it all in the letter I put in with the parcel, back at Christmas.'

'Oh,' says Rosalind.

'Is that all you've got to say, "Oh"?'

'I'm sorry, James. I never read your letter.' There is another long silence. 'I never even properly opened your parcel.'

'What am I going to do with you, Rosie?'

'I don't know, possibly nothing.' There is no sound at all. The street and the dogs are hushed for this.

'I got a wonderful welcome from Margaret.' The reproach is unmistakeable. 'Nothing was too much trouble.'

'I'm sure it wasn't, James.'

'And, apart from the bushfires, Adelaide opened its doors to me, Rosie. People were', said James, 'wonderful. And Lorraine's been wonderful. She came out to the airport to meet me this morning, Rosamund. Six o'clock in the morning, Rosie, and there she was. Flowers, gifts, everything. Her mother sent a fax of welcome. Lorraine actually cried when she saw me.'

'And how did you feel about that, James?' Here is a favourite Dinahism popping out.

'It was wonderful, Rosie. It gladdened my old heart, Rosie, after waiting for you in Sydney and you never turning up. We're none of us getting any younger, Rosamund. I don't know why you don't want to have a good time. I had it all arranged. I had you slotted in, between Margaret and Lorraine, so you all got a share of me,' — he sighed heavily — 'and now look what you've done, Rosie. You've ruined everything. You're rotten.'

'Yes, James.' The old rose at the bottom of the back lawn, visible from the telephone, was covered in small pink flowers, enough to fill a large bowl on the hall table where their spicy scent would filter through the house. I must pick a bunch of those, thought Rosalind.

'You don't even seem to be paying attention, Rosie. I really don't know what to do now. Lorraine's got all sorts of things laid on — '

'I'm sure she has, James.'

'— and she's very jealous, so I might have to give up my contingency plan to spend day and day about with you both. Some wonderful friends of hers, they're really wonderful people, have lent her a cottage so she can take me to stay at a beach somewhere. She actually saved their marriage a couple of years ago. Lorraine', said James, 'is a very wonderful person — warm-hearted, generous, caring, giving.'

'Yes, James.'

'She's a big girl. She has this eating problem, but she's in therapy for that now. She's got this wonderful pubic hair that pokes through her — '

'Yes, James. Thank you. You've already told me that.'

'Anyway, Rosie, I really don't know what I can do about

you now. You've really missed out, haven't you?' There is no answer for this. 'Lorraine's very possessive. She's just popped into the shower so I was able to ring you. I might be able to take you out to lunch next Friday. Lorraine's got some time off, but she has to front up at her office one day to do the rosters. Lorraine', said James, 'has a very good career. Everyone thinks well of her.'

'That's nice, James.'

'Still writing those funny little bits and pieces are you, Rosie? I asked Lorraine about you — I just pretended you were a sort of friend of a friend — and she said she'd never heard — Oh, God, she's coming Rosie. Hello, darling. Come and let me dry that very lovely back.' He hung up.

The cottage has the air of a sanctuary this morning, a jewel of a little dwelling made for artful show, not real life. The Persian rugs march down the bare boards of the hall, past the Gothic cabinet that Benjamin admires so much, lit by an ornamental skylight over the front door. Its glass is the colour of cranberries and casts a bloom, tender as a blush, over everything. The rugs are already rosy with their own faded carmine and vermilion, and the cat prances through this assembly of shabby splendours making for its saucer of milk beside the back door. James, although only about a kilometre away, is locked in the massive arms of Lorraine, incarcerated by possessive fantasies and entwined in her pubic hair. Benjamin may possibly have, by now, escaped from behind the Napoleonic sleigh bed. Apart from all that, it is a quiet and peaceful day.

Dear Blarty Blarty Blah — Rosalind has begun to write some letters, long overdue — *Thank you for your letter about 'The Rose' and also for your kind enquiry about my later work. I was most gratified at your interest. Of course, I would be most happy to allow you to incorporate stanzas 50-130 of my poem 'The Rose' in* Glowing Lights Amongst The Stars.

The telephone interrupts all this activity.

'Rosalind?' It is Benjamin. 'Rosalind, did you get my message from Wally? Oh, good. I've just rung to let you know the bed's now at the house, Rosalind, *in situ* so to speak.' He coughs and Rosalind thinks he is smiling.

'Everything's in place, Rosalind, and Wally's got the B29s all organised. The show's on the road, Rosalind. You've got your concert tonight, haven't you, with that girl you went to school with? Right. Give me a ring when you get home, it'll only be ten o'clock or so, won't it? Nine forty-five? Oh, good. Give me a bell and I'll come over and get you. I'll stay at the office and catch up on some paperwork. I'll wait, Rosalind. Don't say a word, dear.' There has not been a space left to say a word, thinks Rosalind. 'Catch you later.'

But I wonder if I could make one small request. Rosalind continues writing the letter. *Could my complimentary copy be in hardback, please? I would be most grateful if this could be arranged.* The cost of a hardback is higher than a paperback, thinks Rosalind, so James will be paid for a little more by someone else. Compensation. Recoupment. Recompense. Everyone can pay for James.

I also very much look forward to the champagne breakfast launch of the volume. I have enclosed part of the manuscript of 'The Geranium', a later work which post-dates 'The Rose' whilst at the same time expanding on its use of tonal phenomena and symbolism within the framework of the French School.

I must confess to you that my publisher found the work a dated one, and indeed this could be so, but I think myself that, say, stanzas 46-92 have their own brand of charm that is not without merit when viewed in the light of historical literary contexts. I have signed the permission slip you enclosed with your letter and return it with my thanks for including my work in your poetry anthology.

Yours sincerely, Blarty Blarty Blah.

Rosalind now thinks of herself as Blarty Blarty Blah, as well as all the other people. Rosalind now knows that she is just as bad as everyone else and has become a member of the world.

On the way to see the Kaufmanns, Rosalind posted the letter in the box on the corner where an old white dog always sleeps beside the gutter. He is too old for life on the middle line now and sleeps peacefully on the kerb.

The drawings by Alderton have been packed carefully in the brown leather suitcase. The dress patterns it held up till now have been put in a drawer. The jerseys in that drawer have been put in the picnic basket on top of the wardrobe. The contents of the basket have been put in the shed. The inevitable shunting of unimportant possessions is a summing-up of the world, thought Rosalind, with everything and everybody jostling for some sort of place, jittering this way and that.

James wants, and does not want, Priscilla and cannot do without the excitement of that doubt, so provokes other people into moving themselves even as far as Africa. Certainly as far as Wiltshire, Hereford, all points north on the compass. Lorraine has moved herself out of bed before six in the morning to meet him. Her friends, the wonderful people, have probably rearranged their beach cottage, hidden the socks that suddenly look suspect, removed the row-boat from the wash-house, cleared cobwebs from the outside loo, washed down the porch, thrown away last year's newspapers all in readiness for the arrival of James and Lorraine the little (big) marriage saver. And there will be a dialogue to match, thought Rosalind as she stepped over rubbish on the pavement. The rubbish collection was yesterday and the rubbish truck has left its usual inevitable spillage. Empty petfood tins, half eaten fish, fish heads, skeletons of fish, the odd bone or two, crumpled newspapers weighed down by the overnight rain all jostle for space on the road. Everything is heavy with damp, particularly the newspapers which may, thought Rosalind, be those published by Malcolm the bun-eater, the non-rememberer of old friends.

Behind all the false innocence of smiling ladies driving to the airport, mothers sending faxes, dark-haired women putting jerseys in picnic baskets will lie lengthy dialogues of manners that contain no amusement. James will tell Margaret that Lorraine's house/flat/apartment is better than hers. He will tell Lorraine that Margaret took him to more interesting places, that the weather was better in Adelaide, that she is fatter than Margaret. Margaret will be telephoned from Lorraine's place, at her expense (while she is in the shower) and he will say that Adelaide was too dusty and his sinuses are better now, better in this new roosting ground. Rosalind herself has already been told that Lorraine has never heard of her poetry, and perhaps Lorraine has been made to feel inadequate because she has never written any. Who would know? Cheered by the movements thus provoked, James will return to Wiltshire/London/Hereford/anywhere/take your pick.

But not Rosalind. Rosalind is thinking of this as she tramps over the rubbish on the way to the bus stop, the brown leather suitcase in her hand. Rosalind, spinach-grower extraordinaire, appalling pianist, writer of unwanted poems called 'The Geranium' and other similar titles, Rosalind has not moved one millimetre except in opposition. The silence in her cottage has been of her own making, a silence that contains many tiny signs of life. There is the scraping of the climbing roses against the windowpanes when the wind comes from the north, the sound of the cat's purr as it sits on Rosalind's knee, the click of the door on the letter-box as the postman puts interesting letters inside, like the one about the anthology of poems, the tinkle of the telephone as Rosalind ends James's calls. These small signals of another life amidst the silence are as eloquent as laughter, as elegantly discreet as a clasped hand.

The dogs that live on the white line in the middle of the road never bark when Rosalind walks to the bus stop. They do not bite her, but they have bitten other people. The newspaper says so, and some of the dogs have been put down. As she sallies forth with the letter in one hand and the suitcase in the other, they do not bark or growl or snarl because, she believes, they recognise another lost plunderer. This is what Rosalind thinks, but whether this is true or not, who would know? Is it true when people like James say, 'I love you, Margaret,' in the morning and by evening are saying, 'I love you, Lorraine,' for instance? And would say, 'I love you, Rosalind,' the following day, or week or month, or anything. Who would know the answer to any of this?

16

THERE IS ANOTHER concert tonight, the last of the holiday season. The orchestra will play Mozart and Delius.

'But will it be cheerful?' Rosalind has asked on the way to the restaurant. Mozart's overture will be very suitable for the mood of the evening with its ominous use of brass and drums after a slow introduction with everything sweeping towards a brilliant *molto allegro.* But what about Delius, thinks Rosalind, and *A Song of Summer* that is to be played tonight, what about that tranquil opening giving way to an exultant richly scored climax? What about all that?

'Cheerful? Rosalind, you've got a morbid fetish about cheerfulness.' Dinah is tramping along swinging her red tartan umbrella and they have both parked their cars side by side again in the Town Hall carpark (F for full on Rosalind's petrol gauge). 'Why does it always have to be cheerful? A lot of these composers had broken hearts, Rosalind. They led lives of extreme suffering. I feel a lot of it could have been alleviated with antibiotics, a correct diet involving heavy doses of the B family of vitamins, proper therapy and family support.'

'I suppose so.' Rosalind regards the umbrella. 'Is it going to rain?' Has Dinah, apart from all this other knowledge, an intimate understanding of the weather?

'I always carry my umbrella, Rosalind, in case we're attacked. You never know,' says Dinah, 'with the city the way it is.'

'You can be attacked anywhere, Dinah,' says Rosalind and remembers how she came back through the kitchen of the big house on the hill and went out across the quarry tiles of the conservatory to see James leaning against the french doors. 'They told me a lady lived here, by herself.' That was an attack of sorts, a slow war of attrition on peace of mind, repose, self-esteem (as Dinah would say), health, beauty.

An umbrella would not have driven that away.

In the restaurant the same waiter comes to take their order.

'Nice to see you two ladies again. And what do you think you'd like tonight?' He stands there with his pad and pencil in hand.

'Fillet steak, medium rare, with a side-salad. No vinaigrette, no mayonnaise, nothing.' It will be essential to stay thin. 'To follow I'd like a piece of blue vein cheese, three crackers and a cup of black coffee, very strong.' Rosalind has not even read the menu.

'Well,' says Dinah (another brick for James), 'you're certainly in a decisive mood tonight, Rosalind, and I'm glad you're going to have something more substantial. I feel really tired, so I'll just have to sit here for a minute and think about things before I decide.'

After lengthy thought, while the waiter seats another two tables of diners, including a birthday night out for an entire family of Chileans with their grandmother, and a brindled dog left tied to a lamp-post outside, Dinah thinks she might have the fillet steak as well. And the usual claret.

'I'm very indecisive today,' she says when the waiter has gone off into the kitchen. 'I've had a really dreadful day, Rosalind. I've started this class for stress management. So many people suffer from stress these days that I've had to start a class for stress management with mutual support and confessions, which we call unburdenings, from all the members. It keeps the costs down, Rosalind. These are hard times and the economic viability of everything has to be considered, even psychotherapy.'

'Mmm.' says Rosalind. Once more, she does not know what to say.

'But now Henry wants to come, Henry of all people. I thought I'd talked Henry through his crisis.' She thinks for a moment. 'His crises,' she says. 'Henry's had a very stressful life, starting off with the death of his mother when he was only nine. They were walking along the street one day and he was holding her hand, Rosalind; imagine that. And she fell over stone-dead. Anyway, let's not dwell on all these difficulties. I'm just hoping my class will fill a need.'

'Have you got many people for it?' Rosalind is hardly paying attention. The Chilean family is making so much noise. There is much shouting and laughter and corks are popping out of bottles of Première Cuvée. The waiter has taken a life-size rag doll from one of the children and has hung it up on a coathook beside the door, and the brindled dog has gone to sleep outside.

'You must be joking, Rosalind. I've been inundated. I got two new ones today, and', says Dinah, 'that's just the tip of the iceberg. I shouldn't be telling you all this, but you won't be able to identify any of these people. It's really got on top of me.' She pours herself a glass of claret. 'Are you sure you won't have any of this? You can have a glass if you like. No? Well, stay with the water then, better for you. I'm really exhausted, Rosalind. I think the wine's gone to my head already.' She sinks back in the chair with the glass of wine, nearly spilling, in her hand. 'The first extra one I got today was this woman, Rosalind, aged forty, single, never married, caught in this terrible relationship with a man who doesn't even live here. I think he lives in England and periodically he comes to see her and he just wrecks her life, or she saves up and goes to see him in some miserable little flat in the north of London somewhere. Last time she was there the sink was blocked, Rosalind, the whole time.'

'And on the fifth floor, too,' says Rosalind. 'Or probably on the fifth floor. They have those huge blocks of flats all over London. Everyone lives up in the air.' Rosalind coughs. The remark has been a mistake.

'She's got this eating problem, Rosalind. You'd just never believe how much she eats. If we could just get her self-esteem level up a bit we might be able to get her into a state of self-realisation. If she could self-actualise, Rosalind. And what was that you said about the fifth floor?'

'Nothing,' says Rosalind.

'You're so penetrating.' Dinah is pouring more claret. 'It's being a poet. You see things, Rosalind. You'll be quite shocked when I tell you the flat was actually on the fifth floor.'

'Well, well, well,' says Rosalind (another three bricks).

'And to further complicate the problem she's going to miss the next two classes because this man's actually coming to see her. Now just what sort of emotional mess will I have to clean up after all that?'

'Those Chileans seem to be getting a bit rowdy,' says Rosalind. What else is there to say?

'And there's this other very tragic case I've had loaded into my class by an ear, nose and throat specialist who shall remain nameless. Her deafness is entirely psychosomatic, Rosalind, and she's another tragic figure, aged forty-five, no qualifications, lived with this very wealthy man for nine years, and now he's announced he doesn't want to live with her any more. He says he's fallen in love with someone else —'

'Oh, has he?' Rosalind brightens.

'— and he's gone off, Rosalind, after living with this poor woman all that time in her own house with all her own furniture. He's thrown the tenants out of some house he owns and he's gone to live there, Rosalind, and now she's found out that he's had all this antique furniture in storage all those years. Including' — Dinah taps with her spoon on the table because by now her dessert has arrived — 'some fabulous bed that's worth a fortune. And now I have to fit her into my class, Rosalind, because she's filled with stress-related misery: all the best years of her life wasted on this man, her child-bearing potential lost, reproaches from her parents. Rosalind, the mother's got senile dementia, and the woman herself, well, I ask you, what's she got to look forward to?'

'I don't know.' Rosalind is eating the cheese. 'Would you like some of this cheese, Dinah? What was the apple pie like tonight?' So, she thinks, Roberta is forty-five.

'It was fine, Rosalind.' Dinah is very abstracted, and dinner seems to have gone by in a moment. The Chileans are blowing out the candles on a birthday cake and the dog has woken up. 'It's all made me feel very tired, Rosalind. And that woman I mentioned with the eating problem, she's got a further source of emotional trauma. Henry had to field her call today, I just couldn't face it.

'She rang up in a terrible state because she suspects that this manipulative man who intermittently takes over her life whilst giving nothing, this man, Rosalind, has some other woman right here, Rosalind, actually in this city.' There goes the spoon again on the table. 'Exactly here, Rosalind, in this city at this exact moment could be some other woman also waiting —'

'Perhaps she isn't waiting.'

'Rosalind, I've told you this before. You've got this very bad habit of interrupting. She suspects, anyway, that he's got some other woman right here. Can you imagine that?'

'No, I can't,' says Rosalind.

'That's the sort of thing I've been hearing all week, and it's got on top of me. Have you got the programme for tonight? What's the music? If it's Skriabin I'm going to scream.'

'Overture from *Don Giovanni*,' reads Rosalind, 'Mozart. And Delius's *A Song of Summer*.'

'That sounds a pleasant, undemanding offering. That's all I can face at the moment.' Dinah has put her left elbow on the table, cupping her forehead with a hand. 'She actually confessed last week, this poor fat woman, that every time she goes to see him she leaves something behind so she can return at a later date to collect it. It's pathetic, Rosalind, and grotesque. Last time, for instance, it was a pair of pink satin shoes.'

'Pink satin shoes?' Rosalind's coffee cup remains in mid-air, the hand holding it trembling a little. 'A high-heeled court, rather scuffed at the back of the heels? Ankle straps with one buckle a later replacement in a slightly different shape? Size 10C?'

'Rosalind,' — Dinah's head is still in her hands — 'there speaks the ex-journalist, the poet, the weaver of fantasies. Why can't some of these people see their lives as a verbalised and endured fiction, Rosalind, just like you? I'd be out of work. I'd be happy. I could work in my rose garden all day.

'Just think, Rosalind,' says Dinah as she orders coffee and a chocolate, 'out there somewhere in that dark and mysterious city is that woman who's waiting for this man to arrive —'

'From all points north on the compass,' says Rosalind.

'— exactly, Rosalind.' They both stare out of the window of the restaurant into the street. There is a bus stop almost directly outside, and nine people are waiting there for transport to a far-flung suburb. 'And also out there,' says Dinah, 'somewhere in this exact city, Rosalind, is another woman who's the third party —'

'The third, mysterious party,' says Rosalind.

'The third, mysterious party in this other triangle involving the woman with no qualifications and the man who's lived with her for nine years and has now moved into his own luxurious dwelling from which he has flung, and I do mean flung, a diplomat and his family. And that woman,' — Dinah stares out into the street again — 'she's out there too. I haven't got room for any more people in my class, but imagine their burden of stress, Rosalind.'

'Yes,' says Rosalind. Yet again, what else is there to say? 'Dinah, it's nearly half-past seven and the concert starts at eight. I think we should hurry.'

'You didn't tell me about that appointment you had today,' says Dinah as they both hurry over the road to the Town Hall. 'Rosalind, wait for me, you're striding along so fast I can't keep up. You're not going all nostalgic again are you? You're looking very sad.'

'I'm fine, Dinah.' Rosalind is shouting now across a lane of traffic. She is standing on the pavement beside the Town Hall, and Dinah is still in the middle of the road. 'They bought all the pictures, it's a company, Dinah, not just one man, and I have to go and see them next week about a job.'

'Oh, Rosalind.' Dinah is still standing in the middle of all the traffic. 'Isn't that good news!'

'It won't be good news if you get run over.' Rosalind returns to the white line between the lines of cars. 'I've known you since I was five. Run, Dinah, run.' What if there were no happy remnants of the past, thinks Rosalind. No peaceful recollections of childhood, no stalwart markers along the way, no good-hearted signpost in a lost landscape, no Dinah.

'Well, here we are then,' says Dinah. They have reached

the foyer safely, and Dinah has already begun to say hello to people. 'Hello Geoffrey and Mary. Yoo hoo, Louise. Hello Barbara.'

Eric Kaufmann had said, 'Well, here we are then,' when the lift stopped on the fourth floor in that shabby, old, sandstone building down in the middle of town where the red-light district was just beginning with a smattering of massage parlours, hairdressers and chemists. 'We're really not in the market for buying up large,' he said as he opened the door to his office, 'but you seem to already understand that.'

'Yes.' She spoke very slowly, drawling out the words as if they might have been written on old paper, hard to read, harder to speak. 'I think we all understand that. I think we all run very tight ships,' and she thought of how the coffee from the second usage of the grounds was always considerably weaker, but still had some taste. How the expensive teabags could not be used a second time, but the cheap ones could, and still gave a cup of something brown. Brownish.

'Sit down, Mrs Wentworth.' There was a small, cream tweed sofa in the reception area with cushions thick enough to be comfortable and not thin enough to hint at misery, but the effect was sensibly austere. The Smither she had sold them back before the crash was nicely placed on the other side of the room. 'I'll just call Sheila. She works here with me three days a week.'

It had been a pleasant hour with the Kaufmanns, she thought now, going up the stairs to the concert.

'Hello Grace. Hello, Marion. Hello George.' Dinah is in full spate again. 'Hello, Alistair.'

'I suppose we'd better explain what we do here, Mrs Wentworth,' Eric Kaufmann had said, 'and then you'll understand what we want the drawings for. No, don't bother getting them out. I'm sure if you recommend them they're worth buying, and they can't do anything but increase in value on the wall, isn't that so?'

'Oh, yes,' said Rosalind. 'It's perfectly true.' And it was. Perfectly, perfectly true.

He tells her that the whole world is running a tight ship these days, and everyone is sorting through houses and jewel boxes and things are being sold.

'Realisation on capital assets is what we call it,' said Eric Kaufmann, 'but we like our clients to keep a stable, if modest, base of possessions they can realise on if times get tough. But we can't have too much capital tied up. My wife does her best to advise them about the sorting, but we don't have your specialised knowledge. I mean, if we've got a client who needs capital and, say, he's sold the Goldie and flogged off the W.G. Bakers to get it, then what's he going to buy, in a more modest way, to ensure he still owns art as a growth investment? And that', he said, 'is where you come into it, Mrs Wentworth. We were very, very glad you telephoned. Someone said you'd gone to live in England and we're so pleased you didn't.'

'England?' says Rosalind. 'I just went there for a while.' There is a silence. 'I studied art at the Tate. But I came back.' Another silence. 'I came home.' The suitcase of little Aldertons lies at her feet and her silence is construed as refusal.

'Don't say no just yet,' said Mrs Kaufmann. 'I really love that drawing you sold Eric once for my birthday.' She had a teatray ready and poured tea. 'Milk? Sugar? Would you like a biscuit, Mrs Wentworth? I said to Eric, didn't I Eric, anyone who can sell him something so nice, well she'd be just the person we want. She's quiet, I said, and she knows about pictures. Didn't I say that, Eric? You'd be better off thinking about her, I said, now that she's started up again, rather than the glossy brigade. I don't trust the glossy brigade, do I Eric?'

'No, darling. Well, Mrs Wentworth, what do you think?'

When tears fill an eye they will filter away again within the eye socket, thought Rosalind, if a person who owns those eyes sits very still and looks down and drinks a cup of tea. They will leak away slowly through the cranium and they will cleanse a brain, soaking down a painful throat into the kernel of a heart.

'Yes, indeed,' Dinah is shouting at someone over the heads

in the crowd on the top landing. It is five to eight. 'Mozart had a wonderful heart, even if it was broken, he had a wonderful heart. Mozart had a heart as big as the world.' The claret has definitely been a bit much for Dinah. 'Rosalind, is my face red?'

'Of course it isn't, Dinah.' It is, but never mind.

'Rosalind, hurry. Hurry.'

Tap, tap, tap. There is the conductor with his baton. They are just in time.

'Clap, Rosalind, clap.'

The programme has been changed. It is *Music for the Royal Fireworks*. Handel at his best. The music's overpowering splendour is as eloquent and telling as a cold cheek, the tilt of a mutinous head, a sharp shoulder turning finally away from the last echoes of London. Music and paintings, paintings and roses, roses and the cat, the cat and Benjamin, Benjamin and Dinah. That's all, that's all there is.

Other New Zealand Titles Available In Vintage Editions

Holy Terrors and Other Stories by Amelia Batistich
Man With Two Arms and Other Stories
by Norman Bilbrough
Strangers in Paradise by Jonathan Eisen and
Katherine Joyce Smith
To the Is-land by Janet Frame*
An Angel at My Table by Janet Frame*
The Envoy From Mirror City by Janet Frame*
Owls Do Cry by Janet Frame*
The Carpathians by Janet Frame*
The Pocket Mirror by Janet Frame*
A Population of One by Alice Glenday
Strained Relations by Gaelyn Gordon
True Stars by Fiona Kidman
Wakeful Nights by Fiona Kidman
Finding Out by Elspeth Sandys**
Love and War by Elspeth Sandys**
The Peace Monster by John Smythe
Always the Islands of Memory by Noel Virtue*
The Redemption of Elsdon Bird by Noel Virtue*

*Available only in New Zealand
**Available only in Australia and New Zealand